Smith's
MONTHLY

Every Month Original Novels, Stories, and Articles

USA Today Bestselling Writer
Dean Wesley Smith

TABLE OF CONTENTS

Smith's Monthly Issue #5

The Writings and Opinions of
Dean Wesley Smith

Introduction

Now For Something a Little Different

SINCE THIS IS MY MAGAZINE and the fine folks at WMG Publishing are letting me roam off into doing different forms (within reason), I figured I would have some fun. So I'm doing an issue with a novel and a couple of stories that have a little hotter sex in them.

Now, don't worry, these stories are far from erotica. A long ways, actually, so no worries there. But there are sex scenes (or at least hinted at sex in one) in two of the four stories and in the novel.

The novel in this book, *Sector Justice*, is pure science fiction, but it has sex scenes. Most science fiction with sex scenes tends to end up over in the romance subgenre areas, even though Phillip Jose Farmer brought sex into the science fiction genre with the

ground-breaking novel *Flesh* back in the early 1950s.

Sure, you see it in some stories and some books in science fiction, but for the most part, science fiction is a "sweet" genre (in romance terms) where the love scenes sort of fade off and let what happens in the sex scene to the imagination of the reader.

Remember the famous scene of James T. Kirk putting on his boots in *Original Star Trek*. And that was almost too much for some viewers and readers. Science fiction, for the most part, (inside the walls of the literary field of science fiction) has kept sex to "putting on your boots."

Mostly, as a science fiction writer over the years, I have done the same thing in my stories and novels. But then I started writing mysteries and thrillers where real sex can happen. And then I wrote some romance where they actually grade a book on how much sex the book has in it, from "sweet" (pulling on your

Thanks for the Support

Dean Wesley Smith

boots) to "hot" meaning just this side of full erotica.

Nothing in this issue gets to "hot" levels, but a few places I sort of get in the neighborhood.

Also, as a form of playing with this issue, I have three stories that actually were published under pen names or my name and the publications went out of business almost instantly after publication.

All the rights were reverted and it wasn't until just lately I went back and looked at them again and realized I liked them. All three of them, actually. Two are science fiction and the other is a western. The science fiction stories have a little sex in them, so the varied genres fit perfectly with *Smith's Monthly* and the sex scenes in two (actually only hinted at in one) fit perfectly with the novel in this issue.

And now these stories can finally have a few more readers. They had almost no readers at all when they first came out.

Also, in this issue, I'm starting something new. I've been writing brand new stories for every volume of the *Fiction River Anthology Series*. I figured now, after doing that for a year, I would spotlight stories that I wrote that have only been in *Fiction River*, starting with the first volume that came out a year ago.

I won't do this feature every month, but I'm proud of all the stories I wrote for Fiction River and would like them to get some new readers.

However, if you are not subscribing to *Fiction River*, you are missing some great stories by a lot of great writers from around the world.

Thanks for putting up with my craziness. I hope you are enjoying the ongoing volumes of *Smith's Monthly* as much as I am writing the stories and novels and putting out the volumes.

Dean Wesley Smith
January 6, 2014
Lincoln City, Oregon

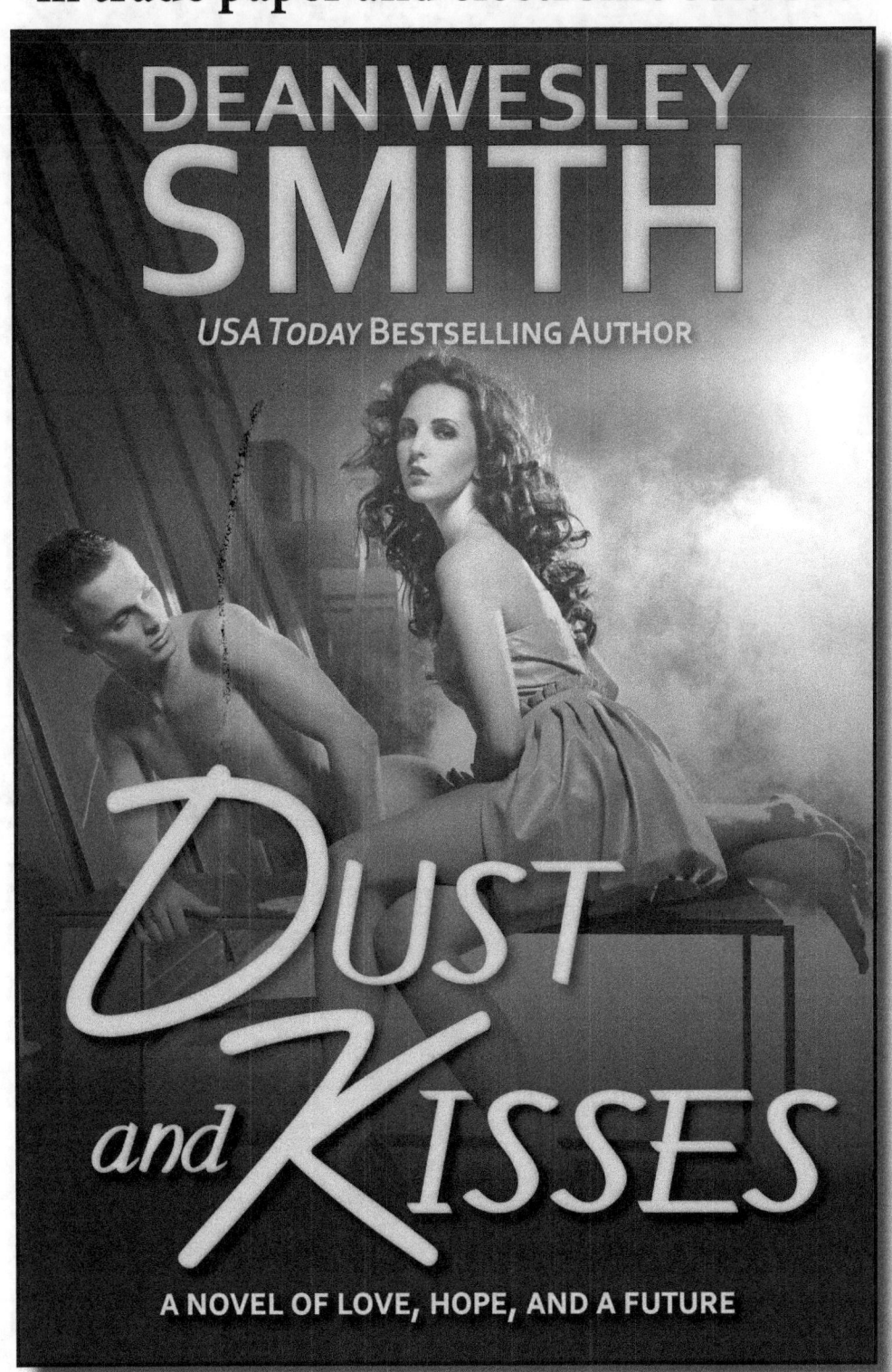

DEAN WESLEY SMITH

USA *Today* BESTSELLING AUTHOR

Dust and Kisses

A NOVEL OF LOVE, HOPE, AND A FUTURE

USA Today Bestselling Writer

DEAN WESLEY SMITH

IF SEX IS ALL A DREAM, THEN WHO CLEANS UP THE MESS?

Science Fiction With a Twist...

*USA **Today** **BESTSELLING WRITER** turns science fiction on its head with a strange sexual journey through space.*

It seemed like such a simple cargo run between systems for Sabrina and her husband. No passengers, lots of great alone-time for a couple in love to enjoy each other. What more could they ask for?

But then the cargo rebelled. And you thought sex caused a mess before.

(Note: This story appeared once before in an anthology from a company that went out of business when the book appeared and only authors in the book saw the story. But I liked this story, so here it is again. This does have sexual content.)

IF SEX IS ALL A DREAM, THEN WHO CLEANS UP THE MESS?

SABRINA KNEW she was dreaming when the vast green ocean of smooth water that covered the blue planet rippled like someone had dropped a stone in it, obscuring her reflection, turning her from a young woman to one with wrinkles and shimmering skin. Then the ripples sucked back in on themselves, as they can only do in a dream, and the ocean became smooth again, showing her almost-true face in the reflection as she drifted through the air.

She had long hair in this dream, not short and cut tight against her scalp like she had kept it for the last four years. And her nose was shorter, just like she'd always wished.

And her hips were narrower.

And she was naked.

And hungry.

She could see fish swimming down under the water, smiling up at her with the face of her old history teacher back in college on Earth. She could eat one of them, but she doubted they would taste very good, since she had always hated his classes.

Ahead she could see a small island, with two large trees and a man standing under one tree. The next instant she stood beside him under the other tree, the shade making her nipples hard and goosebumps form on her arms. The man was her husband, Lyman, and he was naked as well. He was taller than her, and looked even more handsome than she thought he looked normally. His blue eyes seemed to shine with extra light, and his dark hair blew in the breeze.

She realized she was hungry for him, not food.

"Sabrina," he said, "you're naked and dreaming and thinking about sex and I like your hair longer and your nose shorter."

"I know," she said as a giant fish six feet long flopped up on the shore between them. Instantly it started to smell foul, as if rotting and burning at the same time.

It stared at her with one fish-eye, as if daring her to get near it, to get past it to be near her husband. She tried.

And tried.

But no matter how hard she wanted sex with her husband, she couldn't get past the smell to be near him, to touch his body, to feel him inside her, to let him touch her shorter nose.

The stench became like a cloud, filling the air, choking her, forcing her to her knees. This was quickly becoming a nightmare, not a dream. She had to wake up.

Like swimming for the surface of a deep ocean, she fought to come out of the sleep. She blinked and opened her eyes, staring at the ceiling over her bed. Thank heavens she was awake.

But the smell was still there.

Rotting fish and burning trash.

"What...?"

She tried to push the dream back and clear the sleep from her head. She was in their private cabin on board their charter ship, the Sweet Adele. They were on a five day run to the colony on Daring Three. No passengers this time, just three plastic crates of cargo. High paying cargo, but cargo.

They were the only two on board, but if there had been a major problem with the ship, or a fire on board, the alarms would have ripped her from the bed. Clearly the ship's sensors didn't think the smell was a major problem.

Lyman was beside her, tossing and turning as if in a nightmare. He had kicked the covers down to a point just below his waist, exposing his firm stomach, hard chest, and just a hint of pubic hair. She liked making love right after they woke up. And over the last four days of this trip, they had made love a lot. But just like in her dream, that smell wasn't going to allow her to pull that blanket even lower at the moment.

She grabbed his shoulder and shook him. "Lyman! Wake up. We have a problem."

He didn't want to come awake.

"Lyman!" She shook him really hard that time. "We have a problem!"

He jerked and opened his green eyes. "Wow, that was a weird dream..." Suddenly he sat up. "What's that smell?"

"That's the problem," she said.

By the time he had on his pants and shoes, she had put on a halter top, a pair of shorts, and her shoes and was headed out the door. In the main corridor that ran the length of their thin, long ship, the smell was even worse. It choked her and she covered her nose in a useless defense.

"Has to be coming from the cargo," Lyman said.

She turned and headed for the cargo bay with Lyman right beside her. With every step it felt as if she was climbing a steeper and steeper slope, slick with slime and goo. The air seemed to get thicker and thicker, holding her back.

Finally she stopped and leaned against the bulkhead, not wanting to breathe in any more of the foulness that surrounded her. The cargo bay door was still a good twenty paces ahead.

Lyman stopped beside her, his face white and sick-looking.

"What do you think is holding us back?" she asked, barely managing to keep the snack she had eaten before going to bed in her stomach. The smell was so bad now, it was as if she had put her head inside a rotting fish, and then stuck pieces of it up her nose.

"I have no idea," he said. "Let's get back to the control room."

She nodded. They had access to the security cameras there, as well as environmental suits. Together they turned around and headed away from the cargo bay.

Suddenly it seemed as if the air was pushing them, helping them move faster and faster down the corridor, as if they were in a strong river and the current was rushing them toward something. It was the strangest thing she had ever felt.

By the time they reached the control room at the other end of the Sweet Adele's long central corridor, the smell was very weak, the intensity of it gone from everything but memory. There was no way she would ever forget that smell. She may never eat another fish as long as she lived.

Lyman shut the door to the control room behind him, clearly hoping to keep the smell out. She doubted that would work. The control room was as comfortable to her as her living room in her parents' home when growing up. Over the past five years she and Lyman had made the Sweet Adele their home, making hundreds of runs in this area of space, ferrying passengers and cargo. And lots of strange things had happened, but never anything like this.

Usually they took on up to a dozen passengers, ferrying them from the Bank System to the interstellar jump hub in the Dawson System. But two days ago a man named Garren Fore had hired them to take three large crates to Daring Three, a small, out-of-the-way colony world. He had paid full price for the ship, and added a nice bonus for on-time delivery.

He had demanded that no passengers be taken, as if anyone was in a rush to go to Daring Three anyway. He just wanted the three crates to be the only thing aboard and was willing to pay for it, which had been fine with Sabrina and Lyman. They had both figured to spend the time catching up on work and making love. And for the first four days, they had done just that. It had been wonderful. Now it seemed their cargo wasn't going to be so trouble-free as they expected.

Lyman moved over to the communications panel and punched up the security images of the cargo bay. The three crates were no longer secured ten paces apart. Somehow, they had moved together and merged, as if they had always been one unit.

A pool of liquid covered the floor around them. The same color as the ocean in her dream. The thought made her shudder.

The rest of the cargo bay looked as if it had been sprayed with slime-like paste. It was going to take a long time to clean up that mess.

"How did they get like that?" She asked, staring at the three crates. Only she and Lyman were on this ship, yet something had moved those crates together.

"I have no idea," Lyman said. He flicked through five different images of the crates, looking at them from all sides.

They seemed to be the standard, hard plastic crates used to ship everything from food to medical supplies. Except now they were fused together somehow, the hard plastic melted and reformed.

And there was no telling what was going to happen next. Maybe they should have been just a little more insistent on knowing what was in those crates before they started. But the money Fore had offered had been so good, it just didn't seem important enough to push the issue.

The smell in the room was starting to get worse. Clearly they were running out of time.

Lyman moved over and put the environmental controls on higher pressure for the control room. That would help keep the airflow moving outward from them. But she doubted that would do much good, either. It wouldn't be long until the entire ship was contaminated. They had to do something and do it quickly. But what? Against what? A smell?

Sabrina laughed at the thought. She moved to the communications panel and opened a channel to the communications hub on Banks Two. She knew it would be a very costly expense. Any sub-space conversation costs a lot per second, but this seemed to be the time to spend the money. Besides, Fore was going to pay for it if she had her way.

After the standard ten second jump-lag setting up the link, the officer on duty appeared on the screen. "Channel open and tied in. Go ahead Sweet Adele."

"We need to make an emergency call to a Mr. Garren Fore." She gave the officer Fore's communication link information and waited as the screen went blank.

Lyman moved over beside her and stood with his hand on her shoulder. Clearly he agreed with what she was doing. As far as she could see, they had no other choice. They had to know what was in those crates, so they could figure out a way to fight what was happening.

When Fore's weathered and wrinkled face appeared on the screen and saw her, he actually paled and swallowed. "Is there a problem with my cargo?"

"You tell me," she said, sending him the image of the cargo bay and the three fused crates. Then she said, "We can't get near them for some reason, and the smell is enough to choke a pig."

Fore looked almost angry, not at her, but clearly at himself. "This wasn't supposed to have happened."

"No kidding," Sabrina said. "So how about starting from the beginning and tell us exactly what is in those crates and what is happening."

Fore nodded. "Ever hear of Pelagic Prime?"

She nodded and glanced up at Lyman, who clearly had also heard of the planet.

"The water-world in the Bella System," Sabrina said.

"What is in the crates are a dozen Elucidations from Pelagic Prime," Fore said.

"Fish?" Sabrina asked. The idea stunned her.

"Very special fish," Fore said. "Telepathic fish for a scientist on Daring Three."

"Telepathic fish?" Sabrina almost laughed, but somehow managed to contain it. Around them the smell was getting worse.

> *"Your ship will survive," Fore said. "I'm more worried about you two."*

"So what's going on in our cargo bay?" Lyman asked, leaning down beside her so his face was captured on the com-link camera.

"The Elucidations are mating," Fore said simply. "This wasn't supposed to start for another ten days."

"Wonderful," Sabrina said. "Smelly fish sex."

Fore said nothing.

"And they have the power to fuse plastic and hold us away?" Lyman asked.

"They do," Fore said. "Their telepathic and telekinetic abilities are fantastic when they are mating."

"Nothing gets in the way of their having sex, huh?" Sabrina said, not really wanting to believe what Fore was telling her.

"Basically, yes," Fore said. "It developed as a necessity on their home world. Their power is what we are trying to study."

"But they jumped the gun," Lyman said, "on the mating part."

"And smelled up our ship," Sabrina said.

"Your ship will survive," Fore said. "I'm more worried about you two."

"You want to explain what you mean by that?" Lyman said, his voice cold and angry.

Fore nodded. "In a short time the odor will overcome you. You will either suffocate or fall into a very, very deep sleep from which you will never wake up."

"So we just dump the cargo bay into space," Lyman said.

Sabrina agreed.

"Have you tried that yet?" Fore said.

"No, but I'm thinking we should."

"It won't work," Fore said. "Take a look at the images from the cargo bay. See the slime covering everything. That's a protective cocoon the fish create around themselves during this time. Blowing the cargo hatch would do no good, since that slime layer will hold them in place."

"Wonderful," Lyman said, staring at the screen and the image of their messed-up cargo bay.

"And how were your people on Daring Three going to deal with this problem?" Sabrina asked.

"They are prepared with environmental suits capable of keeping all outside influences out."

She glanced over at Lyman, who caught where she was going.

"We have a full environmental suite on this ship," Lyman said, "built for passengers who couldn't mingle with our normal air. Would that help?"

"Completely self-contained?" Fore asked.

"Completely," Lyman said.

They had added in the suite in case they needed to transport any medical patients. They hadn't had to use it yet other than as a normal passenger room.

"It would keep you alive for a while," Fore said.

"We can program the auto-pilot to take up a standard orbit when reaching Daring Three," Lyman said. "Can your people take care of your cargo at that point?"

"We can," Fore said, "if you give me the information on how to open your cargo bay doors from the outside when your ship arrives. My people will be able to remove the Elucidations to a safe place."

Sabrina felt even more shivers run up her back. "And just what are we going to be doing in the mean time?"

"Sleeping," Fore said, his dark eyes not blinking.

"And why would we be doing that?" Lyman asked.

"Because you will have no choice," he said.

"Oh," she said.

"How much time do we have?"

"Can you smell anything?"

"Yes," she said. Clearly Lyman's attempt to set up a counter-flow of air out of the control room wasn't doing much good.

"The effects of the Elucidation mating spreads as time goes on," Fore said, "and becomes far more intense. The quicker you get into that suite, the more chance you have of survival."

Sabrina had a very clear memory of trying to push toward the cargo bay in that smell. Fore clearly knew what they were dealing with. And there would be time later for making her believe there was such a thing as telepathic fish.

"Got it," Lyman said.

They both set to work as each minute the smell grew more and more intense.

It took Lyman ten minutes to completely program the auto-pilot for the approach and orbit of Daring Three, then place a back-up program in the computer, plus send Fore the details of how to override all ship's systems if necessary.

While he was doing that, Sabrina was giving Fore the codes for entering the cargo bay area from the outside, as well as three other hatches, and then she scrounged together some medical supplies and extra food for the environmental room.

The smell was choking the corridor outside the control room when fifteen minutes later Lyman shut and secured the double airlock door to the environmental room, locking them inside.

She sat down on the bed and looked around the small cabin. There was a closet, a sink and bathroom area, a dresser built into the wall, and a large bed. She could almost imagine the sound of the environmental systems behind the wall to the right recycling all their air. They were going to have to be in here for the next twenty-seven hours while the Sweet Adele set its own orbit around Daring Three and strangers boarded her and took off the fused crates.

In her entire life she had never felt so helpless.

Lyman moved over and sat down beside her. "Jailed on our own ship."

"Yeah," she said. "And by telepathic alien fish with bad body odor."

"And too much sex drive," he said, smiling at her.

"There can never be too much sex drive," she said.

"Why'd I know you'd say that?" Lyman said, putting his arm around her and holding her.

His body felt wonderful holding her. Until that moment she had not realized just how much this situation had scared her. For some reason, even jailed on their own ship, when in his arms she felt secure. And safe.

They sat like that for a few moments, then Lyman pulled away and headed for the bathroom. She stretched out on the bed, staring at the ceiling. The next twenty-seven hours were going to crawl by, that was for sure. She just didn't believe that they would be forced to sleep the entire way.

A few moments later Lyman lay down beside her and she snuggled against him.

"What are we going to do for twenty-seven hours?" she asked.

"Oh, I have a few ideas," he said, squeezing her, "for at least as long as we are awake.

She smiled at him, then kissed him hard to let him know she liked at least one of his ideas. And if this kept up, she planned on being awake the entire time.

Then she snuggled against him, feeling safe.

She closed her eyes, trying to make herself relax.

A moment later she was asleep.

And dreaming again.

This time she was alone in her dream, back on the island in the middle of the vast green ocean. There was no smell, no fish, and no Lyman. Just water and sand and palm trees.

She moved to the edge of the water, looking down at her reflection in the glass-like surface. She was naked. Again her hair was long, her waist narrower, and her nose shorter. When they got out of this fish mess, she was going to have to grow her hair long. Clearly these dreams were telling her she wanted it that way.

There wasn't much she could do about her hips though. Or her nose.

"Nice ass."

She turned around to see Lyman standing naked behind her.

"You fell asleep as well?"

"Seems that way," he said. He glanced around. "I like this island better without the smelly fish."

"Yeah, me too," she said, moving up to him and pressing her naked body against his.

If this was a dream, it was the best-feeling dream she had ever had. His body hardened against her, his skin seemed to almost melt into hers. Every inch of her skin felt alive under his touch.

His hand went to her breasts, stroking them, making them feel wanted and cared for, then moved to her crotch.

At his first touch the orgasm overwhelmed her as she lost herself in the movement of his fingers.

Back and forth, back and forth.

The orgasm was small and sharp and wonderful, like a sampling taste before a big meal.

Behind them the waves started to roll up on the beach, lapping at the sand, matching the movements of his hand and the pulses of her orgasm.

After her mind cleared, she kissed him hard, letting him hold her up as the ocean calmed.

Then she took him by the hand and led him back toward one of the palm trees where a blanket lay covering the sand. Even in her dreams she was being practical not wanting sand in places where sand shouldn't be.

She pushed him down on the blanket and started kissing him, first on his lips, then his neck, then his chest, then his stomach, then his hard penis.

Above them the clouds rolled over, rumbling and boiling like angry watchers as she brought him, and herself, nearer and nearer.

After what seemed like only a few moments, yet at the same time was just the right amount of foreplay, a full hurricane pounded down on the island, whipping the waves up over them, snapping off the palm trees, yet never touching them on the blanket.

She could feel he was about to come, so she intensified her actions with her mouth on him, and her own hand on herself.

As his first explosion filled her, she had her second orgasm.

The wind picked up the island, spinning it through the air over the ocean as wave-after-wave of orgasm shook them both.

On the blanket she could feel nothing but the pleasure of her own orgasm, and her husband's pulsing hardness.

The moment seemed to last for hours and hours, all wrapped into the seconds, confused as all time is in dreams.

Finally the island dropped back to the water and she crawled up and lay beside him, stroking his chest softly. He held her, not letting her go, making her feel safe and warm and cared for.

"I like this dream," she said to him.

"I like to dream with you," he said.

He rolled her over on her back and knelt between her legs. The waves on the ocean around them had just begun to calm when he slid inside her, pushing her down into the blanket and sand with all his weight.

Suddenly a massive wave crashed over them both as she lost herself in the feel of his hardness inside her.

He filled her with life, with energy, with desire.

The wave pulled them off the island and under the water, letting them float to the soft ocean floor as he kept pushing into her, then pulling almost all the way out, then pushing in again.

Above them the storm raged, but the ocean protected them, made them feel safe and secure and together as they made love.

She could feel her husband's movements getting more insistent, and at the same time another orgasm was building for her as well.

Under them the floor of the ocean pushed them upward, closer to the storm raging just above the surface.

Lyman moved faster and faster, pumping into her.

She met his every thrust, pushing back, harder and harder.

Until finally she was coming again, even harder and more intensely than before.

The ocean bottom shoved them into the storm, thrusting them into the air, up through the clouds, and into the intense blackness of space.

The pulsing of her orgasm matched Lyman's.

All the stars around them pulsed with her orgasm.

Bright.

Dim.

Bright.

Dim.

The orgasm lasted and lasted, seemingly for all time.

Galaxies crashed, and then were reborn around them.

Stars went nova, new systems were formed.

Finally, as the universe cooled and their orgasms faded, they spun back toward the ocean planet. They dropped onto the island, landing on the beach, on the blanket next to the calming ocean.

She looked up into her husband's face and had nothing to say. What could you say after sex so great that the Big Bang paled in comparison?

He moved off her and lay down on the blanket. "That was nice."

"Nice?" she asked, looking over at his smiling face. He was clearly teasing her.

"You want to see nice, try this," she said. She climbed on him, straddling his hard penis, letting it sink inside her once again, only this time she was in control. And she would take him to parts of the universe neither of them could ever imagine, even in this dream.

She started to move on him, her gaze locked on his, when suddenly he vanished.

She was empty, kneeling on the blanket.

"Lyman!" she shouted, the panic filling her heart.

"Sabrina!"

She could hear his voice, but it seemed like it came from a long distance away.

She stood and looked out over the glass-calm surface of the ocean. Why had he left her? Where had he gone?

"Sabrina!"

His voice carried over the water.

"Wake up!"

The ground shook and then she realized the dream was about to end. She didn't want it to end, but she had to see what Lyman wanted. Then they could come back. They had plenty of time before they reached Daring Three.

With that thought she opened her eyes.

Lyman was staring down at her, smiling. Beside him stood a strange man she didn't know wearing a protective suit of bright silver.

"Good," the man said. "She's going to be all right." He turned and keyed in a com-link. "All clear."

"Am I still dreaming?" she asked, her throat dry.

"No, you're not," the man said, smiling at her.

"We're in orbit over Daring Three," Lyman said. "We made it!"

"And the fish?" she said, sitting up with Lyman's help. Every muscle in her body seemed to ache.

"Being taken off the ship now," he said. "But we had to be awake to make sure we weren't taken with them."

"Taken with them?" she asked.

The man nodded. "I'm sure Mr. Fore will explain it to you when he arrives. Something about your minds being lost."

"Nice of him to mention that possibility," she said.

The guy in the silver suit laughed.

"So we were asleep and dreaming for twenty-seven hours?" She couldn't believe that was possible.

"Yeah," Lyman said. "Strange, huh? But wonderful." He smiled at her, a twinkle in his eye. Clearly he had had the same dream.

She could still feel the beach, the wonderful sex, the exploding orgasms. She leaned in and kissed her husband as hard as she could. She wanted him to crawl up inside her, to take them both back to the dream.

He kissed her back, hard and passionately, the real feeling of him now even more wonderful than the dream.

The man in the silver suit laughed. "I'll excuse myself now," he said. "The effect of the dream will fade with time."

Lyman broke the kiss and turned to the man standing in the doorway. "How long?"

"A few hours," the man said.

"Time enough," Lyman said.

She couldn't agree more. "Pull that door closed behind you."

The man in silver nodded. "Will do. Just no sleeping until we get the Elucidations to the surface."

They both laughed.

"Trust me," she said. "Sleeping is the farthest thing from our minds."

As the man in the silver suit pulled the door closed, she turned back to her husband and gave him a long, hard, kiss that was the start of a wonderful adventure in sex, time, and space.

Two hours later, as they lay there in each other's arms, she asked, "You ever thought of getting an aquarium for the ship?"

His laughter started them both all over again.

~

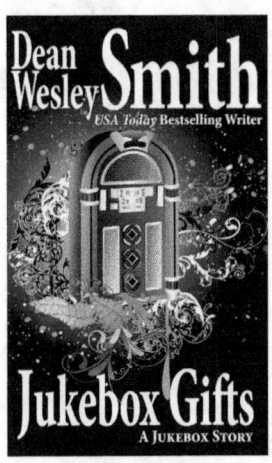

USA *Today* Bestselling Writer

DEAN WESLEY SMITH

THAT LOST RIDDLE

A Poker Boy Story

SINCE THIS ISSUE has all sorts of new features in it, including some sex in science fiction, I figured why not continue to be strange. So I have decided to include my Fiction River *stories, one per issue, until I catch up to* Fiction River. *From that point, it will be one every other month.*

I am proud of the stories I had in Fiction River *and I wanted them to be here as well as the months go along. "The Lost Riddle" came from the very first volume,* Fiction River: Unnatural Worlds.

Poker Boy finds himself taken by his boss, Stan the God of Poker, to Reno on a surprise mission for the team of superheroes. But little did they know that the puzzle wasn't the mission, but something far stranger.

THAT LOST RIDDLE
A Poker Boy Story

OUT OF THIN AIR I heard Stan, the God of Poker say, "Knock, knock."

It wasn't a bad joke. It was how he asked to come into my private doublewide trailer up in the woods in Oregon. It seems that when Stan teleported, he couldn't just drop in outside and then use the door to actually knock on. But he was a God, and my boss, so I supposed he could do just about anything he wanted, even make bad "knock-knock" sounds in thin air in my living room. I was only Poker Boy, a lowly superhero. Not much I could say about it.

I pushed aside the cold fried chicken I had been eating while sitting on my old green couch and watching the evening news out of Portland. "Come on down."

Stan appeared beside my couch and glanced around, shaking his head. He always did that when he came here. He just didn't understand why someone with as much money as I had (and as many superpowers) would keep an old, 1970s-furnished doublewide trailer in the Oregon Coastal Mountains, even if it was within a half mile of a casino.

It was the green couch and chair and shag carpet that did it for most people, not counting the fake wood paneling on the wall. I figured if I waited long enough the styles would come around.

The last time Stan had come here he suggested I put a felt painting of dogs playing poker on the wall. I was considering it.

My girlfriend and sidekick, Patty Ledgerwood, aka Front Desk Girl, couldn't figure out why I liked this place either, now that she knew how much money I really did have. I discovered I had a vast amount when Patty made me go through it and lay it all out for her. I hadn't bothered to total it in a decade. I just kept adding to it.

Even though I could afford a couple dozen mansions, I liked this old place, even though Patty said it smelled of faint mold and pine trees. It reminded me of my early days as a poker player and superhero. The old furniture and funky smell sort of kept me grounded. I said that to Patty once and she just shook her head and muttered something about how the place kept me actually in the dirt.

Needless to say, we spent most nights in her wonderful and very large apartment in Las Vegas, furnished with the best and most modern furniture, thick carpet, and views of Las Vegas that were tough to beat.

I usually only came up here while she was working and I was waiting for a tournament to start. Instantly jumping from Las Vegas to the mountains of Oregon was one of the many advantages of being able to teleport.

Stan didn't say anything after his disgusted look at my place. He was wearing his standard tan sweater, tan slacks, and loafers. He looked so nondescript, he could blend in anywhere and no one would notice him. I had a hunch if he stood in my trailer long enough, his sweater and slacks would turn 1970s green.

I took one more bite of the cold chicken leg, then stood and headed for the coat hanger beside the front door to get my black leather coat and black fedora-like hat. They were my superhero uniform that helped make me Poker Boy.

Stan only came here to get me when something was going wrong somewhere. Never a good sign. So the coat and hat were going to be needed for something very soon.

"So where to?" I asked as I slipped on my coat.

"You look like you need a drink," he said.

"What?" He knew I didn't drink. Never had and I sure couldn't see myself starting now.

I was about to say something about going back to my chicken and news when Stan jumped us to position beside a large white-marble pillar with people walking by. There were slot machines and a nearby restaurant. I could feel the power from the casino around us flowing into me.

The air smelled of prime rib and faint cigarette smoke. It took me only a second before I realized we were on the second floor, the mezzanine level, of the Eldorado Hotel and Casino in downtown Reno, Nevada.

To my left along the interior mall-like area was the Silver Legacy Hotel and Casino and beyond that the Circus Circus Hotel and Casino.

This interior mall area stretched for a very long three blocks and must have a couple dozen restaurants, shops and gift stores along its wide corridor. It was a nice place considering Reno's weather in the winter, allowing people to move between the three casinos without ever going outside.

I had always liked this interior mall and the feel of it. Some people said it reminded them of a huge cruise ship, only without ocean views and people getting seasick.

I glanced around. No one had noticed our arrival so I figured Stan had jumped us into a blind camera area.

"Back with your girlfriend in a moment," Stan said and vanished, leaving me alone.

I had no idea what the problem was, or why we were in Reno, but if he was going for Patty when she was still at work, I knew it couldn't be good.

I stepped away from the stone pillar and let my poker senses take in everything around me. A few people upset at losing, and one couple went past not happy, headed for the Silver Legacy. I caught part of a conversation about how the guy was angry with his wife flirting with another man. He was telling her so in no uncertain terms. It wasn't hard to miss, even without extra poker senses.

But I could sense nothing that would cause Stan to jump us to Reno and into the Eldorado.

Across from me was a brewpub full of younger patrons laughing and drinking. I'm not sure exactly when I started thinking of adults around age thirty as younger, but I did. Since I have been told that as a superhero, I have basically stopped aging at thirty even though I am over forty, I have no idea how jaded I was going to get by the time I reached one hundred.

Or two-hundred-plus like Patty. She still hadn't told me her real age. She just shook her head and said it didn't matter every time I asked. She didn't look a day over thirty either, but knowing there might be a few hundred years in age difference sometimes actually bothered me.

I felt a hand on my shoulder and the calming sense of Patty's touch. That was one of her super powers and I loved it.

And her. More than I wanted to admit to myself at times. We just fit together in seemingly every sense.

I turned around to look into her beautiful brown and very worried eyes. She was still dressed in the uniform of the MGM Grand Hotel front desk. A black skirt, white blouse and MGM dark vest with their hotel emblem on the right side.

Her long brown hair was pulled back tight as she kept it while working.

"Any idea what's going on?"

I shook my head, keeping my poker senses on full. I didn't quite have a "Spider-Sense" like Spider-Man did in the comics, but I had a pretty good ability to know when danger was approaching and right now I could feel nothing.

"Where is Stan?" I asked.

"He went to get Screamer," she said.

"This can't be good," I said.

She nodded.

A moment later Stan appeared next to the stone column in the dead camera area. Screamer was with him looking just as puzzled.

Screamer had the ability to touch someone and get into their mind and their thoughts. He didn't have a distinctive look, more like Stan with the ability to blend into just about anywhere. He usually wore old jeans and a sweatshirt with the UNLV logo on it and tonight was no exception.

Screamer had gotten his name from his ability to put images into other people's heads. He often worked for the police and could put images so bad and so real into a suspect's mind that he could make the most hardened criminal scream. What he did could never stand up in a court, but he had solved a lot of crimes over the years.

And he had helped this team save the world a few times as well.

"All right," Stan said. "Let's go."

He turned toward the short staircase leading down around an ornate fountain and into another section of the Eldorado Hotel and Casino mezzanine level.

> *If we survived whatever we were facing, we were going to need to have a talk about her powers.*

"What are we doing here?" Screamer asked a moment before I could.

"Going for a drink," Stan said, his voice almost lost in the sounds of the multiple fountains.

Patty just shook her head and I followed them, keeping every sense I had on full alert. And that was a lot of senses, so many in fact I hadn't named them all. But the one right now I was trusting the most was my danger awareness sense.

And it was flat coming up blank.

We went past a gift shop, down another short flight of stairs, and toward what looked to be a combination bakery counter, restaurant on the right, and bar in the back on the left, tucked against the wall.

Suddenly Patty said, "Sherri."

Her uniform morphed into a black dress, her hair flowed into a perfect shape around her head, and black high heels replaced her tennis shoes she wore while working.

All in the space of one step.

I had no idea she could do that.

None at all.

And we'd been together now for a few years. If we survived whatever we were facing, we were going to need to have a talk about her powers.

"Oh, no," Screamer said as Stan headed toward the bar past the huge counter full of very tasty-looking pies and cakes and cinnamon rolls coated an inch deep in white frosting. The entire area smelled of fresh bread, making my stomach rumble and me wish I had taken a few more bites of that cold chicken.

"Come on, Stan, why?" Screamer asked.

Stan said nothing. Just kept walking.

Stan reached the bar and pulled up a barstool. Screamer sat on his left, Patty took the spot on his right, and I took the spot next to Patty.

I could still sense absolutely nothing wrong, but from Patty's sudden change and Screamer's comment, they were clearly sensing something I wasn't.

And that scared me more than I wanted to admit.

We sat there in silence with the sounds of the distant casino echoing faintly in the background. It must have only been a few seconds, but it felt like an eternity.

The bar was a normal wood bar, pretty wide, and even though it looked rustic, it was polished as smooth as glass. We were the only customers sitting at it. There were three empty stools to my right. It felt really, really strange to be sitting at a bar. I just never did this.

Bottles of varied booze lined the ornate back bar, blocking most of a mirror that made the area seem bigger. The top of the back bar was also a rustic ornate wood as were all the decorations on both sides of it.

This kind of bar could have been in any one of a thousand places. It actually seemed a little out of place with all the desserts in a huge counter ten paces behind us. It felt like it belonged more in an Old West saloon in a movie. A long ways from the smell of baking bread and ringing modern slot machines.

I was about to say something when a door into a back room swung open and a stunning woman emerged carrying a few bottles of vodka. She wore tan slacks, a white short-sleeve blouse, and an apron with the Eldorado Hotel logo on it. Her pitch-black hair was pulled back tight and I caught a glimpse of a dark tattoo on her shoulder and upper arm.

And she might have been one of the most beautiful women I had ever seen.

"Hey, Stan," she said, smiling in a way that could knock down just about anyone with its radiance.

Now my warning senses were going off and going off strong. If she was sitting across from me in a poker tournament, I would be very, very careful even being in a hand with her. She had power. More than likely she was a superhero or maybe a god.

But I caught no threat at all of danger from her. Just warnings about her power.

Stan nodded and didn't return the smile. "Sherri," was all he said.

She put down the bottles, wiped her hands on a white bar towel and slipped a bar napkin in front of Stan.

"Great seeing you," she said. "I suppose Mom sent you and your team here."

"She did," Stan said, again nodding.

"Well, I appreciate you coming," she said, smiling. "Thanks."

I wanted to shout out "Mom?" but then realized the only woman who could order Stan, the God of Poker around, was Laverne, Lady Luck herself. I now had a hunch suddenly who I was facing. I hadn't known going into a previous mission that

Lady Luck had a daughter, so I suppose it shouldn't surprise me that she had two.

Or more for all I knew.

When this was over, I really needed to ask some very pointed questions about the family trees of some of my bosses.

Sherri put a bar napkin in front of Screamer, the smile turning a little sad on her face.

"I miss you," she said.

He only nodded just slightly, his gaze holding hers.

She missed him?

What in the world was going on? If this Sherri was Lady Luck's daughter, having both Stan and Screamer have strange reactions to her didn't seem like much of a good start to whatever we were facing here.

She shrugged and moved to a spot in front of Patty. She slid a napkin in front of her and smiled, the smile actually reaching her eyes. "Patty Ledgerwood I presume. I've heard so many good things about you and your work. You look stunning."

Patty smiled, blushed, and said nothing.

Sherri slid a napkin in front of me, her smile turning to something I couldn't read.

"So this is the famous Poker Boy I've been hearing so much about."

I kept my poker face and only nodded slightly.

She laughed. "You people sure aren't much for idle conversation, are you?"

"We're here," Stan said, his voice very controlled. "I don't understand why you are here, or what you need from us."

"I work here," she said, smiling. "I have now for about four years. Moved here from the Atlantis Casino. I worked there for ten years. Remember?"

She looked at Screamer and he just nodded.

She went on. "The management here keep offering to make me a bar manager, but I like keeping my hand in the drinks and talking with the customers."

Even though Stan had the best poker face that existed, I could tell he was surprised by that. If this was Lady Luck's daughter, I was surprised as well.

"And I didn't ask you to come here," Sherri said. "That was Mom's idea. She said you four might be able to help me with my lost riddle."

Stan said nothing, Screamer just shook his head, and Patty just smiled softly and stared at her.

Wow, was there a lot of history between these four. Clearly it had all happened long before I was born. And since Stan had been married to one of Lady Luck's daughters, more than likely he wasn't pleased to see this one either. So it looked like this was going to be up to me to figure out what she was talking about.

"So what's the riddle that your mom thought we could help you solve?" I asked. "And I assume I am talking with a daughter of Lady Luck. Correct?"

"Sherri," she said, giving me that beaming smile that I had no doubt melted some of the icing off a cinnamon role in the case behind me.

"The Queen of Clubs," Screamer said, his voice soft.

"Dear husband," Sherri said, a slight touch of hurt going to her eyes, even though she kept smiling. "You used to not like anyone calling me that name."

I was trying to deal with the fact that Screamer had been married to Lady Luck's second daughter at one point. Now all I had to do was figure out why

Patty had a problem with her and I might have a clue what was happening.

"So the riddle?" I asked, pulling her attention back to me. "What's so important about it?"

"It's lost," Sherri said over her shoulder to me as she moved fluidly down the bar to pour some drinks for a waitress that had come up to the waitress station in front of a bar well.

Sherri seemed to move faster than anyone I had ever seen, yet the waitress never once looked up. After only a moment, which I guessed had something to do with her slipping slightly out of time to do the drinks, she came back toward us wiping her hands on a bar towel. "Can I get any of you a drink?"

My three teammates sat silently, so I said, "Sure. Bloody Mary mix with no vodka."

"Celery?" she asked as she moved to the well again.

"Nope," I said.

As she finished my virgin drink, I studied her. Not one sense of danger, nothing from her, and she wasn't blocking me in any way. In fact, I wasn't getting that much sense that she actually had many powers at all, even though I assumed she was a god. Could it be that Lady Luck's daughter was only a superhero like I was? That didn't seem possible.

As she put the drink on my bar napkin and again wiped off her hands, I asked her a simple question. "What's so important about finding or solving the riddle?"

"It will lead me to a second key holding the Four Faces of Janus."

"Oh," was all I said.

Stan just shook his head.

Screamer sort of snorted in disgust and Patty again didn't move.

We had already gone into Elysium, the capital of the ancient race of the Titans, to rescue Sherri's sister, Helen

DEAN WESLEY SMITH

USA TODAY BESTSELLING AUTHOR

*M*ONUMENTAL *S*UMMIT

A SCIENCE FICTION NOVEL OF THE OLD WEST AND TRUE LOVE

the Queen of Hearts, who had gone there to get one of the keys that held the Four Faces of Janus.

Supposedly, legend says that when the four keys are combined, they will open the time lock and allow the Titans to return to their rightful place in time and space. Or something like that. Mythology and facts were sometimes hard to tell apart for me these days. I really, really needed to ask more questions about all this.

One thing I did know, the Titans' major city existed in the same location as Las Vegas, only many, many eons in the future. So their coming back to this time would be a pretty large problem that I doubted anyone wanted to face.

"Are all your sisters looking for a key?" Stan asked.

"Sure," Sherri said. "It's sort of a hobby for all four of us. We're giving the keys to Mom for safekeeping when we find them. We have no intention of bringing them together, especially after seeing the wonderful city the Titans are living in."

"And you four have only found the one key, right?" I asked, trying not to be too stunned at Lady Luck having four daughters. I really, really, really needed to talk with someone about who had been married to whom and who was a child of whom.

"Just the key that you four helped my sister return with from Elysium," Sherri said, "although I feel that if I could find the lost riddle, I would be able to retrieve the second one."

Her bright smile had now vanished and she was clearly thinking about her problem. And I had zero idea what she was talking about when she said a "lost riddle" and my glowering team was sure no help at the moment.

"How can a riddle be lost?" I asked, slightly fearful I was walking into some trap.

Sherri just shrugged. "Lost in time, maybe. Never written down. Lots of ways a riddle can be lost."

"So it's just called "The Lost Riddle?" I asked.

She nodded.

Now all four of us were just looking at her as she headed back down the bar to the right to serve drinks to another waitress who had arrived at the station there.

"Someone want to tell me what's going on?" I asked.

"I think she's finally lost it," Screamer said, shaking his head sadly.

"She's fantastically beautiful," Patty said. "More than I even remember."

I stared at my girlfriend for a moment, realizing she hadn't been mad at Sherri, she had just been in some sort of fan-girl state with her.

"She's serious, all right," Stan said. "And she's as sharp as she ever was, trust me."

"So why do you hate her so much?" I asked Stan.

He laughed, softly, something I rarely heard him do. "I don't hate her. My wife, her sister, thought I fell in love with Sherri and caused all sorts of problems that led to me leaving Helen."

"You didn't?" I asked. "Fall in love with Sherri, that is?"

Again Stan just laughed. "I don't even really know her, to be honest. And Sherri's been married to Screamer here for a very long time."

"Over two hundred years," Screamer said.

"And she left you?" I asked.

"No, I left her," he said. "When I

acquired this new power and could read all her thoughts every time I touched her. Staying together wasn't fair to either of us until we figured out how to deal with it all. We never got a divorce. It's been ten years now."

"So you are still married?" Patty asked, looking at Screamer, who nodded.

"Oh," was all I could say again.

I had been working with this team now for some time and seen the inside of Screamer's mind more than I wanted to think about, and he had kept all this blocked from me. Clearly he had gotten pretty good at walling off parts of his own thoughts.

"She's so beautiful," Patty said, almost sighing. "We have to help her."

Now both Stan and I were shaking our heads at my girlfriend. Everything was screwy about this assignment and it was making me slightly annoyed. No one was in danger, I wasn't saving anyone, not even a dog, and I wasn't playing in a poker tournament. So far all I could see was a complete waste of a perfectly good evening.

Sherri again came back to a place in front of us. "Will you help me?"

"A couple more questions," I said. "So you need this riddle to find the Janus key?"

She shook her head. "I know where the key is at."

"So why do you need the lost riddle?" I asked, almost afraid of the answer.

DEAD MONEY could be the start of a new thriller genre— the political poker thriller.

—Sheldon McArthur, former owner of Mysterious Books in Los Angeles

Available Now
from all your favorite booksellers in trade paper and electronic editions.

"Stan," Sherri said, smiling at my boss, "If you wouldn't mind taking us all out of time for a moment, I'll answer Poker Boy's question."

He shrugged and an instant later the sounds of the casino stopped around us. And so did everyone and everything else.

I loved being able to step between an instant of time. One of my abilities was also to take myself and others out of the natural time flow. But Stan was a ton better at it and wouldn't have to strain to hold this for hours.

Sherri pointed to a place in the air behind her and an image like a three-dimensional movie appeared.

"That's new," Screamer said, looking puzzled.

"Learned it from you, actually," Sherri said, smiling at her husband. "It's a projection from my mind."

"I can't do that," Screamer said.

Sherri looked almost longingly at her husband. "We both have our new powers. I would love to talk later."

I was starting to get the clear understanding that she wasn't a god, but only a superhero like three of us at the bar. And she was learning new superpowers as she went along just as all superheroes did.

She turned back to the image she was projecting in the air as everyone in the casino remained frozen in their instant of time around us.

The image showed what looked like an old ghost town from a height of about a thousand feet in the air.

"Virginia City," Sherrie said. "South and slightly east of here."

The view came down and focused on some old buildings, then flew inside like a bird going through a wall. "Yellow Jacket Mine," she said. "Part of what most people think of as the Comstock Lode."

The traveling view of the image floating in the air went straight down, under some water and finally came into a flooded huge cave.

Sherri went on narrating the tour that was coming from her own mind. "The Yellow Jacket Mine broke into this huge cave and couldn't contain the flooding and had to retreat. No pump could ever clear it. It's over three thousand feet under Virginia City and the water temperature is over one hundred and fifty degrees."

At the bottom of the huge cave was a stone stand with a clear glass bubble covering it and protecting what looked like a very old key from the water.

"That's the second Janus key," Sherri said, her voice wispy.

"Why couldn't these stupid keys ever be hidden above ground?" I asked, shaking my head. My warning senses were going off big time just looking at that key so far down underground and underwater.

"So why the lost riddle?" Patty asked, the spell of Sherri's beauty clearly now broken by the little tour underground.

The image of the submerged cave vanished and Sherri just shrugged. "Not a clue what the riddle does," she said. "Or even what it is or why it's lost. I just know it's attached to this key in some fashion. And we don't dare touch the key until we understand what the riddle is all about."

I just shook my head. "This is a very strange hobby you and your sisters have."

Sherri laughed high and light. "Don't you think I know that? But after you guys helped my sister get the first one, Mom thinks it would be a good idea to get all four of them and get them really protected. So she's trying to help us."

I didn't want to say that having a key three thousand feet underground in one-hundred-and-sixty degree water wasn't already pretty protected, but what did I know? Lady Luck thought this was important for some reason. And she was Stan's boss and Stan was my boss, so by that reasoning I thought this important as well.

Stan let us slip back into the normal stream of time and the noise from the restaurant and distant casino slammed back into use like a tidal wave. And the wonderful smells from the restaurant came back as well, making my stomach rumble again.

At the bottom of the huge cave was a stone stand with a clear glass bubble covering it and protecting what looked like a very old key from the water.

"Okay," I said, trying to grab onto something that made sense in all this. "Tell me when I get this wrong."

Stan and Patty nodded and Sherri and Screamer just sort of looked at each other.

I ignored them and started trying to check off what I knew. "The four keys each have one side of the face of Janus on them. Right?"

Sherri and Stan both nodded.

"Apart they keep the doors locked, the Titans in the future, and the war between the Gods and the Titans stopped," Sherri said.

"Got that," I said. "And no one wants to start that war again."

"Exactly," Stan said.

"Does this Janus still exist?"

"No," Sherri and Stan said at the same time. They clearly did not like that question and I made a note to ask what happened to him at a later date.

"So why would anyone associate a riddle with a key?" I asked. "And then lose all record of the riddle? I've only been around this superhero and god world for a short ten or so years and I've come to realize that all you folks have very long memories."

"Good question," Stan said. "But the battle between the Gods and the Titans was long before any of our times. Long before Atlantis."

I nodded to that. I still have never asked exactly how many years all this stretched back. Another question for another time in my history lesson.

I leaned back and just stared up at the back bar. No one else said a word and Sherri moved back down the bar to serve another waitress with a tray full of dirty glasses and a long order of fresh drinks.

I tried to ignore my rumbling stomach and my desire for a cinnamon roll and just think.

On the back bar were a number of bottles of Jack Daniels, all with different colors and added names on the labels.

There were other bottles of the same brand, but different types back there as well. I stared at that for a moment and then it suddenly hit me what we were dealing with.

Being able to put things that made no sense together to make sense was one of my super powers, it seemed, and if I was right, I had just done it again.

"Stan, could you call Laverne to come and help us?"

He nodded and a moment later, without him moving, Lady Luck appeared, taking the empty stool to my right.

In my fondest dreams as a poker player, it never would have occurred to me that I would be sitting at a bar with Lady Luck herself.

Sherri finished the orders and came down the bar as her mother appeared.

"You want your usual, Mom?" she asked, smiling. Clearly the two of them had a good relationship.

"Later, honey," Lady Luck said. "First I want to hear what Poker Boy has to say about all this."

For the first time in a long time I wished I actually drank. I had a hunch I could use one right now. I took a deep breath and turned toward one of the most powerful gods that existed and asked the question I needed to ask.

"Do the keys have names besides one, two, three, and four?"

Lady Luck looked at me for a moment, then laughed and said, "I don't know, but I know who to ask."

She vanished.

I decided I could breathe again. It felt good.

I took a sip out of my Virgin Bloody Mary as Patty touched my leg and sent a calming sense through me.

"You think the key might have a name?" Sherri asked, clearly puzzled.

Stan just smiled and Screamer sort of smiled. They had seen me ask these kind of questions before that got right to the heart of a problem.

"Just an idea," I said.

It seemed like forever, but then suddenly Lady Luck was again sitting at the bar beside me.

And she was laughing.

"The one you all retrieved from the Titan's city under Vegas was called Mystery. The two that have not been found yet are called Enigma and Dilemma."

Then Lady Luck smiled at Sherri. "The one you found, dear daughter, is called Riddle."

Sherri clapped her hands together and did a little dance as she laughed and smiled. "It's not protected!"

"I'll get it," Lady Luck said, smiling at the joy her daughter felt.

She vanished and then a moment later reappeared holding the key that had been under three thousand feet of Earth and very hot water. She wasn't wet at all.

She started to hand the key to her daughter who held her hands up. "I don't want to touch it. Just get it safe and sound."

"I will," Lady Luck said.

Then she turned to me. "Once again, Poker Boy, thank you. And to your team as well for taking the time to help with this."

It never got old having Lady Luck thank me for helping her.

Never.

Then Lady Luck looked down the bar at Screamer and smiled. "Talk to your wife. If you two got back together, she'd make a great addition to this team."

"Mom!" Sherri said, but Lady Luck was already gone.

For the first time Stan really laughed. And hard. And that also was a rare thing as well for the God of Poker.

"Great seeing you again, Sherri," Stan said. "And listen to your mother. We could use you." Then he vanished.

Sherri actually blushed.

Patty smiled at Sherri and then at Screamer and touched my leg. "Come on,

I'm dressed up and I think I need to do some dancing."

"Dancing?" I asked, looking at her. In all our time together she had never told me she liked to dance. Ever.

She winked at me and squeezed my leg just a little higher and I got the message. "Oh! Dancing."

A moment later we were in the living room of her apartment in Las Vegas, leaving Sherri and her husband alone in a crowded casino in Reno.

"Wasn't she beautiful?" Patty asked as she headed for her bedroom.

"Sherri?" I asked. "She was all right, but not as beautiful as you by a long ways."

"You sure know how to say the exact right things," Patty said.

She looked back over her shoulder at me and smiled a "dancing smile" as her dress vanished, leaving her totally naked and me totally speechless.

~

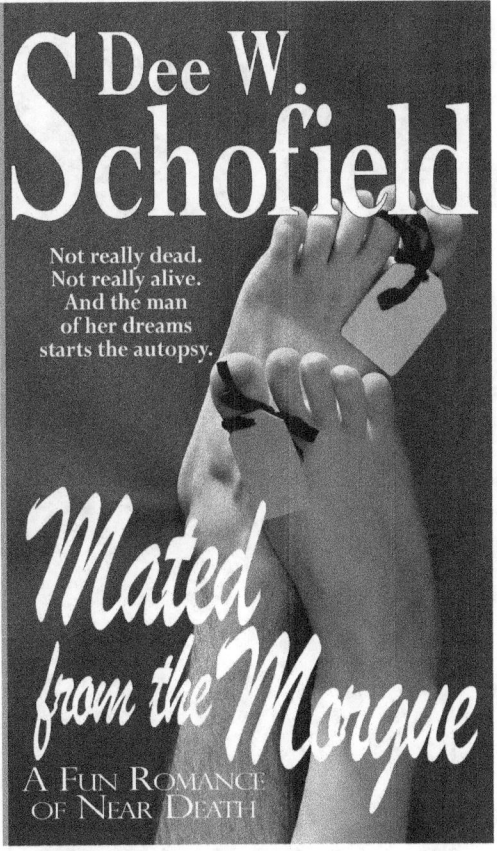

USA *Today* Bestselling Writer

DEAN WESLEY SMITH

THE LIFE AND TIMES OF BUFFALO JIMMY

Chapters 13-15

What Came Before...

Nineteen-year-old Boston native Jimmy Gray had been traveling with his parents and older brother, Luke, headed west to find a new home and new riches.

Before even reaching Independence, they were attacked and robbed by Jake Benson and his gang. Jimmy's parents were killed, his brother wounded.

In one of the wildest towns in all of American history, Jimmy Gray, a sheltered, educated son of a banker from Boston, suddenly finds himself very, very much alone.

But then, through some luck, he finds other young men about his age and down on their luck who might be able to help him.

Together, the five of them head west after Benson.

They end up hunting buffalo as he always dreamed of doing, but then they are hit with a massive flash flood and Jimmy is left alone, his friends more than likely dead.

THE LIFE AND TIMES OF BUFFALO JIMMY

Part Thirteen
ALONE AGAIN

THE MORNING LIGHT was barely allowing Jimmy to see the narrow side canyon around him. The air was bitingly cold, and Jimmy was soaking wet from the long night in the rain. He needed to get dry and warm quickly, before he got sick. He knew, without a doubt, that this kind of cold and wet could kill a man out here in the wilderness faster than any wild animal.

Faster than a killer like Benson.

Jimmy had to get dry and warm up as soon as he could, somehow.

In the faint light, he slowly eased himself and his two horses down off the rock ledge he had reached during the flood. The canyon was no more than a hundred paces across and the walls were as tall as three Boston banks. The stream flowing through the bottom of the canyon now was only a fast torrent, not at all dangerous-looking. But he could see the water-marks up the rock walls where the water had been last night in the flash flood. He had been lucky to survive. He had no idea how the rest of them could have.

Yesterday, there had been an easy path through the rocks. Now the way down to the main canyon and the wagon trail was completely blocked by boulders and brush and walls of mud. In one place, the water was flowing under some boulders that were far too big to get a horse over. It was clear he wasn't getting down the canyon and back to the river that way, at least not with two horses. He was going to need to find another way out.

He took a deep breath and shouted, "Zach! Long!"

His shout echoed among the rocks and then died under the sounds of the stream.

Nothing.

No one shouted back.

He had to keep believing they were alive. He had lost his parents, and left his sick brother Luke in Independence. He couldn't lose his friends as well. He had to find them.

Or at least find their bodies.

He shivered and felt light-headed. The cold and wet was clearly getting to him. He had to keep moving, find a way to get dry.

He headed back up the side canyon, sometimes wading in deep mud, other times climbing over rocks, looking for any trail up and over the steep rock walls. Finally he found a path that he could get the horses up to a ridge line and then work his way around and back down to the river.

At the top, in the morning sun, he stopped, took off his wet clothes and wrung the last of the cold water from them, letting the sun warm him as best it could so early in the day.

He had some mostly dry extra clothes in his saddle bag, so he put those on, then put on his light coat, and then put back on his heaviest coat. He would be sweating this way soon enough, but that was what he needed to do to get warm.

An hour later, as the warmth of the sun had him warmed back to normal, he headed back down into the wide valley that ran along the side of the North Fork of the Platte River. It took him almost three hours to go the few miles down to the trial, the riding was so rough.

No wagon companies were in sight in either direction. With one look at the wagon trail, Jimmy knew why. Every stream that flowed out of the hills above the river had flooded last night in the storm. And now the trail was cut with deep gashes, sometimes up to the height of ten men deep. Those streams would take time to work wagons through or around. The next company through here was basically going to have to build a lot of new trail.

The river itself flowed dark brown with mud and much higher than it had yesterday. There was all kind of debris floating in the river, and as Jimmy watched, the canvas top of one wagon floated past.

Jimmy rode back to the mouth of the canyon he had been trapped in, then on foot he searched the length of the huge gash in the ground from the canyon wall to the river's edge, looking for any signs of his friends.

Nothing.

More than likely, they had been swept into the river. Maybe a couple of them had made it out downstream.

He headed down the trail they had come up yesterday. The going was slow, as he had to pick his way over one washed-out gulley after another. But finally, he reached a half dozen men working out ahead of a wagon company, trying to find or build a new trail through the area.

Jimmy talked to all of them, asking if they had run across any boys about his age along the river.

"Nope," one man said. "Just a number of dead horses and cattle floating past. Sorry."

Jimmy sure hoped those horses were from a company of wagons up the river farther. He didn't want to think about any of them being his friends' horses.

By the middle of the afternoon, he gave up his search and turned back west. He might as well go on to Fort Laramie. Maybe the rest of the Wild Boys would be waiting for him there. More than likely, if they had searched for him and couldn't find him, that's what Zach would have them do.

They would be there. He had to believe that.

Part Fourteen
BENSON SHOWS UP

FINALLY, ALONE AND TIRED, Jimmy came face-to-face with the killer of his parents.

With the light just barely tinting the sky on the morning of the second day after the flash flood, Jimmy had worked his way into the settlement beside the military buildings of Fort Laramie. There were a large number of saloons spaced with even more general stores than Independence had. He knew the stores sold expensive supplies for those who needed them at this point of the trip west. This would be the last major re-supply stop until the west side of the Nevada Territory. Entire wagon trains full of supplies had left Independence ahead of the main rush of settlers to stock these stores.

The town was laid out on a gentle slope, and to one side were hundreds of Sioux Indians camped in groups of lodges. Long had told them that his people would be here, trading with the settlers, but Jimmy was still surprised to see that many camped that close to the town and the military buildings.

On the other side of the town were a good three hundred wagons filling a hillside and a wide valley. Smoke drifted lazily through the crisp, clear air from all the morning campfires.

Jimmy had rode into the mostly still-dark town, moving down the main street looking for any sign of his friends or their horses.

Nothing.

Luckily, he had saved what was left of his father's money when scrambling for safety in the flood. He needed a new tent and bedroll. He pulled his horses up to a general store that was just opening.

Suddenly, the man he hated the most walked out of the saloon right beside the store.

Jake Benson stood right there in front of Jimmy on the wooden sidewalk, not more than twenty paces away.

Jimmy sat in his saddle, stunned and frozen. That man had shot Jimmy's mother in the back. Jimmy could feel his anger building like a pot ready to boil. He wanted to run at Benson screaming and shouting and just beat the man to death with his fists, but he knew he wasn't big enough or strong enough to do that to Benson.

And besides, Benson had a gun and his men were with him.

"Just follow him until I can join you," his brother Luke had said. "Then we will take care of him together."

Jimmy made himself take a deep breath, then he dismounted and eased around to the other side of his horse so he was hidden from Benson. He had been lucky the killer hadn't spotted him.

Jimmy hands were shaking, his breathing shallow and swift. Benson scared him to death, and made him fantastically angry at the same time.

Benson laughed at something another man coming out of the saloon said. Then Benson and his three men mounted up and started toward the edge of town, heading west. There was no sign of the man Luke had shot.

Jimmy mounted back up as well. Staying far enough back as to barely still see the four men in the distance, he rode along behind them.

An hour later, it was clear that Benson and his men were on the wagon trail, moving at a steady walking pace, following a company of wagons that had just pulled out.

Jimmy turned around. At least he knew where Benson was headed.

West.

For a gold mine.

Now Jimmy had to find his friends. He could afford to wait around Fort Laramie for three or four days and still catch up with Benson. The killer and his men had had a five or six day head start on him out of Independence and Jimmy had caught him this time. He would catch the killer again, he had no doubt.

Jimmy couldn't let Luke and his parents down. He had to keep following Benson, even if he had to do it alone.

The sun was cresting over the hills as Jimmy got back into town and tied up his horses in front of a general store. As he was about to climb up onto the wooden sidewalk and go inside, he glanced down the street.

Zach!

Jimmy couldn't believe it. His best friend was standing against the wall of a saloon with his back to Jimmy. Zach was clearly watching the trail coming in from the east, the trail that Jimmy had come in on three hours earlier.

Jimmy wanted to shout and jump for joy. He couldn't believe Zach was still alive. He headed down the sidewalk with a smile on his face that hurt it was so big.

He walked up behind Zach and then said in his most serious voice, "Is Truitt working wagons again?"

Zach spun around, then smiling, he grabbed Jimmy by the shoulders and shook him. "You're alive. I can't believe it. You're alive. C.J. said you would be."

"And you didn't believe him?" Jimmy asked, smiling just as hard.

"We searched that entire area, but we couldn't get back up the canyon, and by the time we went around to an area on top of the hills to look down into the canyon, there was no sign of you."

"We?" Jimmy asked. "Is everyone all right?"

Zach nodded, smiling. "Banged up a little, and the horses have some cuts and scrapes. That stream just dumped us out onto the bank of the river like so much garbage. Long has been taking care of the horses and they're going to be good as rain. But we lost some of our provisions and gear. We've been living on what's left of the buffalo meat, camped down near the wagons since yesterday."

"Well," Jimmy said, "Let's go get everyone. I think I have enough left of my father's money to get whatever new gear we need. I lost some of mine as well."

"You managed to save your father's money from the flood?" Zach asked.

"Sure did," Jimmy said, "and a pack horse."

Then Jimmy got serious. "This morning I saw Benson."

"Where?" Zach asked, clearly stunned. "What did you do?"

Jimmy patted his best friend on the shoulder. "Let's head back to the camp. I'll tell everything over breakfast. We have plans to make and a gold mine to get back."

Zach laughed. "Oh, I can't tell you how much I love the sound of that."

"Yeah, me too," Jimmy said. "Me too."

Part Fifteen
A NEW TEAM MEMBER

WITH LONG tending to the slightly injured horses, the four of them went back into town that afternoon to get supplies for the trip west. It was going to take every dime of the money Jimmy had left to re-supply, especially in Fort Laramie.

As Jimmy was helping Truitt and C. J. carry gear out of one store, he came out to find Zach, who had been guarding the horses, sitting on the edge of the wooden sidewalk next to a young man who looked to be around Jimmy's age of twenty. The man was writing in a notebook. He had on a tall black hat and his long dark hair flowed out from under the back of the hat.

Across the street, two drunks were taking wild swings at each other and then falling into the mud. As Jimmy watched, the guy seemed to be writing down what he was seeing, stumble-by-stumble, blow-by-missed-blow.

Zach glanced up to see Jimmy watching.

"Meet Joshua Mark," Zach said. "Future journalist and storyteller."

"Call me Josh," the man said, glancing up at Jimmy. "You two got separated in the big storm, didn't you?"

Jimmy glanced at Zach, who shrugged. "I didn't tell him."

"Saw your meeting this morning," Josh said, still writing down what was happening with the two drunks across the street. "Figured it out for myself."

"Pretty sharp," Jimmy said, surprised. "You with one of the wagon companies?"

"Nope," Josh said. "I'm just trying to head out west. I'm going to be like Mark Twain and write down stories about the west and then sell them."

Jimmy stared at the side of Josh's face as he wrote down how the fight had ended, with one drunk falling against a horse rail and knocking himself out. This guy was clearly very, very smart. Jimmy had had a number of years in school, but he couldn't write anywhere near as well or as fast as Josh was doing.

"Who's this?" C. J. asked as he came out of the store and dropped down on the edge of the wooden sidewalk besides Josh. He noticed what Josh had been doing and said, "Hey, can I read it?"

"Sure," Josh said, handing C. J. the pages held together with a strip of leather. Josh pointed to a place on one page and said, "Start there."

"You have family?" Jimmy asked, starting to like this guy more and more every second. He was clearly very smart, maybe even smarter than C. J., if that was possible. And they were going to need smart if they were to do anything with Benson when they caught up with him again.

"Nope," Josh said. "Just me. Parents died, no one else."

"You got a horse?" Zach asked.

"Nope," Josh said. "I was just going to walk along with one of the trains, maybe work for some food along the way when I could. That's how I got this far."

Jimmy motioned that Zach should follow him back into the general store. As Zach stood, C. J. said, "This is really good. You have more like it?"

"I sure do," Josh said, smiling.

Inside the store, Jimmy turned to Zach. "Are you thinking what I'm thinking?"

"We're headed into some really rough country," Zach said. "We're better off if there's more of us riding together."

"And the mine?" Jimmy asked.

"I have a hunch," Zach said, smiling, "that there's going to be more than enough work and gold for all of us."

"I agree," Jimmy said, thinking about what it would take for Josh to join them. He likely had his own gear, and they had an extra horse. They only needed one packhorse.

Jimmy looked at Zach. "Let's ask him if he is interested in joining us."

"Who's going to join us?" Truitt asked, coming up with a handful of spices in cloth bags and a block of salt.

"The man outside with the tall black hat," Zach said. "He's as sharp as a drapery tack."

"The guy doing the writing?" Truitt asked, glancing out the front door.

Jimmy nodded, looking for any sign that Truitt might not like the idea.

"Great by me," Truitt said, turning around to go back to shopping. "I have a hunch that where we are heading, we're going to need all the help we can get."

Jimmy laughed. "That settles it, then. Three votes win."

Zach pointed back out the door at how C. J. and Josh were laughing over something. "I'm betting you'll get a fourth vote real easy."

That night, around a warm campfire of buffalo chips, Truitt cooked them a great meal and the six friends talked late into the darkness.

By the end of the evening, Jimmy was very glad they had met Josh.

By mid-morning of the next day, they were headed west.

Four of the eighteen legs to reach California were behind them.

The easy four.

To be continued next issue...

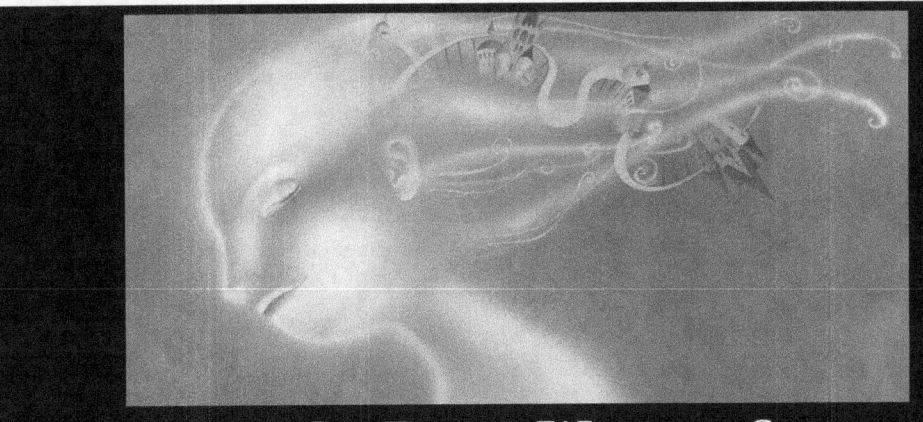

Poems by Dean Wesley Smith

She Laughed

In the apartment complex through the trees
a woman laughed,
high, like a bell ringing,
calling out to the world to come enjoy with her.

I imagined a woman with that laugh
to be beautiful, maybe thin,
maybe even a model,
with a perfect body to match the perfect laugh.

But it is freezing cold outside,
my windows and doors are closed tight.
Yet I could hear her through the walls of her apartment,
through the trees, through the walls of my office.

If I could hear her, up close her laugh must be loud,
annoying,
more like a donkey baying
after someone kicked it.

Distance and two walls
made the laugh pretty and enjoyable.
Distance and walls made an ass into a beautiful woman.
I wish I would have learned that when I was dating.

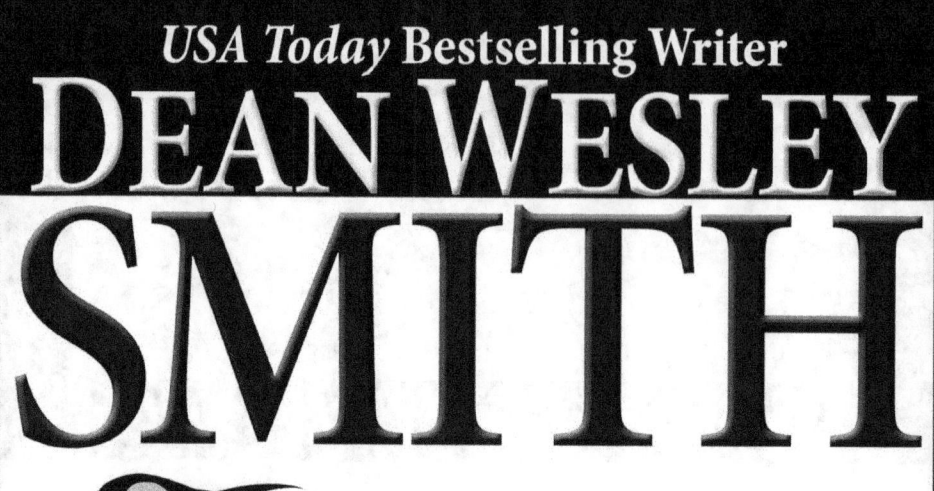

USA *Today* Bestselling Writer
DEAN WESLEY SMITH

A Thunder
Mountain Story

STAND FOR HOME

Keeping with the theme of this issue for the short stories, I wrote this western for an anthology that got no distribution. No one saw it. Plus I wrote it as a partial collaboration with another writer under a pen name.

With the permission of the other author, who had only added in the sex scenes, I removed the sex scenes, reverting the story back to my original draft which I was pretty proud of, to be honest.

So now, because of this magazine, I get to give this story, in its original form, a new life.

Cora and her husband, Harold, fight for their lives in the rough lands of the western wilderness. A story of survival and defending your home and family.

And as a side note, this story takes place in the same setting as my novels Thunder Mountain *and* Monumental Summit. *In fact, both the reminiscences from Viola Lamb, a real pioneer, and the story opening, takes place on the Roosevelt side of the very real Monumental Summit.*

STAND FOR HOME

"...it was while going up Elk Summit that Barney McGill died. He sat right down on his toboggan and died from sheer exhaustion, and three men were killed in a snow slide just two days before we went over. I saw their supplies beside the trail."

From the reminiscences of Viola Lamb
Thunder Mountain Gold Rush
Idaho, June, 1902

ONE

THE SOUND OF THE HORSES splashing through the cold, rushing stream echoed off the tall mountain walls and massive pine trees.

Cora Danials patted the neck of her gray mount and kept the solid old mare following the white packhorse being led by her husband, Harold. Through habit born from weeks of practice, she started to turn to make sure that the packhorse she was leading made it through the stream, then remembered that horse had gone off the edge of the trail just over the summit earlier this morning.

She shuddered and forced herself to take a deep breath as the scene again flashed through thoughts. It had been like a nightmare happening in slow motion.

The big, black beast slipped, tried to catch its footing on the snow-covered trail, then slipped again, dropping to its knees. The heavy packs seemed to pull it over the edge as it struggled to climb to its feet.

Finally, it just toppled over the edge, the look of panic and terror filling its round eyes.

She had only been five steps away, leading her own horse, but Harold said she could have done nothing to save the creature. The sound of the massive beast rolling and crashing through the brush for a thousand feet below them had been more than she could take. She had simply dropped to the snow and sobbed.

There was no getting to the supplies that had been on that horse. Somehow after a few minutes she had managed to go on, one step at a time, the fear of falling off the side of the mountain squeezing her chest every foot of the way.

Now, finally, they had reached the wide, safe valley floor. More than anything she wanted to stop, rest her back, wash her face in the snow-melt water, but she said nothing. Before crossing the stream Harold had said they had two more miles yet to go before stopping for the night. And since Harold was leading the four of them to the gold mining town of Roosevelt, no on argued.

Besides, the other two worked for Harold. He had hired them and their packhorses to get all the extra supplies into the Roosevelt area. He was to be the area's first postmaster. And, of course, he hoped to do a little prospecting on the side as well.

She wasn't sure exactly what she was expected to do when they got there. All Harold had told her was that the area was rugged and that he would need her help.

They crossed into a clearing, and the sun directly overhead warmed her back. She could have never imagined that a land could be so down-right inhospitable and beautiful as this Thunder Mountain area. The snow-covered ridges and peaks towered so far over her head on both sides that she sometimes imagined that any moment the mountainside might simply fall and cover them all. Growing up on the rolling hills of the Midwest, she had never thought about real mountains. And now actually being in them terrified her more than she wanted Harold to know.

The meadow they were crossing for the moment felt safe and inviting, pushing back the memory of coming over the summit. How they had managed she had no idea. That had been the worst part of the trip so far. Much more frightening than swimming the horses across the angry Payette River, or wading through the mud that was called a trail above Warren. Now this valley floor and beautiful meadow was much better. And if Harold was right, the boomtown of Roosevelt was only ten miles farther on.

"Yo!" The shout came from behind her. "Hold up!"

She glanced around to see Danny, the youngest member of their four-person party, jump down off his horse and move into the brush. He was followed a moment later by Al. She hadn't trusted Danny and Al from the moment Harold had told her he had hired them. Danny seemed to always have a smirk on his boyish face, and Al had mean, dark eyes that seemed to spend far more time staring at her then was proper.

"Now what are they up to?" Harold asked. He dropped off his horse and headed back past her. Harold seemed at home in these mountains, which surprised her. He wasn't a big man, at only five-six, but he was strong and had a level nature and a wonderful smile. She had wished a number of times over the last few weeks that Danny and Al hadn't been along, so she and Harold could have enjoyed a naked swim in one of the lakes they had passed, or made love under the stars. But with two men she didn't trust so close, that hadn't happened, and she was frustrated more than she wanted to admit.

"Stay in the saddle and I'll find out what's going on," Harold said as moved past her.

She nodded, even though she had no intention of staying on this mount one moment longer then necessary. As he disappeared into the brush near the creek to follow the others, her stomach suddenly twisted into a tight knot.

Something was wrong, she could feel it.

Very wrong.

TWO

SHE SLIPPED DOWN off the horse, feeling the tight muscles in her shoulders and strain in her back. Stretching those aches was a welcome feeling after the hours of riding. She pulled her saddle rifle out of its holster and quickly checked it to make sure it was loaded.

Then moving as silently as she could while making sure her skirt didn't catch on anything, she crossed the fifty paces through the grass and brush in the meadow toward the shade of the trees. If something was going wrong, she was going to be ready. And if not, standing in the shade would be much better than sitting on the horse in the sun.

There was still no sign of the three men when she reached the dark area under a massive pine tree. Even the trees in these mountains seemed to tower into the air higher than she could have ever imagined. Nothing was small about this country.

She watched and waited, staring at the spot across the open area where Harold had disappeared, trying to calm the little voice in her head that said something was wrong. But with each passing second, the voice just got louder and louder.

Then finally she saw movement in the brush. Harold appeared first, followed closely by Danny and then Al.

She was about to let out the breath she'd been holding when she realized Danny was too close behind Harold. And Harold's sidearm was missing out of his holster on his hip.

She stepped back behind the tree and deeper into the dark shadows so they couldn't see her.

"Damn," Al said, his voice carrying over the open meadow, "where'd she go?"

"Call her," Danny said to Harold, his voice mean and nasty-sounding.

"So you can kill us both?" Harold said.

"You'll die this instant if you don't call her," Danny said.

She could hear Harold grunt in pain as Danny jabbed him with the gun.

She felt as if someone had slammed a fist into her stomach and knocked every bit of the wind out of her. She had never trusted those two, and now she knew why. They were going to kill her and Harold and take their supplies, more than likely to stake their own mining claim.

"Cora!" Harold shouted.

Cora glanced around. Behind her the brush was thick and the hillside was only a few hundred paces through it. The walls of this very narrow valley were so steep that there was no way out. She either had to go up or down the narrow valley along the stream. Going down was the little town of Roosevelt, but that was too far to get help quickly. Besides, she couldn't run and leave Harold with those two. He would be dead and buried before she could make the ten miles to Roosevelt and the ten miles back. And that was assuming there would even be help in Roosevelt. Harold had told her that often these boomtowns didn't have much law.

She had felt alone since they left Boise, and now that feeling was even more overwhelming. At this moment their lives depended on what she did next.

She brought her rifle up past the edge of the tree, holding it steady on the rough bark of the trunk. She had Al in her sights about three steps to Harold and Danny's right. Her only hope was to shoot Al. With luck that would startle Danny enough to give Harold a chance to escape.

She took a deep breath, as Harold had taught her to do in his hours of making her practice firing this rifle. She had complained when they were doing it, but all he had said was, "You never know when you will need to know how to fire a rifle in the mountains. Better to be prepared than sorry."

How right he had been, but she had a hunch he'd been thinking more about her shooting a bear or moose than a human.

"Cora?" Harold shouted again as Danny jammed the gun in his back.

It was clear they weren't going to wait much longer. They might decide to just shoot Harold and come looking for her.

Al turned so that his chest was facing her directly on.

The little voice in her head shouted, Don't think, just do it!

She fired.

The shot was much, much louder than she had expected under the trees.

Al spun to his right and slammed into the dirt of the trail. She couldn't believe it!

She had hit him!

Harold reacted instantly, twisting to the right and smashing into Danny.

Danny stumbled and went down as Harold turned and ran toward her.

She cocked another shell into the chamber and fired past him, her not-so-carefully-aimed shot kicking up dust beside where Al was fighting to climb to his feet.

Danny started to take aim at her husband's back.

She fired again, past Harold at Danny.

The bullet kicked dirt up on Danny as the bullet tore into the ground beside him.

Danny fired but missed Harold.

She fired again, moving her aim up slightly.

Again she missed, but not by much. The shot ripped a hole in Danny's sleeve.

Danny scrambled for the brush, firing wildly at Harold, but clearly missing. One bullet smashed into a branch over her head. She fired back, again sending dirt spraying up on Danny.

Harold reached her just as Al, holding a bleeding arm, managed to stand and stagger after Danny.

Breathless, Harold ran in behind the massive tree beside her and they hugged like it had been a year since they had seen each other. Never, in the years they had been together did Harold feel so good against her. She didn't want to ever let go.

He kissed her long and hard, then looked at her directly. In the five years they had been together, she had never seen Harold gaze at her with such pride and admiration. He gave her strength she didn't even know she had.

"Now what do we do?" she asked.

He nodded at the meadow. "We get the horses."

"Why not just head for Roosevelt and get help?"

He shook his head. "In this country, those supplies are everything. There's no place in Roosevelt to replace them, even if we had the money."

They peered around the tree. She could see all seven horses were still standing in the open meadow, their supplies still in place. The gunfire hadn't seemed to bother the horses at all.

"You're not going back out there?" she asked, not believing that Harold would risk his life like that.

"I have to," he said, matter-of-fact.

She offered him the rifle, but he shook his head. "You're doing fine. I need you to cover me. How many shots do you have left?"

She thought for a moment, then said "Five."

"Use them carefully," he said, "and make them count."

He looked at her and she knew exactly what he meant. Kill Danny or Al if she had to.

She nodded.

"They'll come at us from the upper side of the valley," he said, pointing to the brush and trees to her left. "Watch there

and I'll see if I can get my rifle and the horses. When I reach them, start moving down along the edge of the meadow and I'll join you near that big tree."

He pointed to a large pine at the lower end of the meadow and she nodded.

Without another word he ducked and moved back out into the meadow, staying low enough to almost be crawling through the grass and brush.

She held her breath and waited for the first shot to ring out, but only the sound of water rushing over rocks filled the valley.

She moved into a position where she could both watch what Harold was doing and at the same time the brush where Al and Danny had gone.

It seemed to take an eternity, but finally Harold reached his horse and stood, pulling his rifle from its scabbard in one quick motion before ducking back down.

She instantly felt better, with both of them now armed. Harold was a much, much better shot than she was.

She moved away from the massive tree trunk that had been her shelter and ran toward the next large pine as Harold started the horses walking slowly forward. Four mounts followed Harold's lead horse, but the other two just stood, grazing on the grass. She was glad that Harold made no move to go back and get them.

Ten running paces and she reached the shelter of the next pine. She paused to catch her breath and listen.

Nothing but the sounds of the stream and the distant cry of a bird.

> *Harold reached her just as Al, holding a bleeding arm, managed to stand and stagger after Danny.*

She was about to step into the open again when a bullet smashed into the trunk of the tree just over hear head, sending bark everywhere. A piece hit her neck as she ducked. An instant later the sound of the shot filled every sense she had.

They had moved around and got almost even with her along the valley wall. She could barely see them on the other side of the thick brush.

She scrambled away from the pine as another shot cut through the air, followed by the sound of Danny laughing.

"Shut up and kill her," Al shouted as another shot kicked up dirt just in front of her.

She got to the shelter of another pine, brought her rifle up and aimed at the only piece of color she could see through the brush; a red patch on Danny's shirt.

Her shot cut through the air at the same time Danny fired.

Danny's shot snapped her skirt around her legs.

Her shot sent both Danny and Al scrambling for cover.

Behind her Harold had the five horses tied together and was leading them at a fast walk toward the tree.

She fired once more at a flash of color in the brush and heard Al swear in response.

With that she turned and ran, moving out into the open and across the lower corner of the meadow. She hoped that Danny and Al were so deep in the brush that by the time they got through it, she would be back with Harold.

Harold had the horses into the trees and she was about to join him when another shot rang out from behind and a bullet passed so close to her ear she felt the heat of it.

Harold returned fire, repeating round after round as she staggered past him and to the safety of a large pine tree.

"You all right?" Harold asked as he continued to fire one shot after another into the brush where Al and Danny were.

"Fine," she said.

"Grab my horse and start down the trail," he said. "I'll keep them pinned down and give you a few minutes head start."

She didn't like the sound of that, but didn't argue.

As Harold reloaded and kept firing, she yanked his horse into motion, giving the other four horses a moment to get up to speed, she started down the trail, working the speed up to a run. She forced herself to ignore the shooting going on behind her and focus on where she was putting each step on the rough trail. The last thing they needed was for her to fall and twist an ankle or get trampled by the horses.

For what seemed like an eternity she kept going, pushing herself as her lungs burnt for breath in the thin, mountain air. Each step was a success, each shot behind her twisted her heart. Harold was back there in a fight and she was running away. Yet she knew that wasn't the case. She was saving what future they had in these mountains.

Suddenly the firing stopped.

The valley now echoed only with the thuds of the horse's hooves on the dirt and her heavy breathing.

She pushed on, her skirt held high in one hand, her other hand pulling on the horse. She had no idea how far she needed to go, but if she had to, she'd run all the way to Roosevelt.

Suddenly the sound of Harold's rifle filled the air again. Five, then six shots, the sound echoing between the tall peaks and fading.

She knew what he'd done. He'd stopped firing, letting them think he'd moved on. And then when they moved, he opened up on them again. It would slow them down some, if he hadn't killed them.

Again the silence of the valley replaced the echoing gunfire.

One foot in front of the other. Running as fast as she dared but not so fast that Harold couldn't catch her easily.

She figured she had gone at least two miles when she finally heard over her own labored breathing the words she'd been hoping to hear.

"Cora, slow up!"

She slowed and stopped, then turned to see Harold running down the trail, rifle in hand. He was also winded, but otherwise looked unhurt.

She hugged him, both of them too winded to even try to speak at first. Even with both of them covered in grime and sweat, he felt wonderful and she again didn't want to let him go.

Finally she leaned back and looked him in the eye. "Can we make Roosevelt?"

"Not before dark with pack horses," he said. "You were moving them just about as fast as they could move. Danny and Al both have their own mounts and could catch us easily, even with Al hurt."

"So what do we do?" she asked, the fear twisting her stomach even tighter than it had before. Getting into another gunfight with those two was not what she wanted.

"We hide the supplies and horses for the night," Harold said, "then tomorrow go for help on foot."

"Hide them?" She glanced at the steep walls of the valley twenty paces to her left and the just-as-steep walls of the other side of the valley a hundred paces away. This valley was like being in a narrow hallway. There was no place to hide anything.

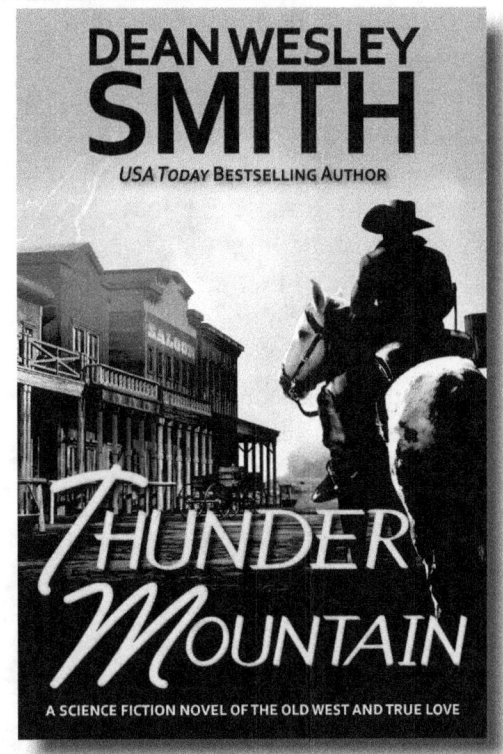

"There's a worked-out mine about a mile ahead up a side canyon," he said. "We'll be safe there for the night."

She looked at her husband, clearly showing the shock she was feeling. "How do you know that?"

He laughed and took the lead of his horse from her hand. "I bought it while we were in Boise," he said. "I wanted to surprise you."

"Well, you did," she said.

Harold just laughed softly and gave her a hug.

It took them less than fifteen minutes to get to the place where a faint trail led off up the canyon. Harold pointed it out, but then kept going on forward on the main trail toward Roosevelt. Finally another hundred paces ahead, where the trail crossed the stream he led the horses through, then doubled them back into the water and headed back upstream.

Core knew what he was doing right away. He was trying to let Danny and Al, who wouldn't be that far behind them, think they had kept going down toward Roosevelt.

Since it was getting late in the day and the sun had already vanished behind the tall mountains above them, by the time Danny and Al discovered they hadn't kept going, it would be getting too dark to backtrack. Right at that moment she was even prouder of her husband than she had been before.

The mine was about a half mile up a very steep-walled side canyon. There was a small, windowless log cabin, clearly not more than a few years old, built against one rock wall, and mine tailings scattered down the hill toward the small creek that wound through the bottom. The cabin sat up high enough to give a very clear view of anything below.

"What's farther up the canyon?" she asked as they dismounted on the flat area in front of the cabin.

"The guy who sold me this claim told me it was too steep to climb," Harold said. "No way out."

She looked at the cabin and then back down the narrow valley. "I was afraid you were going to say that."

"Don't worry," he said. "We can defend this place if we have to." He pointed up the steep hill above the canyon. "They can't come at us from that direction, so the only way to get up to this cabin is the way we came. And with us on the high ground here, they'd be fools to try it."

"So where's the mine?" she asked. She could see all the rock tailings that had been dug out of the hill, and the small log cabin, but no mine opening.

Harold moved over to the large main door and pushed it open, then pointed inside at the blackness.

"That's the opening to the mine?"

He nodded. "Hold on to the horses for a moment and let me see what we have."

She pulled her rifle from its saddle holster again and made sure it was fully loaded, keeping an eye back down the quickly darkening small canyon while holding onto Harold's horse.

The sounds of the stream were faint here, and only the cry of a hawk circling overhead disturbed the intense quiet.

After what seemed like an eternity, Harold came back out and took his horse from her, telling her to stand guard. He then led the horse toward the door, stopping just outside. He unstrapped the packs and pulled them off to one side, then led the horse into the cabin. The sound of the hooves on the board floor echoed louder than she wanted any sound to be from them.

She moved over and sat down on a large rock, intently studying the brush and trees below the cabin, expecting to see movement at any time.

Nothing.

It was almost completely dark by the time Harold got the last horse inside and the packs pulled inside as well.

"I'll watch the trail," he said. "Go take a look at our place, but close the door so the light doesn't show."

"Four sweaty horses in the house," she said. "You sure know how to make a home attractive to a woman."

He laughed. "I do my best."

She was surprised when she got inside the cabin. It was a large room, with a table and counter on the left side that served as a kitchen area. A large bed filled the right wall. The space was lit by a warm, orange light from a lantern sitting on the table.

On the wall directly across from the main door was another large door, slightly closed. She opened it to see the mine tunnel disappearing off into the mountain. The horses were tied in a line in the rock and wood shaft, facing her. Each had some grain and water and they seemed happy enough for the moment.

She glanced around the cabin again. It felt warm and cozy and safe. She liked it at once.

Back outside in the dark it took a moment for her eyes to adjust, then she moved over and sat down beside Harold on the large rock overlooking the small, narrow canyon. "So what happens now?"

"We get a good night's sleep," he said, putting his arm around her and pulling her close.

It felt good. "What about Danny and Al?"

"This is a pretty hidden canyon, and I doubt they even know it's up here," he said. "Plus, another half hour and there won't be any moving around in the brush. Too dark"

"Plus Al's hurt," she said, thinking about how she had shot him. She didn't regret doing it at all. She just wished she had killed him.

"Yeah," Harold said. "And I think I winged Danny as well."

"Good," she said. "And in the morning?"

"We deal with them."

She didn't like the sounds of that, but had no other plan at all.

They sat there in the dark, watching and listening, Harold's arm around her, holding her. Even with two men chasing them, right then she felt safer than she had since they left the midwest. She was going to love this little canyon, she knew. But first they were going to have to defend it.

THREE

THE NEXT MORNING, when it was just barely light enough to see the edge of the rock area in front of the cabin, Harold gave her a hug and they went out in front of the cabin to get ready.

Even with him beside her she had never felt so alone. There was something about these mountains that just made a person feel small. Yet behind her she had something to defend and she was going to do it in any way possible. Last night they had made that cabin their home, and she wasn't going to let anyone take that home from her if she had anything to say about it.

She had on her coat and gloves and she had put a blanket on the ground near the cover of the big rock she had sat on the night before. From the blanket she had a clear view of the narrow canyon, but anyone coming up would have a hard time spotting her.

Harold was about ten steps to her left, also lying down.

She had her saddle rifle and extra shots, plus an extra thirty-thirty Harold had bought. Both rifles were loaded and ready. Harold had his rifle and his sidearm. It was going to take a lot to get past them.

Harold had said that if Danny and Al were smart, they would take the two horses they had, and the supplies on them, and get out of the valley at first light. But she didn't think Danny and Al were the type to run. Especially with a woman getting the best of them yesterday. She knew they were coming.

It was only a matter of when.

The sun still hadn't quite reached the valley floor yet when she heard them coming long before she saw them. Danny's voice echoed up the small canyon, and the sound of brush cracking on the trail was like small shots.

She forced herself to stay as low as she could, keeping the rifle focused on where the trail came out of the trees and brush about a hundred paces below the mine tailings where she lay.

The rifle felt comfortable against her shoulder and this time when she fired there were going to be no doubts at all.

Danny appeared first, on his horse, staring up through the shadows at the cabin and mine tailings.

She knew he couldn't see her if she didn't move.

She took a deep breath and made herself wait while Danny got farther into the open.

"Take Danny, I'll take Al," Harold whispered just loud enough for her to hear.

Danny stopped and Al appeared, his arm wrapped in a white cloth that had a large red spot on it. Danny had a cloth wrapped around one shoulder as well, which must have been where Harold hit him.

They both stopped and stared up at the cabin, staying on their horses.

"You think they're up there?" Al asked, his voice carrying.

She took a deep breath, focused all her attention on Danny's chest, aimed slightly high to adjust for firing downhill, just as Harold had taught her, and fired.

Harold fired an instant behind her.

The sound of the shots filled the canyon and Danny flipped over backwards off his horse.

Al spun to his left and also fell off his horse.

She reloaded and fired again at Danny as he hit the ground.

Her second shot missed, kicking up dirt near his head, but her third shot caught him square in the shoulder, the sound a thickening thud mixed with the echoes.

Harold had also fired twice more.

The sound of the shots echoed into the distance and then was replaced by the silence of the canyon.

Both horses had moved off twenty paces and stopped. The two men lay there in the rocks and dirt, neither moving.

Danny looked dead, twisted in an unnatural way, his neck sideways and his head turned too far to the side. If her shots hadn't killed him, it looked like the fall had.

Al she wasn't so sure about. If he moved, she and Harold were both going to fire again, since Al still had his rifle right near him.

They waited, trying to see any movement at all from either of them. The silence was almost too much to stand.

Finally, after what seemed like half a day, just as the sun was starting to reach the two bodies, Harold said, "Let's take a look."

Keeping her rifle cocked and ready, she moved down the slope beside her husband, easing up on the two men who had tried to kill them.

She had been right about Danny. He was dead as dead could be, his neck twisted like a chicken's. Harold checked closer to make sure Al was dead. He was. It looked as if his shot caught him right under the arm and plowed into his chest.

She let out a deep sigh and hugged Harold. For the moment they were safe and for the first time on this trip that felt wonderful.

FOUR

IT TOOK THEM the next hour to unpack Danny and Al's horses, then hook rope around the dead men's arms and have their horses drag them up the canyon.

There Harold spotted a sharp rock outcropping and they stacked the two bodies there. Then Harold went back and got a stick of dynamite. He lit it and tossed it into the rocks above the two.

The explosion did exactly what he had planned it would do. The rockslide buried them so deep no animal would ever find them.

An hour after that they had carried water up to the cabin and she had started some boiling for washing. It was going to take her a long time to wash off the grime from those two, and even longer to push the memory back.

When Harold came in, she turned to him. "Think anyone will miss them?"

Harold stepped up and held her tightly. "You heard the stories in Boise. If a local didn't show up to winter there, people thought the mountains got him."

Cora nodded and walked with Harold back outside. The air was warm and the faint sounds of the stream were a nice background. It calmed her instead of scaring her.

She looked up at the peaks while holding onto the man she loved more than anything. The mountains had nearly got her. If Harold hadn't taught her how to use that rifle, if she hadn't had a strong will to survive, she might have slipped off that trail like that horse, or let those two men shoot her.

Harold was worth fighting for.

This new home was worth fighting for. She knew that now. A home was never worth much unless you stood and defended it.

"Regrets?" Harold asked, sounding very worried.

She hugged him and then kissed him hard. "No, I'd do it all over again if I had to."

He sighed in relief and buried his face in her hair. "Can I ask why not?"

She laughed and kissed him again. "I have you and I have all this."

She gestured toward the fantastically beautiful tall mountains towering over them. "That's more than I could have ever hoped for."

He looked at her for a moment, as if her words had surprised him. Then he bent down and kissed her, gently, as if it were the first time.

Which, in a way, it was.

~

DEAN WESLEY SMITH

THE ADVENTURES OF HAWK

Chapters 13-15

What Came Before

Nineteen-year-old Danny Hawk, his uncle, and his best friend Craig, were in Cairo to look for his missing father. Danny had witnessed the death of his only contact in Cairo, Professor Davis, because the professor had Danny's father's journals.

Danny knows that the men who had killed the professor were now after him and the journals. Danny finds the journals and gets his uncle and friend to safety in an airport hotel where he tells them what happened. They decide to keep searching for Danny's father and try to rescue him.

Along the way, Danny and Craig find some help from a street kid named Bud and twins from South Africa who had worked with Danny's father.

They managed to escape the men chasing them for the moment at the airport and head back into the main part of Cairo.

THE ADVENTURES OF HAWK

CHAPTER THIRTEEN

August 20, 1970
Cairo, Egypt

BUD DROVE PAST the small apartment building twice before finally backing the cab into a hidden driveway and stopping in the shade.

The neighborhood around the two-story apartment building looked to be an older residential one, with small buildings packed in tight together. No lawns or shrubs like in the States, just rocks and peeling paint. Some of the houses had laundry hanging in the front or side yards. It was far too hot for anyone to be outside in the sun, so everything felt abandoned.

"I'll keep the car running and if you hear a honk, come running. It will be hard to escape this neighborhood."

"Got it," Danny said. "We won't be long."

"So, what's the plan?" Craig asked as they climbed up the exposed outside stairs to the second floor and faced the wooden door.

Danny dug for the key in his pocket that his mother had given him. His father had sent it to her as a backup, in case something happened to him and she needed to come here. He always kept the rent paid up for months in advance so nothing would be disturbed by the landlord at least.

"We gather up what we think might be important, then get out of here," Danny said. "We'll let the twins figure out if what we got is important or not."

"As good a plan as any," Craig said.

"No talking inside," Danny said. "It might be bugged."

Craig nodded. "Good thinking. I've just got to get more paranoid."

Danny unlocked the door and slowly pushed it open.

There were no lights, so he stepped inside and let Craig follow before shutting the door and flipping on a light switch.

The place smelled musty and unused. At least it was much cooler than outside.

The living and dining areas were almost empty. A wooden table with two metal folding chairs were in the dining room, and a couch that had clearly seen far too much use was the only thing in the living room.

Danny glanced at Craig who was shaking his head at what greeted them.

The tiny kitchen had a few glasses and chipped bowls in one cupboard and that was it. Not even a dirty dish in the sink.

Everything had been cleaned off and wiped down. Danny knew his father was known for being a slob. His mother complained about it all the time, sometimes even going so far as wishing he would leave on another dig so that the house would be clean again.

Danny knew that his father put all his attention into his work. Keeping a clean apartment was just an annoyance left up to others.

If Danny's father had lived here, someone had gone to a lot of trouble to make sure nothing was left of how he lived.

Or any of his personal things.

The one bedroom had a made bed against one wall and a small wooden desk against a second wall. The desk was empty. As was the closet and bathroom. The bed was made like a maid had done it.

Danny wasn't really that surprised. At least not as surprised as he would have been if he had come here first from the airport three days ago. Someone clearly had come in and taken all of his father's things and cleaned the place. The only thing left was a large world map that somehow his father had glued like wallpaper to the wall.

Craig pointed to it after Danny finished checking every corner of the closet.

Danny stepped over to the map. Small "x-marks" had been made in blue ink, at least a dozen of them all over the world.

South America's western coast area had two. One over New York City, three over London and the surrounding area. Another in the Soviet Union behind the Iron Curtain. Even more in Egypt, China, Mongolia, and India.

Danny studied the marks, not having a clue what they had meant to his father. But his father had put those marks on that map for a reason, Danny was sure of that.

Danny tried to pry the map off, but it was glued completely. It would completely destroy the map and the wall to take it off.

The only reason he and Craig were seeing the map with the marks was because the map had been impossible to peel off and the people who had cleaned out the apartment had just left it.

Danny leaned over to Craig and whispered in his ear. "Memorize the exact locations of all the marks."

Craig nodded and both he and Danny stood in the nearly empty apartment for the next few minutes doing just that, like they were both studying for a geography test in school.

After Danny felt like he had the dozen or so marks clear in his mind, he motioned for Craig that they should get out of there.

He locked the door behind them and quickly went through the heat down the stairs to where Bud waited in the running cab.

Bud was clearly happy to see them. "Starting to worry me. Find anything."

"Place had been cleaned out," Craig said as Bud pulled out of the driveway and headed back into town.

"Except for a map glued to the wall with a bunch of marks on it," Danny said. "I just hope we can remember where all the marks were. We need to write them down later, while it is still fresh."

"Yeah," Craig said. "And better yet, at some point figure out what they mean."

Danny couldn't agree more.

"One more stop," Danny said. "But we have to pick up the twins."

"The Pyramids on Giza?"

Danny nodded.

"Well," Craig said, "at least I get to be a tourist before some goon kills me."

CHAPTER FOURTEEN

August 20, 1970
Giza Plateau, Egypt

ONE BLOCK AWAY from the bazaar, Bud parked the cab in a shaded alley so narrow that Danny was amazed that Bud could get the cab backed in and still get the door open. Bud was small enough to squeeze out the door somehow and vanished around the corner, leaving Danny and Craig sitting in the cab, clearly trapped. They were both too big to even climb out the open windows between the car and the walls.

And on top of that, the alley smelled of urine and some sort of fried meat. The two odors did not combine well.

"You ever wonder what has just happened to our nice, normal lives?" Craig asked.

"Most of the last three days," Danny said. "So much for football practice starting next week."

"And the homecoming dance I suppose is now out of the question as well," Craig said, shaking his head. "I was really looking forward to maybe asking Karen. I would have loved dancing with her."

"Slow-dancing," Danny said, smiling at his best friend. "You fast-dance like a monkey."

"It's all the rage," Craig laughed. "Or haven't you heard?"

At that moment, Bud slid back into the car and pulled the car to the front of the alley where Ernie and Ed had room to climb in, Ernie in the front seat, Ed in the back beside Craig.

"Field trip," Craig said as Bud pulled out into the busy traffic, narrowly missing another cab and causing at least three cars to swerve to miss him.

"You have your translations in a safe place?" Danny asked, feeling the backpack on the floor beside his leg with his father's original notebooks.

"Hidden safe and sound," Ed said.

"Don't tell us where," Craig said, holding up his hand. "I think it's better that we just don't know."

Danny agreed.

Bud turned west and headed out a wide highway, picking up speed and making it impossible to talk with all four of the windows rolled down. He was going faster than Danny thought any street kid should be allowed to drive. And just like he had done on the main streets, Bud was swerving in and out of traffic.

Danny just held onto the door handle and let the wind blow in his face from the four open windows.

Ahead of them, the three larger pyramids of Giza seemed to grow like mountains as the road climbed out of the city and up to the sands of the desert. Actually, the pyramids were very close to the edge of the city. Danny had no doubt that in forty years, the city would surround the entire Giza Necropolis. From what he had heard, the smog was already starting to eat at them, and just recently, people had been barred from climbing on the pyramids anymore.

There was no way to describe the awe that Danny felt seeing those huge stone pyramids grow bigger and bigger in front of him. How could anyone have built them? Now he understood that age-old question. Pictures just didn't do them justice and there was nothing in the United States that even compared.

For a few miles, all of them just stared. Craig his mouth slightly open, just kept shaking his head, as if he wasn't believing what he was seeing. Danny understood that feeling.

The most famous of the pyramids was the Great Pyramid of Khufu, the second was the Pyramid of Khafre, and the smaller one, still a giant structure but dwarfed by the other two, was the Pyramid of Menkaue. There were a lot of other smaller pyramid-like structures scattered around the base of the big three. They were called The Queen's Pyramids by many.

Three smaller Queen's Pyramids were between Khufu and the Eastern Cemetery. The Western Cemetery was on the other side of Khufu, and three smaller still pyramids were lined up beside Menkaure.

The entire area was huge. But it was the three monster pyramids that dwarfed everything.

"So, where are we headed?" Bud shouted to Ed.

"The Great Sphinx," Ed shouted back over the winds.

Bud nodded and headed to the east to a parking lot there.

Danny wanted to ask him why the Sphinx, what his father had said in the notebooks that was taking them here, but decided to wait until they stopped so they could talk normally. The idea of rolling up the windows in this hot air was just an insane thought.

Finally, Bud pulled the cab into a place facing the Great Sphinx and shut off the engine. There were only two other cars in the parking area, and Danny could see no other people around at all. The stones and shallow valleys were such that hundreds of people could be in the area and not be seen from the parking lot.

The silence was like a thunderclap to Danny. He was startled by it, after being in the cab and in the city and the bazaar. Out here there was only the wind blowing over the sand and that seemed to suck away noise like a soundproof room.

They all piled out of the cab and headed up the tourist sidewalk.

The Great Pyramid towered over everything, a good fifty stories tall. Danny couldn't believe how large it was. He just kept staring up at it.

Finally, after a dozen steps in silence, Danny finally got his head together and asked the twins, "Where was my father's dig from here?"

"Abusir," Ed said.

"To the south and east of here about twelve kilometers," Ernie said, pointing up the Nile.

Ed nodded. "Your father believed that under the 5th Dynasty cemeteries of Abusir were remains of a much older civilization, dating back to far before King Scorpion in what is called the Archaic Period."

"Far older than four thousand years B.C." Ernie said.

"That's old," Craig said, shaking his head.

"Isn't the Great Sphinx believed to be much older than the 4th Dynasty pyramids built here?" Danny asked.

Both Ed and Ernie shook their heads.

"It was built in the stone quarry for the Great Pyramid, by Khufu's men," Ed said.

"But," Ernie said, "the famous Hall of Records from the legendary civilization of Atlantis is supposed to be buried somewhere near the Great Sphinx."

"Edgar Cayce predicted that would be where it was found," Ed said.

"Your father believes it is here as well," Ernie said.

"Atlantis?" Craig asked.

Ed nodded. "It is believed to have existed before the great dynasties of Egypt, and the survivors from the great disaster flocked to the Nile valley and other places around the world to live and rebuild."

"The Hydra League was formed in the time of Atlantis," Ernie said.

Danny just shook his head and stared up at the ancient pyramids, amazed at what it must have taken four thousand years ago to build them. If he had been sitting at home, on his couch, he would have never believed any of what Ed and Ernie were telling him. But Danny had men from this Hydra League after him

now, and he was facing giant pyramids that he doubted that 1970's technology could build. So he was willing to believe just about anything at the moment.

They moved past the Valley Temple and up a dirt walkway until suddenly the giant cat-like stone figure sort of appeared in front of them, towering over them with the Great Pyramid behind it.

"Oh, wow," Craig said, stopping and staring up at the towering carving. It was a man's head on a lion's body, with huge paws extending away from the body. Clearly the air and time had done a lot of damage to the Sphinx, since its nose and part of its face was missing. But it was still very, very impressive.

"Nose fell off about a thousand years ago," Ed said.

"Napoleon's artillerymen were rumored to have used the Sphinx for target practice as well," Ernie said. "When only its head was sticking out of the sand."

"But for most of its life, it was buried," Ed said. "The sand around its base, in fact, was just cleared away twenty years ago."

Danny's mind just didn't want to accept that the huge stone creature in front of him was even real. But yet it was.

For the first time, Danny was starting to understand his father's passion toward archeology. So many questions, so few answers.

CHAPTER FIFTEEN

August 20, 1970
Giza Plateau, Egypt

"I'M GOING TO keep an eye out for our friends," Bud said. "You enjoy the tour."

The short kid turned and just silently vanished behind a huge stone before Danny could even agree that it was a good idea. He couldn't imagine how the men could follow them from the airport to here, but anything was possible. Better to have Bud watching their backs.

The twins led the way into what they called the "Valley Temple," a series of tall blocks to the left and in front of the Sphinx.

Over what looked like a main entrance to the temple was a stone placed between two other stones. Carved into the stone were a series of hieroglyphs.

Ed pointed to them.

"What does it say?" Craig asked, staring up at the very old writings.

Danny had a hunch what it said because he could see a number of snakes seemingly flowing together.

"What many think it says is simply a blessing for those entering this temple built in the 4th Dynasty," Ed said.

"But Danny," Ernie said, "your father believed it meant something else, and that the stone was put there to mark the entrance or the general location to the Hall of Records."

Ed nodded. "It says, basically, that knowledge is protected by many snakes and the ten great puzzles of life."

"Hydra League," Danny said softly.

"The term Hydra is commonly thought to have an ancient Greet origin," Ernie said. "But the idea of snakes was common along the Nile, and they were often worshipped or feared as evil spirits or powerful gods, depending on the time. So this is not out of place."

"Ten puzzles?" Craig asked.

"This saying," Ed said to Danny, "got your father started putting together what he believed was ten clues called the Hydra Journals."

"Clues," Ernie said, "actually riddles that would lead to the location of the Fountain of Youth. And from there, maybe even the exact location of the Hall of Records."

"The Hydra Journals are a series of riddles?" Craig asked. "Great. I hate riddles."

"These riddles are as old as time, and your father had found three of them," Ed said.

"We have company!" Bud said as he came running around a large stone and skidded to a halt in the sand. "The three guys in the cab from the hotel just pulled up out front and parked next to a tour bus and a few other cars that just arrived. I don't think they saw our car."

"How did they follow us to here?" Craig asked, looking stunned.

Danny felt just as stunned as Craig felt.

"They know the details of your father's work," Ed said.

"This would be a logical place to check out," Ernie said.

"That's right, they may not know we are here," Bud said. "They weren't acting like they did."

Ernie pointed up at the second pyramid, talking quickly to Bud. "The main road comes in on the north side of the Pyramid of Khafre. There is a side road that runs up near the Western Cemetery. Think you can get the cab without being seen and meet us there?"

"I can," Bud said, nodding and again vanishing between the large stones.

"We need to head to the north and into the cover of the Eastern Cemetery," Ernie said.

"Isn't there a causeway the Pharaohs built between here and the Pyramid of Khafre?" Danny asked, remembering some of his reading about these pyramids.

"There is," Ed said. "But it is too exposed and we would be seen easily."

Danny nodded. "Lead the way."

At full run, the boys headed out through the stones, staying as low as they could as they moved behind the Sphinx. There was on open stretch of sand between the back of the Great Sphinx and the first blocks and mounds and small pyramids of the Eastern Cemetery.

Just the run along the length of the Sphinx had Danny sweating and breathing hard. The heat was intense, and he had no doubt that he and Craig couldn't stay out in this very long.

Ernie motioned for them to stay in the slight shade of the back of the Sphinx and quickly climbed up its side, moving like he had done it a hundred times in his sandaled feet. Danny was impressed. Clearly the twins were a lot stronger and in much better shape than they looked.

And they were used to working in the intense heat of the desert.

Ernie found a spot where he must have been able to see back toward the temple and the parking lot. With one quick look, he came scrambling back down.

"The three men are going into the temple," Ernie said. "We have to run now!"

He led the way out into the sun and across the hot sand, with Craig right behind him and Danny following his best friend very closely. Ed seemed to almost be pushing Danny from behind, and clearly wasn't working as hard as Danny was.

Running in the sand was like a football coach's dream for how to torture his high school team. As sophomores, their football coach had had them run sand dunes for exercise one day. Danny had hated that, and he hated running in the sand now.

It seemed to take an eternity for them to reach the tall stone blocks of the cemetery. And when they finally did, Ernie didn't even slow down. He turned to the west, staying between the smaller pyramids and stone funeral structures of the cemetery. He led them toward the southern edge of the Great Pyramid.

Up close, Danny couldn't believe the size of the blocks that the pyramid was constructed out of. They were taller in places than he was. He couldn't believe people used to climb them for sport.

The four of them ran along the hardened tourist path that framed the south wall of the Great Pyramid, then on around to the west side. They ducked into the cover of the Western Cemetery, finally stopping in the shade near the north side of the Pyramid of Khafre.

Danny worked to catch his breath, and he could feel the heat making him light-headed.

"We're going to need water," Craig managed to choke out between sobbing breaths.

"Only if we live," Danny said, his throat feeling like sandpaper had been scraped along the inside of it.

Suddenly, in a cloud of dust and sand, a cab appeared, bouncing off the main road and fishtailing over the dirt toward where they were hidden. Behind the wheel, Bud grinned like a kid enjoying a new Christmas present.

They all piled in almost before Bud had slid the cab to a stop. A moment later, he was accelerating out of the western parking area, headed toward the main road.

Danny had climbed into the front seat this time, and he turned to Bud. "Did they see you leave?"

"Nope," he said. "They were up in the temple area and I doubt they even heard me start the cab."

Danny leaned his head out the window and let the hot wind cool him some. Was this going to be the rest of his life? Staying just a few steps ahead of sure death and the hands of the Hydra League?

He hoped not, but if that was what it was going to take to save his father, then so be it.

"Now," Bud said, shouting over the wind so everyone could hear, "anyone got a problem getting back to the bazaar? I have to get out of this cab before the police spot it. I have no desire to spend the next twenty years in jail while you four go on and find the treasure without me."

"We'd visit you," Craig said.

"Yeah," Danny said, taking a deep breath and trying to get himself to relax a little. "As long as we're alive."

Continued next month…

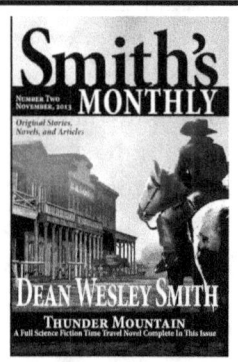

Coming Next Issue in Smith's Monthly

An old murder and a bunch of old detectives playing poker. What more do you need?

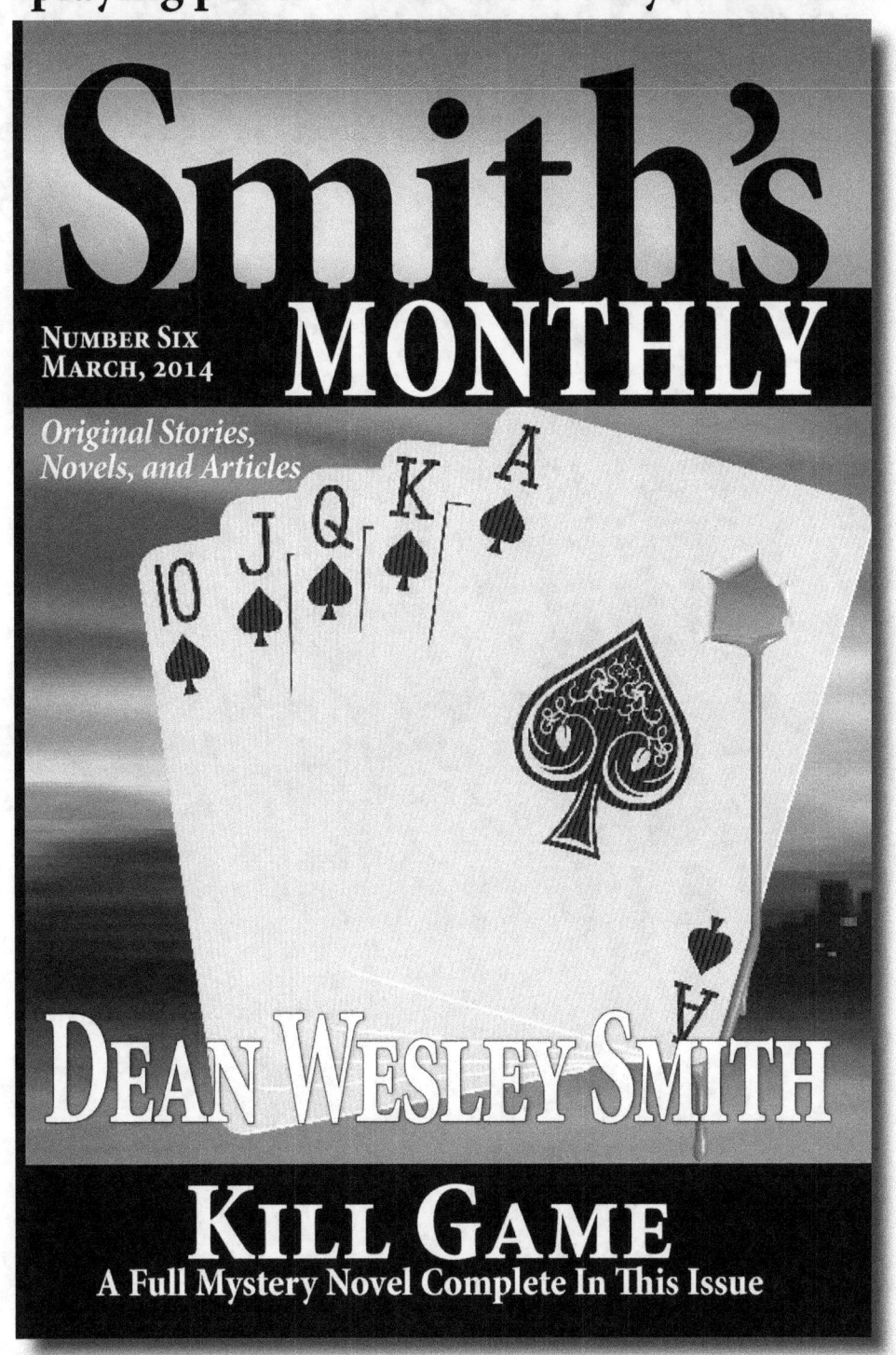

USA *Today* Bestselling Writer

DEAN WESLEY SMITH

LOVE WITH THE PROPER NAPKIN

Who Knew Aliens Could Be So Much Fun

As two of the other stories in this issue, this story had a short flash of a previous life in a small newspaper magazine that died right after this story was published and very few people saw the issue or the story.

And since the story fits the theme of this issue perfectly, I wanted to bring it back to life here.

In romance terms, this is a "meet-cute" story. The alien helps.

LOVE WITH THE PROPER NAPKIN

HELLO, SERIOUS AND BEAUTIFUL woman across the bar.

The drink is my treat and the bartender will point me out. Remember that old joke about an alien being a piece of paper and the paper is making love to your fingers? Well, it just came true for you. Honest.

Don't laugh.

The bar napkin that this message is written on is an alien called a Roggen. It snuck into the human area through the supply section of the hotel here on the station. It has the ability to split itself into thousands of little bar napkins as a disguise to watch and study humans. At this very moment it is making love to your fingers and I can tell from clear across the bar you are enjoying it.

Have fun,

Anna

ps...hope you enjoy the drink.

\#

DEAR ANNA,

Thank you for the drink and introducing me to these great little aliens. What planet did you say they were from? I'd love to go there some day.

Enjoying the feel,
Carla

#

DEAR CARLA,

The alien this is written on says your name is beautiful.

The alien said the sun their planet circles is called BAC 151. Damned if I know where that is.

He said he revealed himself to only a few of us so as to not cause too much commotion around the human section of the hotel. He also likes the beautiful dress you are wearing and I agree with him.

Trying not to stare,
Anna

#

DEAR ANNA,

What do you suppose would happen to the poor alien if I stuck him down the front of my dress? Can he turn himself into anything???? Oh, the possibilities are endless.

Thank you for the nice compliment and I hope you enjoy the drink in return.

Staring back,
Carla

ps...don't you think the bartender is going to mind passing all these notes back and forth?

#

DEAR CARLA,

The bartender loves it. I'm giving the poor kid twenty hotel credits every time. He'll deliver notes until doomsday for that.

By the way, the alien says doomsday for this hotel isn't for a few thousand years. Good to know, huh?

Notice the guy next to me. He thinks I'm weird because I talk to bar napkins. He should talk. His cologne smells like it was scraped off a well-used saddle.

Holding my breath and trying not to laugh,
Anna

ps...is that an empty stool there beside you?

#

DEAR ANNA,

I don't think you're weird. In fact, I kind of like what the bar napkins are doing to my fingers. Would you call it "paper sex?"

Just the thought has me hot.

I'm afraid the seat next to me is taken by my current date, who happens to be off talking to some friends about something boring like rebuilding a cargo ship or something stupid like that. At least he doesn't make me sit and listen to it.

Stroking the alien,
Carla

#

DEAR CARLA,

Did you see that guy who just asked me to dance? God, what are they letting into the hotel these days? Some of these humans belong over in the other sections, I am sure.

The alien told me the guy only wanted to chew on my panties. I guess the alien can read minds or something like that.

He told me the guy next to me wants to do something kinky with ropes. Can you believe that?

Ask your alien a question. Go ahead. He'll tell you inside your head. No one will hear.

Go ahead and try it,
    Anna

#

DEAR ANNA,

My God, you were right. I damn near fell off my stool.

I asked the napkin what your last name was and this little voice inside my ear said "Hartzell." Is that right????

Then I got afraid to write on one of them and the napkin said to go ahead. He said he loved it. I thought I had seen everything the galaxy had to offer. I guess not.

    Gone completely nuts,
    Carla

#

DEAR CARLA,

I was watching and laughing.

Yes, my last name is Hartzell. The alien says you want to know if I'm a lesbian. I'm bi, just like you. (The alien told me...no secrets with these little white things around, huh?) Is this place getting crowded and loud or what?

Is your boyfriend ever coming back? I want to see this guy.

    Waiting and drooling,
    Anna

#

DEAR ANNA,

The napkin says the fool who is my date (or I am the fool for being his) is over at a table by the dance floor talking to a young woman named Brenda Dare. The napkin says this Brenda is totally

drunk, has already spilled two drinks and my date is staring down her dress.

I think he deserves her.

What do you think?

Annoyed,

Carla

ps...this alien napkin says my now ex-date hopes to get both me and Brenda in bed together. Hah! What a joker he is.

#

DEAR CARLA,

How about me? In bed, that is?

How's that for forward?

The alien said my skin temperature went up a half degree just writing that first line. See what you do to me from clear across the bar.

Damn, I wish these napkins were bigger and this bar not so crowded.

Wondering what your voice sounds like,

Anna

ps...the alien said he would be happy to be any size I wanted. Too bad I can't find a man that flexible.

#

DEAR ANNA,

Why don't you come on over? If that jerk of a date returns, I'll tell him to take a walk out an airlock without a suit.

And bring as many of those napkins as you can. This alien told me that with enough of his old self in one place, he could reform quickly into something that just might please both of us.

He showed me an image of what he would look like and I agree.

Stuffing napkins in my purse and pockets,

Carla

#

DEAR CARLA

On my way.

I tipped the bartender a hundred credits to deliver this last note and let us take as many napkins as we can carry.

The alien showed me the same image and I damn near melted off my stool. What do you say we head for somewhere much quieter and far less crowded, such as my room?

Almost too excited to walk,

Anna

ps...the alien told me that the more napkins we take, the bigger he will be able to reform. I've got an armload. How about you?

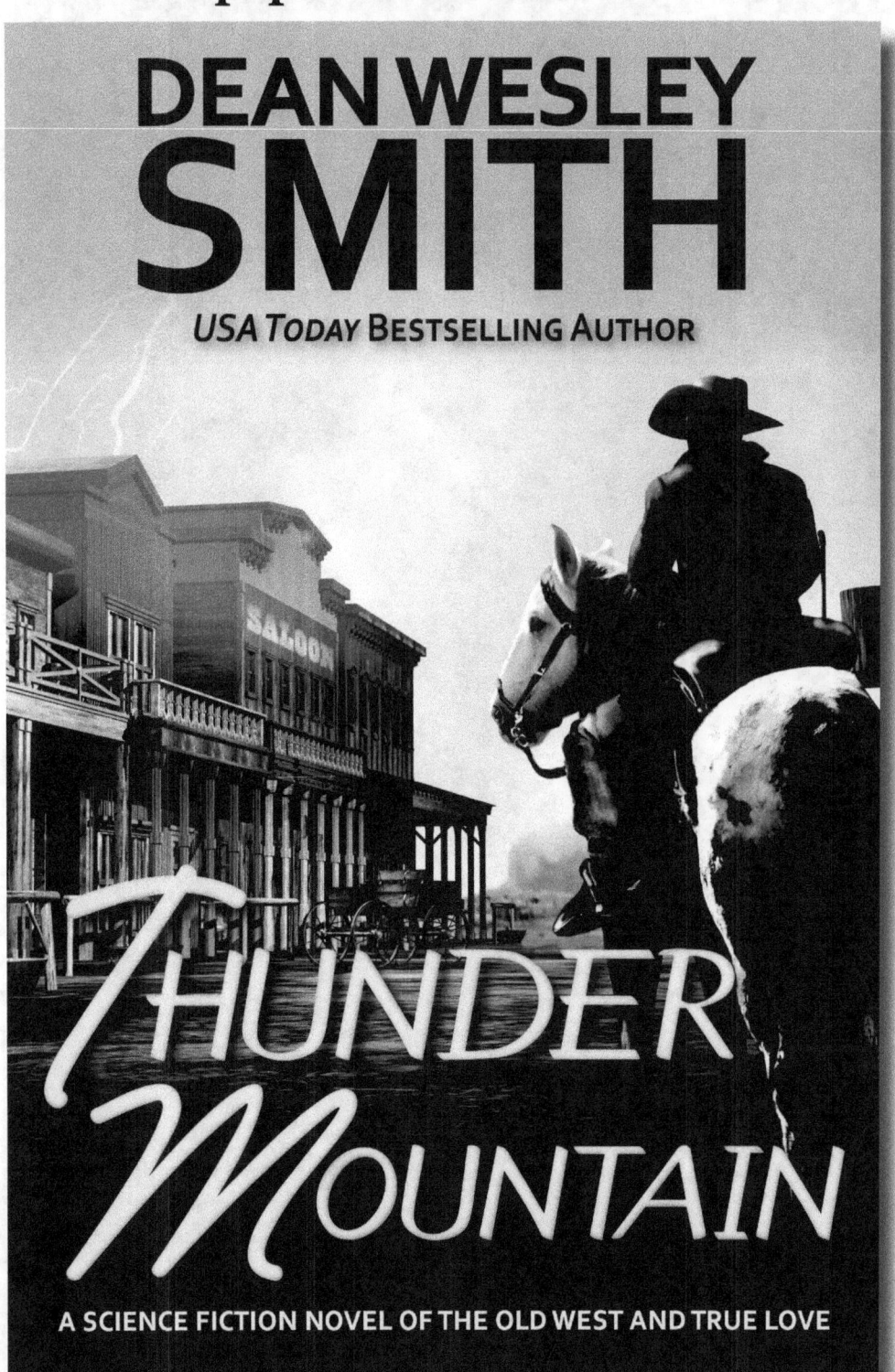

DEAN WESLEY SMITH

USA TODAY BESTSELLING AUTHOR

SECTOR JUSTICE

WITH OR WITHOUT LOVE, THEY MUST SAVE THE GALAXY

USA Today *bestselling writer, Dean Wesley Smith, returns to a not-so-distant future in his acclaimed Seeder's Universe series of novels and stories.*

Mattie Silks must team up with the most unlikely of partners to save the sector from a ruthless dictator. Her only problem, besides saving the galaxy, comes from the man she must work with. She can't keep her hands off him.

And he can't seem to keep his hands off her either.

But with or without love, the two of them must save the galaxy.

SECTOR JUSTICE

CHAPTER ONE

MATTIE SILKS SLIPPED through the milling crowd of the Bodie Station shopping mall and put her back against the wall of what looked to be an arcade of games to keep the kids of the shopping adults entertained. She then moved down along the wall to an area between the arcade and a dress shop divided by a small group of strange trees whose leaves seemed to move in an unseen and unfelt breeze.

At five-two, crowds bothered Mattie just about as much as anything bothered her. As a trained enforcer, one of the best in Sector Force Three, she feared almost nothing physical, if she saw it coming. But in crowds, she couldn't see over the top of anything and with all the movement it was hard to sense when something dangerous was about to attack.

She liked having her back against a wall. That way she could see, but often would never be noticed. With her lack of height in a society that thought six foot tall almost short, she was noticeable in a crowd. Against a wall next to some decorative trees, she just looked normal and could blend in.

In fact, her tan slacks, tan vest over a plain blouse almost blended perfectly with the paint of the wall. She had on hard-toed, but comfortable, flat shoes that she could both run and fight in. Over the years she had stopped a few fleeing criminals with a simple kick.

She studied the people going past. Not a one of them seemed to even glance her way. Perfect.

Standing that close to a kids' arcade also helped her blend in since her blouse kept her breasts pressed close and her thin frame made her sometimes seem more like a teenager. She had often used teenage disguises to get close to a target.

The people streaming past were all dressed for vacation in bright colors and flowered patterns, many wearing shorts as if this station was a place in the tropics somewhere. It seemed like a painter had tossed into a flowing river a bunch of bright, primary colors that weren't blending.

Every human on every planet looked the same. The mythical Seeders who planted humans on every habitable planet many thousands of years before made sure of that. But Mattie could see the variations in different planetary cultures in how many were dressed. Clearly this station was a resort for fifty or sixty closest cultures in this edge of this sector. She saw no person who looked to belong outside that small area.

And the noise level of all the people talking and laughing as they went past was a constant background that seemed to be muffled by the high ceilings.

She let herself relax just a little, let some of the tension ease from her shoulders and legs. A wall to her back, blending so that no one was noticing her, this was a perfect place to wait.

She was waiting for Carson Bernard. He was one of the best, if not the best, investigator Sector Force had. Her orders were for them to team up and track down who had been threatening Sector Force and some of the planetary leaders in this area.

Carson had gotten a few weeks head start, telling her to stay at the Sector Force headquarters until he got a lead and he would contact her.

She had only known him for a few years since he joined Sector Force, coming from the private sector, but she liked him. He seemed to have an uncanny ability to find people and missing items, even in areas of space distant from where he started.

Carson could somehow see links that others couldn't see, trace invisible lines through the cultures of hundreds and hundreds of planets without ever leaving a trace himself. He worked like a ghost when tracking and researching and Mattie admired that skill more than she wanted to admit.

It was going to take all of his skills to discover who was trying to bring down Sector Force. Everyone in Sector Force headquarters was worried, since there was enough information to know the threat was real. Just knowing that someone was out there with the resources and desire to bring down an entire Sector Force had everyone on edge.

Sector Forces for all nine sectors of the galaxy had been set up, so it was said, by the Seeders, the race that had planted humans throughout the galaxy. Each area of the galaxy needed a police force that functioned even over the planetary governments, and the Sector Forces were that force.

Trust was a rare thing among enforcers. Now, to Mattie, it seemed nonexistent with this imagined threat coming at them. The people of Sector Force were her family. She had been raised to be an enforcer. When everyone in a family couldn't trust anyone else, things had to be fixed and fixed quickly.

Carson had sent her a message after three weeks to meet him here, on Bodie Station on the distant edge of the Third Sector. He had information on who was behind the threats and they would jump from here to take care of the problem.

It had taken her almost a full week of travel from the Webb System and Sector Force Headquarters just to get to Bodie Station. This place really was on the edge of space, or at least space that she knew. She had never been to another sector. She had no reason to go to one and didn't much like the idea of being stuck on a ship that long.

Extremely fast ships were rumored to exist, but she had never seen one or knew anyone who had access to one.

For some reason, she expected the people here to be different after so much distance from her home, but this space station attached to a massive hotel and resort complex, was the same as any hundreds of others she had been in around the sector.

Only cleaner.

A lot cleaner.

Bodie Station and the hotel complex attached floated in space at an angle to take spectacular advantage of a curtain of blue and gold and red nebula dust cloud from an ancient exploded star nearby.

After being here for only a few hours now, she could already understand why people came to this place. Beautiful

Some Classic Poker Boy Stories
Available at your favorite booksellers.

views, clean surroundings, and everyone seemed relaxed and calm.

Now all she needed to know was if the food was good and this place would be one to remember.

Around her, everything sparkled, from the polished brownstone floors to the high windows overhead that showed the distant nebula. The entire mall was filled with earth-tones and plants of all types and sizes.

If she wasn't on such a dangerous mission, she might have stopped a few days here and enjoyed herself, taken advantage of a few of the advertised special spas.

She loved a good massage, especially when done by someone who knew what he was doing. During a massage was one of the few times she ever felt she relaxed.

She watched the people stream past in their bright colors and summer wear, both looking for Carson and any sort of danger. Near the center of the big mall area she faced was a forest of trees towering a good fifty feet into the air. Benches surrounded the trees and a wide stone path twisted through them.

Through the passing crowd she could see couples in love sitting on those benches. Some were laughing, some just sat holding hands and watching people pass as if waiting for someone to join them.

Because she had been born and brought up as an enforcer, she had never really had any serious relationships. Not that she wasn't slightly open to one, but she had learned early on in life that trusting anyone that closely for that long a time required something really special. So far, she hadn't found it.

She hadn't given up, but she sure wasn't looking either.

Mattie leaned back against the wall, the hardness of the surface giving her some comfort as she watched the crowds of tourists move back and forth and in and out of the stores.

This could be nothing more than a normal day on any shopping space station or any planet-side mall. People were people were people and no matter how many light years of space she crossed, that never seemed to change much.

Somehow the mythical Seeders made sure of that.

She glanced at a big decorative clock on a wall near one store. Carson was late. That worried her a little, but not that much. This was a big station and he said he might be delayed along the way. If he wasn't here today after an hour, she was to rest, enjoy herself, and meet him at the same time tomorrow.

She didn't really want to do that. She wanted to get going, get this mission on the way. After this long a journey, she didn't need to rest much more at all.

Finally, from the far end of the open area of the station mall, she caught a glimpse of Carson. His six-three lanky frame seemed to move more like parts were not connected just right. His long, thin face seemed to stretch just a touch too far between his thinning black hair and his jutting chin, making him look almost skeletal in nature. And he clearly used no tanning or sunning booths since no one had skin as white and sickly-looking as his.

He had on his normal black dress slacks that were too short by any fashion sense, a brown belt that held the pants too high, and a colored plaid shirt that didn't match anything else he had on. That attire was all normal for Carson.

He seemed to have always looked that way and people joked that he had been raised in plaid diapers and baby clothes that didn't match.

Still, Mattie was actually glad to see him, even though she would be responsible for his safety from here on out. He wasn't an enforcer and she doubted he even knew how to fight. His skills were in tracking things that could not be tracked to places no one knew even existed.

And he was stunningly good at that.

As he came toward her with the crowd, his gaze constantly darted around, his head turning side-to-side, looking in both directions as if afraid of something.

That put Mattie on alert at once and she did a quick glance around the mall looking for anything obvious.

Nothing that she could see at a glance.

She looked back at Carson as he strode closer. He hadn't seen her yet and more than likely wouldn't until she said something or appeared in front of him.

But striding beside Carson was a man that had likely already seen her. He seemed to be with Carson and even though his head didn't turn at all, Mattie had little doubt that he was seeing everything around him. He was powerful, very dangerous, and flat-out the best-looking man she had ever laid eyes on.

He was Carson's height, had wide shoulders that moved like an athlete would move, and powerful waist and legs. His brown hair was long and pulled back into a ponytail and he wore similar clothes to hers: tan slacks, a shirt that matched, and a long black coat that reached the floor and swirled behind him as he walked.

He took her breath away and scared her to death at the same time. What was he doing with Carson?

About fifty paces away Carson had yet to see her, but clearly the man in the coat had. He nodded to her just slightly, then tapped Carson on the shoulder and with a nod of his head indicated to Carson where Mattie was.

How in the world did that stranger know what she looked like? Something was very, very wrong here. No one had told her there would be anyone else but her and Carson on this mission.

She eased away from the wall and into a more prepared fighting stance as Carson saw her and broke into a huge smile that took his long, thin skeleton face and turned it almost into a pumpkin-like shape.

As the two approached her, the man in the coat hung back just a half step and was clearly scanning the crowd for danger around them.

She did the same but saw nothing to worry about at all in the flowing colors of tourists.

Except the man in the long dark coat.

She could barely keep her eyes off him and his chiseled features. What was wrong with her? Her stomach had tightened into a knot and she could feel herself starting to sweat. No doubt her reaction time and instincts were going to be slower as well if she didn't watch out.

> ## *He was powerful, very dangerous, and flat-out the best-looking man she had ever laid eyes on.*

Just before Carson got close enough to speak, the man in the coat caught her gaze and they stared at each other. God, he had deep green eyes that didn't seem to miss a detail.

She loved green eyes.

Then he glanced away, again scanning the crowd.

Oh, man, was that guy trouble. In more ways than she wanted to think about.

The mall had suddenly gotten ten degrees warmer.

"Mattie!" Carson said, smiling so hard his face truly did look like a badly carved and bleached pumpkin. "Wonderful that you made it. I was worried."

"As was I for you," Mattie said, smiling back at her friend.

Carson stopped just a few feet in front of her and made no move to try to hug her or even shake her hand. He knew the protocol of Sector Force members in the field and followed it perfectly. The other man stopped just to the right of Carson and moved slightly to put his back more toward the wall.

Smooth and trained. That scared Mattie even more since he clearly wasn't trained by Sector Force. She would have known of him and his name. And she had no doubt that if she had met this man, she would have remembered.

Carson turned to his companion. "Red Simms, meet Mattie Silks."

Red bowed just slightly and smiled a light smile that no doubt she would remember in many fond and private fantasies in coming years. When he smiled, he showed a little of his white teeth and his perfectly tanned skin seemed to glow even more.

Again their gaze held each other.

She really, really, really needed to get control of herself here.

She said nothing to him, breaking away from a gaze she really wanted to get lost in.

"Carson, I was told to meet just you here."

He nodded and smiled, again twisting his thin face into something like a twisted child's balloon. "But while you were in transit I discovered that some of my traces had been tracked back to me, so I was given permission from Sector Force to get some more protection."

Out of the corner of her eye she saw Red shift slightly.

"I can protect you," she said.

"I know," Carson said, nodding. "But you just got here. I have been here for almost a week now."

She suddenly felt a great deal of alarm.

"A week?"

He nodded. "A week tomorrow."

She didn't like the sounds of that. If someone had traced back to him, they would have had enough time to get here. He was a sitting target in crowds like this. Meeting here now was becoming the worst thing Carson could do.

"You are from the Sector Force?" Red asked, his voice low and cold.

Carson nodded. "We both are," he said.

"You didn't tell me that," Red said to Carson, clear anger showing in his voice.

"I'll explain it all later," Carson said, shrugging it off.

Mattie stepped forward slightly and turned toward Red to counter his anger. This was not a man she wanted angry with her, but she had no doubt she could take him if she needed to.

"What is your problem with the Sector Force?" she asked him, keeping her voice low and controlled.

"That is my business," he said, staring back at her.

"Fine," she said. "Please keep it that way."

She turned back to Carson. "We need to get you to safety. Red here clearly doesn't understand the level of threats we are facing."

It was as if she had slapped Red. He eased back and scanned the room again quickly.

Carson suddenly looked very worried, again his head turning from side to side looking for threats Mattie was sure he couldn't see even if they were coming at him.

Carson then reached into his pocket and handed her a data stick. "Everything I have learned about the attackers is on that stick. The same data is also hidden in my clothes in my room and I have given Red another copy for safekeeping."

Carson again glanced around, then he went on. "Mattie, we must stop these people. Not only are they a threat to Sector Force, but to entire systems of humans if they are allowed to gain control."

Again Red gave a slight jerk of surprise. Clearly Carson had told him nothing of the threat at all.

She pocketed the stick and nodded. "We'll have time to talk when I get you to a safer location."

Out of the corner of her eye she saw a woman pushing a baby carriage move toward them, but the woman didn't seem right. It took only an instant for Mattie to spot the gun under the blanket in the carriage.

"We have an issue," Red said, staring to the right of Mattie. She glanced in that direction and saw two men in suits, clearly pretending to discuss something, also headed their way. It wasn't hard to

see the guns making an imprint on their business suits.

"Woman with baby carriage behind you," she said.

Red nodded.

So much for getting Carson to a safe location. There was an arcade full of children to her left, a planter to her right, and a wall behind her.

It had been a good place to stay out of the way for her while waiting, but a horrid place for a firefight. No cover at all.

"Carson," Mattie said, her voice completely under control and firm, "when I say drop, you move instantly and crawl behind this planter. Understood?"

He started to say something but she shook her head.

He gulped and nodded.

"They know we've made them," Red said, pulling out two guns from under his long, flowing coat.

Mattie had two as well, one tucked under her blouse against her back and another strapped under her left pants leg.

"Get down, Carson!" she said as she pulled the gun out of the back of her belt.

Carson did as she said and she moved slightly in front of him and crouched to protect him even more.

Red fired first, taking out one man before he had his gun even halfway out of his holster. The sound of the shot echoed through the large mall and stunned everyone to a moment of silence.

Mattie took out the woman with the baby carriage just as she raised her gun to fire.

Red dropped the other man after he got off one shot.

Two more men ran at them from the direction of the center trees with guns drawn, firing.

A projectile from one of the guns embedded into the wall behind Mattie's head and she took out the shooter with three perfectly placed shots in his chest.

What they were all firing couldn't break through any wall or viewport, but they were still very, very deadly. Maybe more so since they spread on impact.

The other man got off two more shots before both Red and Mattie downed him.

The mall had now turned into a screaming, shouting mess as everyone ducked for cover and the sounds of the shots echoed off the walls and high ceilings and windows.

No one else seemed to be rushing at them.

"You all right?" Red asked.

"I am," she said, giving the screaming crowds close attention as they ran from the bodies and to the safety of the stores. It took only a few moments before the entire mall area was mostly clear except for some people cowering behind benches and trees in the middle of the mall.

Finally she said, "We're clear, Carson. Let's get moving, get you to safety."

No answer, so she spun around. Carson was sitting on the ground, leaning against the planter, a single small hole in his forehead. Mattie knew exactly what that soft shell had done to the inside of his skull.

"Damn it!" Red said softly, staring at Carson.

Then Red just stood, his back to the mall, and kept muttering softly, "Damn it, damn it, damn it."

Mattie scanned the big empty mall one more time for danger, then turned to Red. He was still standing over Carson as if he had known him his entire life, as if they had been friends or family.

He hadn't leaned down to touch Carson or anything because there was no doubt Carson was dead.

Clearly Red was a man used to seeing death, just as she was. Carson had been someone she had known at the Sector Force for a few years. She was mad, yes, upset, yes, but not completely devastated as Red seemed to be.

She wanted to say something to him, but she was mad at him as well for letting Carson come to this open and deadly killing field.

A moment later a couple dozen station police in deep blue uniforms and guns drawn stormed in the doors. She put her gun on the ground at her feet and Red did the same with his two guns, never taking his gaze away from Carson.

Then they both raised their hands.

Everything had been filmed, Mattie was sure, and her membership with Sector Force would clear her since it was self-defense. But she wondered how much trouble Red was going to be in, what his background was.

She had no idea and right now she didn't much care. He had put Carson at risk and clearly not known the dangers.

But on the other hand, when pushed, he had risked his life to defend Carson. And that much alone was worth something to her.

CHAPTER TWO

MATTIE SAT in the polished and very clean Bodie Station police interrogation room with its white walls and metal table. It smelled of cleaning solution and some sort of bad cologne.

She calmly and frankly answered all the questions that needed to be answered from the five or six people that faced her at different times.

She waited patiently the time needed for the locals to check her credentials with Sector Force Three, watched the recording of the entire fight to explain to the locals what was going on and what had happened from her point of view, from the moment Carson and Red entered the large area to the moment the fight was over.

She told them nothing other than she worked with Carson and the threat was against him, which was why she was here in the first place.

Seeing Carson again smile at her with that huge pumpkin smile made her sad. Seeing Red again just made her shake her head.

As they went through the recording a second time she watched Red. He never flinched under fire and never missed. He was good, of that there was no doubt.

And extremely well-trained and experienced.

But it sure didn't explain his reaction to Carson's death. Someone that good, that well-trained had seen a lot of death, just as she had. His reaction was not a normal one.

But with what she faced in her coming mission, the question of his reaction was going to have to wait.

After the recording, she answered the same question a dozen times put to her a dozen different ways. No, she had no idea why they were after her and why they would want her or Carson or the Red person dead. She only met Red just a moment before the fight broke out. Carson had told her he feared for his life, but had not said why.

Finally, after three hours they let her go, asked her to stay on the station while they investigated more and then gave her all her things back, including the data disk that Carson had given her right before he died. It was more than likely encrypted so even if they had tried to access it, they would have had no success.

At the moment they refused to give her back her guns, but that didn't much matter since she had others carefully hidden in her luggage and clothes. Luggage she hadn't even unpacked yet, but had simply stored in rental lockers near the docking port.

She had no idea what was going to happen to Red and honestly, even if she found him so attractive as to be sinful, she had no desire to see him again anytime soon. Part of her blamed him for Carson's death even though she hadn't been able to protect Carson any more than Red could.

In the police station she made arrangements to have Carson's body taken care of and his personal belongings shipped back to Sector Force headquarters. It was all that she could do for him at this point except complete their mission and make sure those who ordered his death met their own in a very similar, but slower and far more painful way.

She left the police headquarters and, keeping a clear eye on anyone that looked threatening, she headed for the docking area to get her luggage. A safe distance back, two of the local police in tourist clothing did their best to not be noticed while following her.

She gave them the honor they deserved and pretended she didn't see them as well. It was just easier to play along with the local authorities in most cases. You never knew when they would come in handy. Sector Force like her worked alone, were highly trained, and could bring in local help where needed.

Local police and authorities didn't much like Sector Force, but almost every system in this sector had signed onto the treaty allowing them wide powers.

She reached the locker where her bags were stored and opened it, pulling her shoulder bag and light suitcase out.

"You need some help with that?" a voice said to her left.

She knew the voice instantly and was proud that she hadn't jumped in the slightest, even though he had moved up toward her silently from around a corner.

But what she couldn't control was her heart beating faster and the heat in the locker area going up. She really needed to watch herself around Red. He had an effect on her that no man that she could remember had ever had before.

"No thank you, Mr. Simms," she said. She kept her voice as low and as cold as she possibly could. She purposely did not look at him for fear of her own reaction and her attraction to him. Instead, she made sure her bags had not been tampered with in any way, then slung the one over her shoulder and picked up the second one.

She turned and started off toward the hotel resort section of the Bodie Space Station and, even though she didn't want him to, he stepped into pace beside her.

His long black coat made faint swishing sounds as he walked, but his boots made no sounds at all on the hard surface. The man was good at moving without being heard. That impressed her, among many things that impressed her about him.

She glanced back. The two police officers following him had now joined the two following her. They had a real parade going on here.

"I'm sorry," Red said, his voice low and soft.

She just kept walking, keeping her eyes forward and scanning for possible problems. Red was trying to apologize, but she was damned if she was going to let him.

"How long had you known and worked with Carson?" he asked.

It was none of his damn business, so she just kept walking.

She could hear him take a deep breath, almost like a shudder, like he was trying to come to grips with something he didn't want to face.

"I knew Carson since we were in the fifth grade together," he said. "He was my best friend ever since."

Now she looked over and up at him.

He was even more stunning than she remembered and her reaction was just as strong. But his gaze was directed forward and she could see the pain in his eyes.

"That's why he called me when he thought he might be in danger," Red said. "He knew I would protect him and I didn't. He just never told me the scale of the problem he was facing."

"I don't think he actually completely understood it himself," she said. "If I had realized there was any chance they had traced back his investigation, I never would have agreed to meet him like that, out in the open."

"He was so damned good at covering his tracks," Red said, nodding slightly. "I would have never expected it either.

Whoever you were going after is good, very, very good. And not afraid of anyone or anything, clearly."

"Your best friend?" Mattie asked, looking at Red for a moment as they walked. She wanted to see if there was any chance he was flat telling her a lie.

She didn't trust anyone at this moment, least of all him.

He nodded, not looking at her and again she could see the pain.

Clearly real pain.

"We made a hell of a team for years," he said. "Muscle and Brains. That's what our friends and family called us. I have no idea how I'm going to comfort Karen when I see her next time."

"Karen?" Mattie asked.

"His wife," Red said. "I contacted her just a few hours ago, but she didn't respond."

"I didn't know he was married," Mattie said, feeling shocked and even more saddened by Carson's death. "More than likely Sector Force contacted her the moment they learned what happened and have her under protective custody in case anyone goes after his family as well."

"Good," Red said, nodding.

"I'm sorry," she said, stunning herself that now she was the one doing the apologizing. She never did that, ever.

He only nodded.

They walked in silence together through the large ornately decorated hotel lobby to the front desk and she registered in a top-level suite. Chances

> *"I knew Carson since we were in the fifth grade together," he said. "He was my best friend ever since."*

were she would be here a few days and she deserved as much.

As she turned away from the desk and walked toward the lifts to take her to her suite, Red walked with her.

She wasn't sure what he was thinking, but she knew that right now, even as wonderful as he looked and how attracted to him she felt, she wanted to just spend some time alone and try to figure out what went wrong.

And she needed to go through the information that Carson had given her to really understand the threat.

As they neared the lifts, he stopped and turned to her. "I'm in Suite 1290. I'm going to review the information that Carson had that got him killed. If you would like, we can meet for dinner and talk about the next step in finding his killers."

She had completely forgotten that Carson had given him the same data as he had given her.

"I work alone," she said as the lift opened.

He stood his ground and nodded. "I know that. All Sector Force enforcers do. But I can tell you this much. I am going after my friend's killers. I'm going to track them down and make them pay. And there is nothing going to stop me."

He pointed across the large foyer at a restaurant seemingly hidden in what looked like a forest of some sort of oak trees. "I'll be in that restaurant in three hours having dinner. I know you work alone, but that doesn't mean we can't both help each other in the planning once we both understand what Carson got into."

She nodded and got on the lift.

The last thing she saw as the doors closed was his strong back as he turned and walked away toward a different set of lifts, his long black coat swirling silently around him.

He was so handsome in his long coat and strong stride that her breath caught.

Part of her really wanted to work with him, part of her really wanted much more than just work. But she had told him the truth. She worked alone and more than anything else, she first wanted to find out what Carson had found that had gotten him killed.

Then, and only then, would she consider her options.

And if Red had a part in those options, even for one night.

CHAPTER THREE

THE SUITE WAS LARGER than some homes she had seen. Everything, every detail seemed to be soft and plush, with thick tan carpet, thick blankets on the huge bed in the bedroom, and wonderful thick towels stacked beside a large hot tub just off the main room.

There were two different seating areas in the huge main room, both with overstuffed chairs and couches that were in varied soft hues of tan and brown. One seating area faced a large screen on one wall, another faced a massive fireplace of light and tan stone that towered over one part of the room.

Another screen covered a wall near the foot of the massive bed in the bedroom and yet another screen was tucked off to one side so it could be seen from the hot tub.

The entire room had the very faint smell of vanilla and baking cookies. A nice touch that made her realize she hadn't eaten anything in hours. She was going to have to do something about that after she learned what was going on.

A number of desks were placed into various areas of the suite and she piled her luggage on one of them.

All the softness of the colors and fabrics were designed to counteract the most impressive aspect of the suite: The ceiling. Or better put, the lack of ceiling.

Above the warm room was nothing but the rich blues and browns and reds of the swirling clouds of what looked like a curtain amid the stark and cold blackness of space. Even as tired as she was, the view stunned her.

The colors of the nebula curtain seemed impossibly vivid and bright, as if illuminated from behind by a hundred stars.

With the lights low, it would be easy to just feel like a person was in the folds of the nebula.

The area near the hot tub seemed to be completely open to space with windows that looked out in three directions and up at the nebula curtain around the station. A person could sit in the tub and seemingly float in the clouds of colors that filled the surrounding space.

Now she really understood why someone came to this resort. In all her travels around this sector, she had never seen anything like this before.

All she really wanted to do was sit in that hot tub full of slightly-too-hot water, order room service, and then fall into that huge bed and take a very long night's sleep.

But there wasn't time for that now.

She needed to know what was going on, why Carson had been killed, and she needed to know it now, before she did another thing.

She moved over to a control panel on one wall and quickly found the switch to make the ceiling go opaque. Then she took a small device from her bag and did a quick scan of the room, the bedroom, and the bathroom area for any hidden listening or camera devices.

As she had hoped, the suite was clean.

That was an advantage of not making a reservation. No one knew what room she was going to be in or when or even if she planned on staying in this resort.

At some point she would have to go to Carson's room and get his stuff, but she would cross that bridge when she needed to.

She plugged the scanner into another small device from another pocket of her bag and clicked it on. The two of them together blocked all attempts to listen or watch anything going on in this room.

Then she pulled the data stick from her pocket and plugged it into her data pad.

She sat down on the soft, deep couch, put her feet up on the coffee table and perched the data pad on her lap and slowly started through the information that Carson had found.

Forty minutes later, her hands shaking, she finished. There were parts of that information she needed to watch again, maybe even two or three times, but first she needed to take a shower and get something to eat.

She clicked the intercom to the main desk. "Connect me to room twelve-ninety please."

Red answered after a moment with a curt, "Yeah."

"Forty-five minutes in the restaurant," she said.

"Okay," he said flatly and hung up.

She had a hunch he had just gone through the same data she had and was feeling the same way about it all. This was one job she couldn't tackle alone and she knew it.

And she guessed he knew he couldn't do it alone either.

With this task, she wasn't afraid to admit it. There was far, far too much at risk. And if she had to, she would call in more Sector Force agents.

She quickly set up her data pad to encode all the information on Carson's drive into something that could only be deciphered at Sector Force Headquarters. Then she sent it.

It would take the Sector Force Three hours to go through it and even longer to study the data and get prepared in case she called them in.

Then she sent off an urgent query for as much information about a Red Simms as they could provide. That part would take hours to get back to her, but at least after dinner she would know more about the man that she was going to have to work with.

It was going to be her and Red trying to save both the Sector Force and many more lives through the known sectors. It was no wonder Carson had called his friend to come and help protect him. Now she too was going to need all the help she could get.

It was going to be two of them against what seemed, from what Carson found, to be an army possibly with a fleet of ships. She wondered if Red was going to be willing to even go against those odds. She had a hunch he wouldn't even hesitate.

She had that much of a sense of him.

She turned and strode toward the bathroom. She needed a hot shower and a change of clothes and then a good dinner with the most handsome man she had ever met.

If she was going to take on a suicide mission, she might as well be fed and have great company.

CHAPTER FOUR

RED HUNG UP the phone and stared at it for a moment before turning back to watching the last of the data that Carson had found. The information that had gotten him killed.

Clearly Mattie had gotten completely through the information and had come to the same conclusion he had come to already. They were both going to need help, and maybe a lot of it.

And they were going to have to work together. Something about that idea both excited him and worried him. He wasn't one to trust anyone, let alone a Sector Force Three agent, but she had to be the most alluring and attractive woman he had met in years.

He stopped and stared off into space at the oranges and blues and reds in the curtain pattern of the nebula.

The room around him was a beautiful two-bedroom suite with a huge living room, huge hot tub, and an enclosed deck with a private heated swimming pool that allowed the guests to swim under the stars and the fantastic colors of the nebula filling the sky overhead. It was the largest and most expensive suite in the entire complex and he could care less at the moment.

He had originally booked it when Carson called. He had been thinking they would sit around and talk and enjoy it. Money didn't matter to Red, since he was one of the richest men in this sector, and maybe many sectors, thanks to his family money and some really well-timed investments of his own. Plus the business that he and Carson had started had made him yet another fortune.

But right now, instead of enjoying all this and the beauty that surrounded this incredible suite, all he could think about was losing his best friend, how stupid he had been to let that happen, and how angry he was at everything. All he wanted to do was punch things, but he had learned a long time ago that made no difference at all.

If he had just brought Carson to this suite, kept him here, instead of allowing him to go out into such a public place as that shopping area. And if Carson would have just told him a little more of the problems he had discovered. It had taken a lot for Carson to call him and ask for his help.

And Red had failed him completely and totally.

He took a deep breath and forced himself to stay controlled.

Red clicked back on the information from Carson and finished the last fifteen minutes of it. Basically, what Carson had discovered was that the plots against the Sector Force Three command and agents were staged by what seemed to be an organization bent on taking over entire systems of planets. Maybe even most of Sector Three. And it seemed this army of people had a fleet of ships as well.

For some reason, this organization felt as if the Sector Force organization and their scattered agents was one of their only major threats. They seemed to have no fear of any local or system-wide government. They had more than enough forces to take care of single systems.

But sector-wide organizations with the ability to control and send out highly trained agents scared them to death for some reason. Red had no idea why.

He had hated the Sector Force and had for a long time. It was Sector Force that had broken up the partnership he and Carson had had over a great five years.

He forced himself to contain that anger as well.

When Carson had walked out on their business, Red had turned over the day-to-day operations to someone they both had trusted and gotten drunk for six days. He and Carson had only talked rarely the year after that, but over the last year they were patching things up, getting their friendship back.

But in all the conversations, Carson had never mentioned he had gone to work for the Sector Force. Not once, not even a hint. More than likely he was afraid of what Red would say.

And he would have been right.

Red shut down the information coming over his data pad and tucked the data stick into his pocket. He had no doubt that Mattie would have already sent off the entire thing to Sector Force Three headquarters in the Webb System, but he doubted any Sector Force agents would be out this far on the edge of the sector, or could get here soon enough to help them.

At least not from the timeline that Carson had discovered.

He had already sent off the same information to his people, but it would take them a few hours to analyze everything.

Red had a couple of ideas to maybe buy them a little help, but he doubted Mattie would like the ideas in any fashion, if his sense of her was right.

He had already sent off instructions to his people back home to dig up as much information about Mattie Silks as they could and get it to him quickly. But even quickly was going to take hours at least on that as well.

And he had them searching in everything they could find, every detail about the organization Carson had talked about. He had never heard of anything like that before and that bothered him more than he wanted to admit.

He glanced at the time. He had thirty minutes before meeting Mattie in the restaurant. He needed to wash off some of the police grime and try to go into the evening with a fresh start and a halfway clear mind.

But he had a hunch that being around Mattie was going to do anything but keep his mind clear. There was just something about that fantastically beautiful, fantastically dangerous small woman that fogged his mind and made him want to just ignore everything else.

But for the moment he couldn't do that. He had to stay focused.

He owed Carson, and he was going to make sure the people who killed his friend paid a very, very heavy price.

CHAPTER FIVE

MATTIE SAW the two station police who were assigned to follow Red sitting outside the restaurant pretending to not care. What a horrid assignment, to follow two people who could ditch them in a moment even on their own space station.

Her two keepers had actually come down the elevator with her. She hadn't spoken with them, but she knew they were smart enough to know the score. More than likely they had seen the tapes of the firefight and knew just how deadly she and Red were.

She only had one gun hidden on her tonight, very well hidden, actually. She had no doubt Red had done the same.

The restaurant was sheltered in what seemed like a forest to one side of the vast lobby of the resort hotel. The trees looked to be oak and were as real as anything she had ever seen. There was even a faint forest smell that mixed with the fantastic smells coming from the hidden kitchen. Her stomach actually rumbled as she entered between two large trunks of trees.

Red sat alone at a table near a window that looked out into space and at the curtain nebula. One thing she had to admit, the views from this place would never get old.

Red turned and saw her as she wound her way through the tables and trees. He gave her that same half-smile he had given her the first time they met. And again it snapped up the heat around her and twisted her stomach. It was lucky that smile didn't melt the leaves off the trees and start a forest fire.

"Down girl," she whispered to herself as she moved toward his table.

He had on a casual dress shirt and slacks and had his long dark hair pulled back tight off his face. Without the hair and the stunningly perfect body, he could almost pass for a regular businessman.

She had picked tan dress pants, a white blouse, and a tan business jacket. She too could pass for a businessperson here for an important meeting.

Her heart fluttered as he actually stood when she approached, towering over her. No one did that, yet he had, as if she were royalty of some sort.

Thank heavens he didn't reach for her hand, but instead indicated a chair facing him across the table. She wasn't certain what kind of control she could maintain if he actually touched her.

Why did they keep the heat up so high in this place anyway? She knew her face must be flushed but she pretended nothing was wrong or different.

He really had an effect on her. Part of her liked the feeling, part of her was really annoyed at it. She had other things to focus on at the moment.

"Thanks for joining me," he said, his deep voice actually letting her know that he was sincere.

"You saw Carson's information?" she asked, deciding to jump right to the point.

"I did," he said, staring at her with those fantastic green eyes.

"What do you think?" she asked, staring right back.

He just shook his head. "I think we have our jobs cut out for us. But first I think we need to eat. I'm starved."

She nodded. "I agree," she said.

"About which part?" he asked, smiling.

Damn that smile of his could kill a person without even trying. Did he even know what he was doing to her?

"About both parts," she said, managing to smile back at him.

He motioned for a waiter who was standing off about ten paces to come over.

She watched the motion. Clearly this was a man who was used to getting what he wanted when he wanted it and controlling the people around him. More than likely there was money behind him, a lot of money.

She would know soon enough. The Sector Force research people were very, very good. They had to be.

It had been one of the things that Carson had done so well.

They spent the next ten minutes as they ordered and their drinks arrived making small talk about the hotel, the restaurant, and the views. Then, as the waiter left, he smiled at her again.

"I suppose you are having me investigated as we sit here," he said, smiling.

"Of course," she said, slightly surprised he had brought up the topic in that fashion. "And I suppose you are doing the same for me."

He nodded. "So what would you like to know now, here at dinner, before you get the cold report from your people."

She sat back, staring into his deep green eyes. He was serious.

"You're going to be truthful?" she asked.

"Considering what we are facing, and that I just lost my best friend, I see no reason not to be."

She nodded. She still didn't trust him in any fashion at all, but this would be an interesting test.

"How rich are you?"

"Beyond stupidly rich," he said, shaking his head as if he really was annoyed and almost embarrassed about how much money he had. "I earn more every day, every minute, than I could ever spend."

She nodded. She had figured as much.

"So you don't belong to any organization?"

He shrugged. "Not in the strict sense of the word like Sector Force. But Carson and I started a business a number of years back, a protection business for those who think they needed protecting and could afford to pay for it."

Suddenly his last name Simms came back to her. Oh, oh, she was having dinner with that Red Simms.

"Innocence Incorporated?" she asked, stunned.

He nodded.

"You and Carson started Innocence Inc.?"

She wanted to get up and leave the table now. She understood that when Red learned Carson was working for Sector Force Three, he had been stunned. Innocence Inc. and Sector Force Three seemed to have an uneasy truce of sorts, on two sides of the same job. They seldom tangled, but when they did, it had not been pretty.

"We started it after a friend of Carson's was framed for a sector crime he had not committed," Red said. "Carson did the research and discovered that the man was telling the truth, he had not committed the crime, had not been convicted of the crime on any planet or in any Sector Court, but a Hunter and the person who hired the Hunter didn't seem to care."

She nodded to that, doing her best to calm her anger and listen. The Hunters were a loosely-based organization that often killed their targets for any reason or price. Sector Force had often tried to take them down, but had always failed. They worked the fringes of law enforcement on the sector-wide level, always for hire.

Sector Force Three had strict standards for their agents. Their targets, as they called those they were trying to either capture or stop, were those who were convicted and clearly guilty of crimes against humanity in one star system or another, but had jumped to other systems or another sector to escape justice. Sector Force agents were the enforcers of justice, for lack of a better way of putting it, on a sector-wide scale.

Sector Force agents made sure the convicted killers and mass murderers did not get away with their crimes no matter how far they ran.

Red went on. "We started our business to defend those who were unjustly accused, who had not committed the crimes, but yet still had a sector-wide arrest warrant on their head. In the first five years of business, we never took a client targeted by Sector Force Three. The clients targeted by Sector Force Three were always guilty."

"Then," she said as he stopped and looked out the window into space.

"Then we took a job from a man named Beacher."

"Beacher the Butcher?" she asked, shocked. She pushed her chair back to leave. She remembered the case and there was no way she could talk to or even have dinner with a man who defended such a killer. Beacher had murdered almost one thousand families, fathers, mothers, and children on his home planet in a botched experiment. He had been tried and convicted and sentenced to death before he escaped and fled. There was no doubt as to his guilt.

Red nodded and went on. "Beacher, when he hired us, sent us false data, false records, false everything. We took the defense, took his money. It was to be the first time we were to go up against the Sector Force Three. But then Carson discovered the truth, dug out what really happened and presented me with all the evidence."

"What did you do then?" Mattie asked, keeping her voice low and controlled. His next answer would be the key to everything, of that she had no doubt.

"I attempted to give Beacher back his money, but he would have none of it. He was going to hold us to our contract with him to defend him." Red shrugged. "So

I killed the bastard myself. Dumped his body into deep space."

Mattie stared at the handsome man across from her. That was the last thing she had expected him to say or admit to her, an agent of sector law.

Red went on with his clearly painful story. "Carson and his financial team raided all of Beacher's assets, shut down his corporations, and gave all the money to charities on his home planet. When we were done, Carson decided we had come too close to being duped. He thought we should shut down Innocence Inc. I did not agree. It was the only real fight we ever had in all our years of friendship."

Red looked off out the window, his eyes vacant. "Carson quit. I had no idea he had gone to work for Sector Force Three even though he had no need of the money, but in hindsight it makes sense. Justice was all Carson ever cared about. And Sector Force Three is all about true justice."

Mattie just sat there, staring at the handsome man, shaking her head. The Sector Force Three had labeled Innocence Inc. a problem organization simply because of the Beacher case. No assassin had ever been able to track Beacher and everyone knew his companies had dissolved. Everyone thought Beacher had got away because of Innocence Inc.

Mattie chuckled to herself.

"What's so funny?" Red asked, turning on her, clear anger in his green eyes.

"Someday you might want to set the record straight on all that," she said, smiling at him. It might get your company some cases sent your way from Sector Force Three, the ones we know are false charges."

He shrugged and went back to looking out the window. Clearly he was a man who didn't much care what people thought of him. She liked that more than she wanted to admit. It made him even more handsome if that was possible.

But the loss of his friend was clearly hurting him.

"We'll get the bastards," she said.

"And how do you propose we do that?" he asked, looking back at her.

She smiled at him. "Somewhere in Carson's data, the data your people are sending you, and the data Sector Force researchers are sending me, there will be a way. We just have to put our heads together and find it."

He nodded and then with one more look out the window, he turned back to face her directly, his green eyes holding her gaze. "Deal," he said, smiling.

Once again the temperature in the room went up a few degrees. She couldn't pull away from looking into his eyes and he couldn't seem to look away either.

They were saved a moment later by the arrival of the wine and some wonderful-smelling bread.

She hadn't realized how hungry she was, in more ways than one.

CHAPTER SIX

MATTIE HADN'T ENJOYED a meal as much as the one with Red in a long, long time. At least it was great after she got over the shock of the fact that he was the Red Simms, the founder of Innocence Incorporated, which everyone at Sector Force disliked.

And after he had proven to her that he had actually killed the hated mass murder named Beacher.

He had simply handed her his tablet with a picture of Beacher's body on it. One hole through the forehead, two in the chest. Classic. The man was clearly dead.

She had asked him if she had permission to send this and his other records on the death and destruction of Beacher and his organization to Sector Force Three and he only shrugged. She loved the fact that he didn't care about what others thought of him, but if they were going to work together, better to have what tainted his name and organization with Sector Force Three out of the way.

She sent the picture and some other information he gave her off to Sector Force headquarters right from the table. She got that done between the bread arriving and their salads.

Her only note with the picture was "We were wrong about Innocence Inc. and their involvement with Beacher. They didn't protect him, they killed him. It all should be in Carson's records as well if you dig deep enough."

Then she relaxed into the wonderful dinner and conversation with the swirling blues and reds and oranges of the nebula out the window on one side and the forest of deep green and browns over and around them. Just the setting alone made her relax some.

The main course was a white fish native to a local nearby system sautéed in a light butter sauce with a side of sweet-tasting green stalks she had never seen or tried before. Light and tasty and perfect. It melted in her mouth. During the meal they talked about her being raised on Webber, the home planet for Sector Force Three. Then they talked about his parents and family.

She was surprised that for a rich family, they had seemed to be pretty normal. He had one younger sister who worked in the family business with his father.

She discovered, much to her relief, that he had no relationships at the moment, but had been close to marriage once. All he would say about it with a shrug of indifference was that it didn't work out. And not working out had been a good thing for him.

To Mattie, he hadn't seemed broken up about the memory of the relationship at all or maybe it was so far in the past he no longer cared.

That fact made her very happy. And when she caught herself thinking that, she shut the idea down. They were working together. They needed to keep it professional.

She had a hunch that wasn't going to happen. Not the way she was feeling about him, and the way he clearly was feeling about her. As far as she was concerned, it was lucky they didn't have wild sex right in the middle of the table in the restaurant.

That would have shocked the four security men trailing them.

She and Red talked about Carson after the main course while waiting for dessert. They both described how they had met Carson. Red seemed very interested about how she had met him and how she had admired and liked him a great deal. That made him smile fondly for some reason.

Finally, as they finished their dessert of a red berry cobbler covered in a white sweet sauce of some sort, Mattie got to the point about their coming mission. "From what you read of Carson's research, how long do you think we have?"

Red ordered another bottle of wine, then turned his green eyes on her before answering. "A couple days at most. It depends on where these fleets of ships are located and what they are exactly."

She nodded. "I'm hoping someone in Sector Force headquarters or DI has heard of them. Carson's notes didn't seem to shine any light on their possible location at all."

"Only that they are a distance out of the sector, in the area called The Emptiness. But somehow Carson thinks they are headed inward, toward this sector and will be close enough to start attacks within two or three days."

"Huge ships?" she asked.

He just shrugged. "Maybe. Or maybe some sort of massive fleet. I have a hunch we're going to find out soon enough."

Mattie was grasping for anything that might help them at this point. It made no sense that if there was a fleet coming in from out of the depths of space, why worry about a single operative like Carson or try to destroy an organization like Sector Force.

Sector Force Three had remained completely non-political in all aspects of its work. And Mattie doubted if anyone at Sector Force much cared who ran which system in which sector and why.

And if they were coming in from that direction, where were they coming from? It was a very long distance to another sector across that emptiness.

Nothing about this seemed to make any sense at all. But it was her job to make sense of it.

She and Red shared another bottle of red wine and went back to small talk, trying to learn more about each other. Clearly he felt it was as important to their coming mission as she did. And he seemed sincerely interested in her background. So they talked of their favorite classes in school, hers being anything physical while he loved the sciences more.

> *"If we are to be fighting this fight together, it is always good to know another master is at your side."*

"Where did you learn to fight?" she asked.

"Groff," he said, casually.

She damn near spit out her mouthful of fine wine.

Groff was a city known for its training of the top martial arts and marksmen champions in the entire known universe.

She had trained on Groff as well. Many in the Sector Force did. If you couldn't manage the training at any point in the two years, they sent you away. It was the hardest she had ever worked in her entire life. But it had turned her into a controlled and finely-tuned machine when she needed to be. But the key was the control it gave each person who graduated.

"When were you there?" she asked.

He told her which two years and she said, "We missed by a year. I was there the two years following you."

Now it was his turn to be surprised. She enjoyed that look on his face.

"And I trained under a Groff master for a number of years in Sector Force headquarters as well to keep my skills toned."

He tipped his glass in respect toward her and bowed slightly. "If we are to be fighting this fight together, it is always good to know another master is at your side."

She tipped her glass and did the same shallow bow in return, showing her respect.

"I agree," she said.

Suddenly she felt a lot better about working with Red. Groff masters were taught complete control in all dangerous situations. She had a hunch they were going to be facing some.

It also explained why he was so cool and collected in the firefight in the mall earlier.

They finished the last of the wine making more small talk before he said to her. "Would you like to get the data from Sector Force and meet in my suite? We can do our planning there. I have it swept and completely dampened from any possible spying."

Her heart skipped and her stomach twisted slightly around the wonderful meal and wine. Could she trust herself to be alone in a suite with this man?

Did she dare do that?

The faint smile and his green eyes answered her question completely. She didn't trust herself in the slightest, but at this point it didn't matter. She was going to need to satisfy the other half of her appetite with this dangerous man before she would ever be able to focus completely on the coming task at hand.

And besides, if she was going to die in the next few days, she might as well die with a smile on her face.

CHAPTER SEVEN

RED COULD NOT BELIEVE he had invited Mattie up to his suite to work on the data. The woman was as dangerous as they came, both in sheer physical power and skills, but also dangerous to him because he just could not stop thinking about her.

He hadn't felt that way about a woman since his fiancé left him nine years ago just as they got out of college. Sarina didn't think he would ever amount to anything. She told him flat out, at the top of her voice, that he would always just coast on his family's money.

And if she hadn't left him like that, said all those hateful things, she might have been right.

Her leaving forced him to take another look at himself, to get into Groff for training in self-discipline. He and Carson had founded Innocence Inc. when he graduated from Groff knowing that innocent people were being framed and convicted and killed or imprisoned for crimes they didn't commit.

At one point he asked Carson to look up Sarina, see how she had ended up. She had married a low-level, but struggling businessman in the recycling business on their home planet. He was working his way up the corporate ladder, undoubtedly making Sarina happy with the struggle.

But now Mattie made him feel young again.

And really alive.

The attraction between them was real, of that he had no doubt. Somehow they were going to have to deal with that aspect of working together. It was clear she was attracted to him as much as he was to her.

It was just too bad Carson was no longer with them to make fun of him. He had always said that Sarina wasn't his match. Red wondered what Carson would think of him being with Mattie.

He shook away the image of Carson lying dead beside that planter and focused on the task at hand. He would deal with the grief of losing his friend later, when there was time to mourn. Right now he had work to do and Carson's death to avenge.

He went to his link with his headquarters and downloaded everything they had sent. No one there had even heard of anything about a fleet of ships coming in from The Emptiness, but they were still searching. But there had been various reports of strange ships seeming to come into the sector from the direction of The Emptiness.

No one had thought that odd at all until he asked about it. There was still one ship docked in the spaceport of the Bodie Station that was of the design of ships known to come in from The Emptiness. More than likely the ship that had brought the group in that attacked them in the mall.

He made note of that to tell Mattie. They might find some clues on that ship of what they were facing if they could get in it. Or at least get the information from the ship the police had found. He was sure they would have searched it if they realized it was connected.

However, the security forces here at the station might not have put that together yet. In this sector so many people traveled in the big interstellar passenger ships.

Then Red went over the notes on Mattie Silks, the woman now heading toward his suite. She was considered the top agent in Sector Force Three, deadly and effective in just about any circumstance.

The people at his headquarters warned him away from her, saying she was far, far too deadly and too inside Sector Force way of life to trust in any fashion.

He didn't trust her, but he wasn't afraid of her. However, he was extremely attracted to her. More than he cared to admit. And if he had any hope of going up against the force that Carson seemed to think was coming into the sector, he needed the most deadly Sector Force enforcer there was at his side.

CHAPTER EIGHT

MATTIE HESITATED for just a moment outside the door to Suite 1290 and then knocked.

This was stupid. She felt like a schoolgirl with a crush about to do something that would get her in trouble.

The information Sector Force had sent about Red was complete and matched everything he had told her over their dinner. And it also linked him and Carson in the way Red had said.

Sector Force knew that Carson had been a founder of Innocence Inc. and been happy to have him join Sector Force. And they had known for over a year that Red and Innocence Inc. were not a threat in any way to Sector Force. In fact, the report said they had often been on the same side, especially with Carson working for Sector Force Three.

Red might not have known what organization Carson was working for, but people at Innocence Inc. did and funneled him information all the time. Mattie had a hunch that Red would either think that typical of his lost friend or be angry.

Chances are he would find it funny and yet be disappointed their friendship had dropped so far that Carson was afraid to tell him something.

No one in Sector Force headquarters had ever heard of anything about a fleet of ships approaching the sector, but they were still searching.

Red answered the door and smiled at her and then stepped back to allow her to come in. He had kicked off his shoes, rolled up his shirtsleeves, and clearly had been working on one couch in the gigantic suite.

Her heart raced as she stepped inside. No man should ever be allowed to be that attractive.

"Wow!" she said, walking in and looking around, trying to keep herself from staring at him. "I thought my suite was huge. This dwarfs it."

He laughed and dropped onto the couch and picked up his data pad again. "Take a look at the indoor pool under the stars and nebula. It's a stunner."

He gestured for her to move up past the hot tub.

She did, trying to give herself a moment to calm down.

The full-sized pool was stunning as he had suggested and all she could do was imagine herself swimming nude in it with him watching.

She was having a hard time even catching her breath. She tried to shake her head to clear it, but it didn't work. Before either of them were going to get any work done at all, this attraction had to be satisfied.

"The water warm in the pool?" she asked, sliding open the large glass door that led from the suite out to the indoor private pool. The smell of the pool and the plants surrounding it hit her like she had walked into a thick, rich garden.

"It's supposed to be," he said, studying something in front of him. "I haven't been here long enough to test it yet."

"Any of your people know anything about that fleet of ships?" she asked, standing half in the doorway to the pool, half in the suite.

He shook his head. "Not a clue," he said. "But they are still searching."

"Sector Force researchers are doing the same," she said.

She took a deep breath of the moist pool area and then looked at the back of Red where he sat on the couch, his long dark hair tied back. They could keep playing this sex game or they could resolve it now and then get to work. Clearly he had no more leads at the moment than she had, so they had time.

She kicked off her shoes and left them just inside the suite on the thick, rich brown carpet. Then she moved out closer to the large indoor pool, leaving the door to the suite wide open.

The bright oranges and reds and blues of the nebula seemed to almost surround the pool, draping over the sky like a giant bright curtain over a window, making her feel like she was standing in space. Thousands of bright stars lit up the rest of the sky around it.

It was stunning.

One of the most beautiful sights she had ever seen in a life full of traveling many sectors of space.

She stood for a long moment, staring upward at the colors and the stars, her stomach twisting like she was a teenager back on her first date. What happened if he wasn't interested in her?

Or rejected her advances?

She shook that thought away and slipped out of the dress jacket she wore at dinner, placing it over a table on the deck beside the pool.

Then she took out her gun and laid it on her jacket.

He still hadn't turned around, so she slipped out of her slacks and underwear, then her blouse and bra, standing there naked on the pool deck.

Talk about feeling totally free.

She had never felt anything like this before, naked under the bright oranges and blues and greens of the curtain nebula and all the stars behind it and around it.

She moved over to the edge of the pool, then with a quick shallow dive sliced the water perfectly, coming up near the other side.

Floating in the water with space all around her was not a feeling she had ever imagined before.

It was magical.

Beyond magical.

Dreamlike.

She swam on her back, leisurely kicking and stroking toward the other end of the pool while staring up at the sky and the bright colors.

As she neared the edge of the pool she could see Red's tall figure and smiling face standing on the edge, towering over her.

"This is amazing," she said, her voice far more breathy and light than she had imagined it could be.

"So are you," he said.

She reached the edge, turned over and pushed herself up easily out of the water right in front of him.

Then she simply reached up and pulled that handsome face down to hers and kissed him like she had never kissed anyone before.

And he kissed her back harder and more intensely than she had ever been kissed before.

CHAPTER NINE

AFTER THAT FIRST intense and wonderful kiss, Mattie pushed back from him, turned and did a shallow dive back into the pool. Luckily it was a shallow dive, because she had very little breath left in her after that amazing kiss.

Wow, that man could kiss. Their lips had seemed to fit perfectly together and he had tasted wonderful, like light cinnamon.

No man was supposed to taste of light cinnamon.

She surfaced and turned toward him, smiling, brushing the water back from her face.

"I'd take those clothes off," she said, standing in the shallow water so that he could see her breasts. "And put that gun over on a table unless you plan on spending a few hours drying it and cleaning it. Because those clothes are coming off you, mister, and you are getting wet very quickly, one way or another."

He laughed, a sound that echoed over the water, a sound that seemed magical under the stars and the beautiful colors overhead.

Her heart was racing so fast, she could barely keep herself under control. She had no memory of ever experiencing this kind of intense hunger and longing for a man.

But somehow she managed to just stand there in the water, pretending to be calm, watching him.

He took too steps to the table with her clothes on it, put his gun beside hers, then unbuttoned and pulled off his shirt.

Again she was suddenly short of breath.

How was that possible? He looked better without a shirt on than he did with one. Not many men she had ever seen were that way.

Under the stars his skin seemed to almost ripple. She wanted to get to know every inch of that skin. Kiss and stroke it all.

He slipped out of his slacks and underwear and turned to face her. He was clearly as aroused as she felt and everything about him was proportioned.

Everything.

She felt like she might never breathe again. She couldn't say anything even if she had wanted to.

He took two quick steps and did a shallow dive into the pool, coming up almost immediately in front of her.

She wrapped her arms over his shoulders and around his neck and he stood in the shallow pool, pulling her up with him.

She kissed him again, just as hard and as wonderful as the first time.

She could feel his intense hardness against her, promising wonderful times ahead as he kissed her back, intense, exploring her lips and mouth with his tongue.

She finally couldn't wait even another second.

She wrapped her legs around him and slid down, letting him enter her with a smooth, single motion.

So perfect, so intense.

They fit perfectly together.

Suddenly, he became the most gentle man she had ever met.

And the strongest.

He held her still, not allowing her to even move on him, kissing her softly on her face, her neck, her arms. It felt like he had six arms and hands holding her, and she loved every sense of the touch.

Moving slowly, making each kiss linger on the spot like it was the most important spot on her body.

He didn't seem to miss one spot on her face and neck and shoulders, the entire time holding her on him, not allowing her to move on him at all no matter how much she wanted to move.

And wow did she want to.

Her entire being felt like it might explode at any moment.

She wanted to move faster and harder than she had ever moved on any man.

She twisted, enjoying the kisses, the feeling of him filling her completely.

But she had to move.

She had to.

She could feel him straining to hold her still.

Then finally he moved her, just slightly up and then back down.

And then once more.

She leaned her head back, staring up at the stars and the intense colors, but not seeing them, and with one more easy movement, she exploded in the most intense release she had felt in her memory.

It seemed to go on for an eternity.

And then he joined her, shuddering as everything he had been holding back released into her, filling her even more.

Her release had started to subside, but then she joined him completely again.

Time around her stretched.

She shuddered twice, then he did as well.

She was amazed he managed to stay standing in the water. She knew she never would have been able to.

She shuddered again a few more times and then leaned back up into him, holding him, kissing his neck and face and lips.

It was her turn and she didn't miss a spot.

And he kissed her, sometimes hard, sometimes gently, never letting himself slip out of her, moving his hands over her, seeming to touch every spot at once.

Finally, with her wrapped around him, her arms around his shoulders, her legs gripping his hips, and him still solidly inside her, he turned and started moving toward the stairs out of the pool.

"And just where do you think you are going, mister?" she whispered in his ear as she nibbled gently on it.

"To someplace a little dryer and softer," he said. Then he kissed her with a passion she had never seen before.

They barely made it inside the door to the soft carpet where he lowered both of them to the floor and turned over onto his back, letting her sit on top of him.

She sat up straight and stretched back, letting herself enjoy the feel of him filling her.

"You are the most beautiful woman I have ever seen," he said, his voice almost a hush. He slowly worked his hands along her waist, up to her breasts, then around her shoulders before moving back to her breasts and down along her hips.

His hands were still wet, but she could feel the hardness in them, and the tenderness. His touch sent shivers through her, causing her to move on him.

He thrust up into her, trying to hold her still, but this time she would control him.

And there was going to be no waiting this time around.

She shoved him back down and started to move on him, faster and faster.

> *"You are the most beautiful woman I have ever seen," he said, his voice almost a hush.*

For a moment he kept his hands moving on her breasts, her shoulders, her back, seemingly everywhere at once. Then he just dropped his arms to his sides and let her take complete control as she picked up her pace until finally a second release hit her, even more powerful than the first one in the pool.

And once again he joined her with more passion and love than she had ever felt before.

She had no idea how long that moment lasted. It felt like it went on forever, and yet was over far, far too quickly.

As the waves of pleasure subsided, she slumped down onto his chest and hugged him. He put an arm around her, breathing hard.

They lay that way on the carpet until they both had caught their breaths. Then she pushed herself back up to look into those wonderful green eyes. He was still inside her, but she could feel his passion starting to subside.

She smiled at him, then quickly kissed him before once again pushing herself back up to sit straight on him.

"Now that was some dessert," she said.

He smiled and laughed. "That it was."

"You ready to get to work?" she asked.

He nodded. "I might be able to concentrate on something besides you, now."

She laughed and stood, standing over him, straddling him, letting him stare up at her naked body from his position on the floor. "We'll see how long that lasts."

He couldn't seem to do anything but just stare up at her. He opened his mouth, but not one word came out.

She held that pose just long enough that he would never forget the view, then stepped back out onto the pool deck, retrieved her gun and clothes, and headed for the bathroom.

The entire time all he did was lay there on the floor, his magnificent body completely exposed as he watched her.

And she loved being watched by him. Far more than she wanted to admit.

Her knees were wobbling and she wanted to just go back and sit on him again, hold him, make love to him all night long.

Somehow she made it to the bathroom. They had work to do first.

But she knew, without a doubt, there would be a next time. And as far as she was concerned, that next time better be pretty damned soon.

CHAPTER TEN

RED JUST LAY THERE on the carpet and watched Mattie move to the bathroom. There was no doubt in his mind she was the most beautiful and sexy and passionate woman he had ever been with.

And maybe the most dangerous as well, not because of her ability to kill someone with a simple hit, but dangerous to his mind. As she had walked to the bathroom, all he wanted to do was ask her to come back.

Yet he knew they had work to do and little time to do it if Carson was right.

The thought of his friend being gone forced him to climb to his feet.

Carson would have liked the two of them together, of that Red now had no doubt.

He moved back out onto the patio, retrieved his gun and clothes and headed into his bedroom, doing his best to push out the fantastic memory of what had just happened and the wonderful images of her standing naked in front of him at the pool.

Or standing over him in the living room.

She knew how to make a sexy memory, that was for sure.

There would be time for more memories if he had his way.

But right now he and Mattie had to figure out what had caused Carson's death and what to do next to stop a possible sector invasion Carson saw coming.

If there was anything they could do.

He cleaned up in the master bedroom bathroom, dried his long hair as best he could, slipped on a clean dress shirt and slacks, and rolled up his sleeves again. He left his gun on the table just inside the bedroom door.

He didn't trust her completely, but at the moment they needed to work together, needed to give and take a little trust to get this job done.

In the process they needed to survive and get to know each other better.

And make some more wonderful memories.

He had just dropped onto the couch when she came out of the bathroom.

She simply took his breath away every time he saw her. No woman had ever done that to him. He wanted to go to her, hold her, kiss her again, but he knew that would not help what they needed to do right now, so he just smiled at her smile and said nothing.

She had left her jacket off and now only wore the white blouse. She also had rolled up the long sleeves on the blouse giving her a look of an office worker after hours.

She put her jacket on the small table near the door and he heard the slight clunk of her gun in the jacket pocket. She also dropped her shoes near the door, picked up the data pad she had brought with her and walked toward him barefoot.

So she was trusting him just a little as well.

That was a good start at least.

And the sex had been a great start.

She moved over behind the couch, leaned down and kissed his upturned face.

He kissed her back until she pulled away, smiling. "Someday," she said, "you are going to have to tell me how you suddenly grow extra arms."

He laughed. "Trained in message therapy," he said.

"Oh, my," was all she said to that and he smiled again at her. She clearly had enjoyed that skill.

Then she came around the couch and sat in a chair facing him. Clearly she felt that a safe distance for both of them at the moment.

He couldn't agree more.

"Where do we start?" she asked.

"I think we have two choices," he said. "We could go through every bit of the data Carson gave us together, seeing if either of us missed something."

She nodded. That made sense, but he knew that neither of them had missed anything.

"Or we could try to get into the ship that brought the attackers here," he said, "see if we can find anything there."

Her eyes slightly enlarged. "You think they had one and it's still here?"

He had surprised her with information she didn't have and hadn't thought of.

"My people tell me it is," Red said. "You think that might be a something important?"

She nodded. "We can try to get in their ship. See what we can see, download any data they have in there and where their last flight came from. It might back up Carson's data. And besides, Carson's data will always be here when we get back. We have entire organizations working on it right now."

"I agree," he said. "But any ideas how we might get permission to board that craft?"

"Smile nicely at the men outside," she said, laughing. "I'll bet their chief of security hadn't thought of that ship either."

Red laughed. "I'll bet you're right. Can you call Sector Force headquarters and pull a few strings?"

She nodded. "I can try."

"Good," he said. "I'll call my people and see if they can help as well. Between us we might get something or someone to budge to let us in that ship."

"Never hurts to try," she said.

"But first we have to stop at my ship," he said. "I have some equipment on board that can sense bombs and other kinds of traps that might have been set for anyone going aboard."

"Of course you have a ship," she said, shaking her head and standing.

"Comes in handy when you want to haul around a lot of stuff," he said, laughing.

"I'll bet."

He headed for the bedroom to get shoes and his gun.

By the time he came out she had her shoes and jacket back on and he had no doubt she was armed and very dangerous.

And that was one of the many, many things he liked about her.

CHAPTER ELEVEN

MATTIE WAS SURPRISED that Red's people had discovered the attackers had come on a ship. She spent so much time on the big intersystem passenger ships, it just hadn't occurred to her they hadn't also arrived in some similar fashion.

When she contacted Sector Force Headquarters, she asked them to check any registry of any odd ships in the port here. And then do whatever it would take to get her permission to get on that ship.

Red had done the same for his people.

She gave him one more kiss on the cheek just before he opened the door to the suite.

"That was fun," he said. "You up for a rematch?"

She just laughed. "When you are and the time is right."

With that he gave her one of his soul-melting smiles and opened the door to his suite.

Again she asked herself how one man could be so attractive, kiss so well, and smell so good at the same time.

Outside in the foyer four of the station police sat. Two were asleep, but jerked awake as she and Red approached. They were all wearing tourist-like bright clothing, but clearly all were uncomfortable in the look. And none of them could hide their guns well under those bright flowered shirts.

She and Red walked up to them. "Gentlemen," she said, smiling at them with her sweetest smile, "we need to talk to your chief of security at once. Can you have him meet us somewhere close to the port, please?"

"But it's late," one of the men said, his voice a half-whine.

"We know," Red said. "But this is a matter of station security. You think that firefight this afternoon was bad, there is much worse coming. We need to talk to your security chief and now."

With that Mattie turned away and Red matched her step-for-step.

It felt wonderful having him at her side. She loved working alone, but this was a feeling she had no doubt she could grow to like.

Behind them the four station security officers thundered along all the way to the lift like a herd of cattle.

She and Red got on the lift and smiled at the four men watching them.

"We're headed to the port," Red said to them. "We do not plan to leave. Have your chief meet us near my ship."

All four men nodded like their heads were on the same string as the lift doors closed.

She could barely contain the laughter until the lift had moved them far enough away from the four officers.

Red laughed with her.

"Those poor men are just not used to something like this," she said. "I'll bet that up until today shoplifting was the worse crime they had seen in a very long time."

"No bet," Red said, laughing as well. "But if something gets wild, let's try not to let them get killed. They all seemed to be married and such snappy dressers."

"Deal on that," she said after she stopped laughing.

She and Red were halfway across the main lobby, walking at a steady pace before the herd of officers behind them began to follow. The restaurant covered by trees was to her right, a few open gift shops were to the left.

There were less than two dozen people in the large lobby.

Then she noticed it. Near the front desk, sitting on a couch, was a man pretending to read some sort of tablet. He had jerked slightly when he saw them coming.

"Man sitting to the left," she whispered without breaking stride.

"Two more near the trees on the right," he whispered. "Looks like the ship had more crew on it."

"Seems that way," she said, scanning the others in the lobby.

"Those are the only three I see," he said.

"I agree," she said. Again they were out in the open, caught in a horrid position.

"We'll be in their crossfire in ten steps," Red said. "Any chance they are just more security officers?"

"Zero," she said. "They are trained military. Dressed the same as the attackers this afternoon. Can you get them both on your side?"

He chuckled and she smiled.

The guy sitting on the couch had his gun out of his jacket when she placed a single shot in the middle of his forehead.

She had her gun put away almost instantly without missing a step.

Red didn't allow the other two to get off any shots either. He dropped both of them with two shots and had his gun back in his back holster before their bodies hit the ground.

The two of them just kept walking toward the port.

After four or five more steps to make sure there were no other attackers lurking in some hidden location, she turned around and shouted back to the four confused officers standing with their guns drawn behind them.

"Sorry for the mess, gentlemen. Make sure your chief of security meets us."

"Think that stupid ship is empty now?" Red asked, shaking his head.

"We can only hope so," she said, touching his arm. "Have I told you how good you are?"

He smiled down at her. "What exactly are we talking about?"

"Oh," she said, turning and smiling up at him, "just about everything."

CHAPTER TWELVE

THEY REACHED THE PORT to be met with the Chief of Security, a man named Lovell. He was clearly ex-military, but a long time past. The soft life of living on a plush station like this had sent a lot of his muscle downward to rest in a fairly large stomach.

But he still wore his uniform well and had managed to get dressed and down to the port without missing combing his thinning hair over a bald spot.

"Thanks for meeting us, sir," Red said, giving the man clear respect. That was a great way to get an official to do something, but Mattie wasn't sure if Red actually didn't respect the man.

"What just happened back there in the lobby?" Lovell demanded.

"We were ambushed again," Mattie said. "Your men saw it all and I'm sure you have it on camera. We couldn't let the attackers get off a shot for fear of them accidentally hitting a bystander or one of the employees."

Lovell just shook his head. "At some point I'm going to need statements again from both of you."

"Understood, sir," Red said. "But first we would like to board the ship that all these killers came here on. You are the only one on the station that has the power to allow us to do that."

Mattie watched him for an instant and knew he was going to let them.

"Are you sure it's now empty?" Lovell asked, his thick, round face showing worry.

"No," Mattie said. "And we're not sure it's not rigged with explosives, either. But we have equipment to scan the ship before we try anything to make sure it's safe and won't blow up half this station."

With that the Chief's face went white. "You have that sort of equipment?" Lovell asked, first looking at Mattie, then at Red.

"On my ship, sir," Red said.

Then he motioned that the Chief move over out of earshot of the other offices with him and Mattie.

She knew what he was doing and it was a risk, but one they needed to take at the moment.

Red, in hushed tones, quickly described to Lovell the basics of what Carson had found and how an attack was probably due soon.

"A fleet of ships in The Emptiness?" the Chief asked. "I thought they were only a myth."

"You know something about them?" Mattie asked.

"Just a little," he said. "Nothing solid at all."

Something still wasn't adding up to Mattie. But at least they were another step closer.

The Chief's face went pale. "You think that's one of their scout ships?"

Red said, "We need to find out, don't you think?"

CHAPTER THIRTEEN

MATTIE WAS JUST AS STUNNED at Red's ship as she was with the suite he had rented. It was sleek and just sitting in the dock looked fast. And it was much, much larger than it looked.

"Wow," she said as she entered and saw the plush blue carpet and light wood walls in the wide hallway that led through the middle of the ship toward a wide recreation room in one direction and toward the front of the ship in the other.

It had a fresh meadow smell. There was faint jazz music playing in the background. "How big is this ship? It feels more like a liner. And do you keep the music playing all the time?"

Red laughed and turned toward the front of the ship and she followed.

"Music and lights come on when I key in my password on the door. It can hold thirty people comfortably with everyone having their own bedroom."

"But you travel in this alone?" she asked. "No crew, no help?"

"None needed," he said. "This is basically my home and normally in port I stay here on the ship. But I had heard about the nebula views and wanted to be closer to where Carson was staying this time."

With the mention of Carson's name she didn't say anything more and neither did Red. But there was no doubt she felt comfortable in this ship. Completely.

Her entire home back at the Sector Force headquarters was close to the size of this ship and, when there she loved it, loved being able to be alone and yet have room to move around. Clearly she and Red were alike in more ways than she wanted to think about at the moment. She had a hunch that would be both good and bad if they survived this coming fight.

He turned and went into what looked to be an equipment room of some sort, only without any windows. This was not the room where this ship was flown, she knew enough about ships and how to pilot one to know that. This room with walls of different machines and control panels and large screens was more like a defense room of some sort.

And more than likely the main communications room and research center. She had seen a room similar to this in the research wing back at headquarters.

He dropped into a chair near a control board and his fingers flew over the panel.

On the large screen in front of him the ship they had targeted appeared. It was clearly a design she hadn't seen before, with swept wings of some sort pointing forward. Spaceships did not need wings, only ships entering or leaving atmospheres in glide mode needed wings.

"Strange design," she said. "Weapons on the wing tips?"

"Designed to be there clearly," Red said. "But not on this one. This is a planetary attack ship modified to be a transport. I'm sending these scans to both my people and Sector Force for our people to analyze as well."

"Good idea," Mattie said. Clearly Red had the two of them completely working together. If she had thought a year ago that Innocence Inc. and Sector Force would both be working on the same thing on the same side, she would have said there was no chance.

She liked this new world much better than her old one. Both organizations had top resources and research and weapons departments. Together they made an impressive force.

Red continued to scan the strange ship. Finally he turned around and smiled at her. "No one on board and no explosives. Just locked up tight, but by the time we get to the ship my computer here will have figured out the lock code for us and the passwords to get into their computers, including navigation."

"Chief Lovell will be happy to hear that," Mattie said.

And he was.

By the time Mattie and Red got every detail of information they could scan about the ship sent off to their respective headquarters and they had walked the short distance to the strange ship, Chief Lovell had pulled up the security vids from the area around the ship. It showed the first five attackers leaving their ship and then earlier in the evening the next three attackers leaving.

He showed the vid to Mattie and Red, then asked, "Is that everyone in there? My port scanners show no more life on board."

"No one left," Red said. "And no explosive traps. These people did not expect to fail, so they just locked up and went about their business."

"Could the ship have a recall autopilot feature?" the Chief asked.

Mattie studied the heavy-set man and suddenly gave him even more respect. This man had clearly served in some special forces and knew many, many of the tricks used by those who worked between the systems.

"It might have, Sir," Red said, "But my ship's computer is now in charge of the computers on board this ship. It is slowly dumping all the information from this ship to both Innocence Inc. and Sector Force for study. It won't allow a recall feature to trigger at this point."

"Great," the Chief said. "And great having your two forces working on this together. Kind of odd, but great to see."

"It's that special a case," Mattie said, giving Red a sly smile.

Chief Lovell nodded. "So let's get going."

"No need for you to go in, sir," Red said, suddenly looking a little worried.

Lovell just scowled at Red. "I have nine dead at this point on my peaceful resort station. Trust me, I'm going in with you."

All Mattie could do was laugh. She was starting to really like this guy. And more than likely he might be of great help down the road. She wasn't so sure of his men in their bright shirts, but the chief clearly knew what he was doing.

CHAPTER FOURTEEN

RED HAD SEEN a hundred ships' interiors similar to the attacker's ship from a lot of different system cultures. Pure stark military furnishings.

There were enough bunks to hold forty men in transport, but only eight of the bunks had duffels beside them. Clearly even the pilot and captain of the ship had no special rank, but slept with everyone else.

The place smelled of a slightly-burnt coffee smell and the dishes from a hurried lunch had been left on the large table in the mess area by the last three here.

It wasn't a large ship, about a quarter the size of his, so it wasn't going to take much time to search.

One room held a substantial cache of weapons, most standard for this sector.

Mattie moved along the weapons, studying a couple, then turned to him.

"These were all bought here in this part of this sector, my guess is from arms dealers. Nothing at all unusual here. Or anything that I haven't already seen."

Red nodded. He wasn't sure exactly what that meant. If these attackers were from someplace outside of this sector, they might have easily gotten weapons here for local attacks like this one.

But it also led him more to believe this was just a local sector political issue and Carson and the Sector Force were being targeted for personal reasons. At least that was his hunch so far. He had another hunch that he and Mattie would know a lot more when they could look over this ship's data from its computers.

The Chief ordered one of his men to go back outside and get help to unload and secure the weapons in the room while Red, Mattie and the Chief headed forward toward the control room.

It was also standard military. Stark gray metal walls and floors and a low ceiling. Nothing at all unusual that Red could see. Three seats in front of major control panels and dark screens, view ports front and on the side, lots of control panels that when activated would show the status of all ship's systems.

This ship might look different from the outside, but Red had no doubt it was pure standard military inside.

And the military was from this sector. Of that he had no doubt either.

Mattie inspected around one direction while he went slowly in the other direction, looking for any sign that this ship was truly owned by a culture outside of this sector.

At the middle she stared up at him with those wonderful brown eyes and shook her head. Her eyes were all business, not an ounce of flirting in them or her posture at the moment. She was focused completely. "Nothing at all unusual. I would bet anything this ship was built in this sector."

"I agree," he said, glad they had come to the same conclusion. He pulled out his data pad and checked to see how the systems download was going.

"By the time we get out of here," he said, clicking off the pad and putting it back under his coat, "this ship's computers will be downloaded to both Sector Force, Innocence Inc., and our computers."

"Mind sending me a copy of that as well?" the Chief asked from where he had stopped near the control room door.

"Glad to, sir," Red said. "Sorry I didn't think to do that at first." He was going to do anything he could to keep the local station authorities on their side. But first he wanted to make sure of the data he was giving to a local authority.

Mattie smiled slightly, just the corner of her mouth rising a little. She understood exactly what he was doing and why.

They headed out of the ship and back onto the port platform. The Chief's people were already unloading the guns and putting them in a transport vehicle. Three of his men were standing guard over the weapons. To Red it looked like the Chief was doing exactly what he could in the best way he knew how.

"Chief," Red said, "Would you mind if we stop by the Security Office and give our statements on the lobby shootings tomorrow morning. It's late. And I can get you a copy of the ship's information by then as well."

The Chief nodded. "That would be fine," he said, looking to Red like he was almost relieved.

"Thanks," Red said.

He and Mattie turned and strode off toward the hotel area of the station. They walked in silence until they were out of any chance of earshot of any officer. And this time there were no security officers following them. It seemed like the Chief now felt they were all on the same side and didn't need an escort. That suited Red just fine.

"Well," he said to Mattie as they left the port area. "What do you think?"

"My gut sense is that this is something personal against Sector Force by someone who is also working to take over a system or two in this sector and has the money and the firepower to do it."

"I agree," Red said. "And that person is using the threat of a large fleet coming in from The Emptiness to cover his tracks."

"Exactly," she said. "I need to get from the Sector Force every major target we missed or that got away over the last ten years."

Red nodded, impressed by how she was seeing this. It matched his opinion exactly. "I'll get my people on it as well. We have a list of those who tried to hire us and that we turned away because they were guilty. Have your people check military targets. From the looks of that ship, the person responsible for all this has military training. It would be how he or she would think."

She glanced at up at him as they reached the edge of the lobby and nodded.

They headed across the large lobby for the lift to his suite. She didn't hesitate and he didn't need to say anything. The restaurant under the trees was long closed and there was only one person behind the main desk and no one else in the lobby.

Around them the lobby had been cleaned up, the bodies gone. Not even any blood on the floor. That was fast.

Maybe just a little too fast.

"The bodies are gone," Mattie whispered. "No blood, no mess. We've only been gone less than an hour."

"I noticed that," he whispered back as they kept walking.

"Damn," she said. "I was hoping for another lap in that wonderful pool."

"So was I," he said.

But she knew they didn't dare stay in their suites now.

Without hesitation they both turned and headed back toward the port.

"Your ship have a pool?" she asked, smiling up at him for an instant before going back to watching every nook and person they approached.

"Nope," he said. "But it has top security, a massive shower with unlimited hot water, and a large bed."

"Good enough," she said, nodding.

He forced himself to pay close attention to everything around them as they walked instead of letting himself get lost in being with her. But honestly, getting lost in her kisses and body was all that he wanted to do at that moment.

CHAPTER FIFTEEN

MATTIE KEPT a very close eye on all the security men as they approached Chief Lovell who was still with his men supervising the unloading of the weapons from the ship.

He was clearly surprised to see them return so quickly. She decided to let Red do the talking since he seemed to know how to manipulate someone like Lovell.

"Chief Lovell," Red said. "We forgot some items in my ship and so we've decided to just stay on board for the evening. I can promise you we won't try to leave."

He nodded slowly. "Any problems with your suites?"

"They are wonderful," Red said, smiling a smile that Mattie knew instantly was fake.

She smiled and nodded right along with him. There was something about this Chief Lovell she didn't like and couldn't put her finger on, but if he made any wrong move, she would have no problem dropping him where he stood.

"Well, have a good evening, then," he said, smiling. But Mattie could tell that the smile didn't come close to reaching his eyes.

"You also," Red said and they started toward his ship down the concourse that was the docking area. Their footprints echoed in the high-ceilinged area.

Red turned his head to look down at her. "Pretend we're talking," he whispered as they walked.

She knew exactly what he was doing. He was keeping an eye on the men behind them out of the corner of his eye.

"Understood," she said, turning toward him so she could see while he looked forward for a second.

They went back and forth like that until they reached his ship.

With his pad he did a quick scan to see if anyone had entered or tampered with his locks since they had been here. They had not.

Maybe they were being just a little too careful. Maybe the security force really could clean up a crime scene in less than fifty minutes. But she was with Red completely at this point. Carson was dead, they didn't know who they were up against, so it was a lot safer to be secure for the night.

They would deal with going back to their suites tomorrow if they needed to.

He secured the doors behind them and then led her to the control room. He quickly showed her his controls, his passwords, and how to fly the ship if she needed to.

She paid very close attention until he was done.

Wow, he was trusting her, more than she had a hunch she would have trusted him at this point. It made her feel good, and it made sense. If they had walked into the middle of a major problem on this station, they might need to get away fast.

"Alarms and shields set," he said, turning to smile at her. "Someone would have to blow up half this station to even make this ship rock tonight."

She again looked deeply into those wonderful green eyes, then reached up and pulled his head down to her height and kissed him long and hard. After a moment they broke.

Her heart was pounding, her breath slightly short.

She smiled at him. "There might be another reason this ship would be a rocking tonight."

He laughed that wonderful laugh that made her like him even more.

"You promised me a huge shower with lots of hot water," she said.

"And that I can deliver," he said.

"You had better deliver a lot more than that," she said, smiling at him.

He laughed again. "I've got to stop giving you so many straight lines."

Then he realized what he had said before she could answer.

He stopped her with another long kiss and then they headed back through the large ship to the main suite area, holding hands like two kids in school.

CHAPTER SIXTEEN

MATTIE STARED AT THE SHOWER that was larger than most bathrooms. "You weren't kidding."

She started peeling off her clothes, putting her gun on the large bathroom counter and draping her jacket over an empty towel rack. She was going to have to wear these same clothes back to her suite tomorrow morning, so she hoped to at least keep them from being too wrinkled.

"When I saw the plans for the ship," Red said as he started to undress as well, "I thought the shower too small because of the size of this bathroom. So I told the designer to just make it twice as big and put showerheads every two feet and on the ceiling as well to make it seem like it was raining. He tried to talk me back, but I wouldn't listen."

"Glad you didn't," she said.

"Problem with a shower that large is that it has its own weather system."

She laughed as she slipped out of her pants and panties and then hugged him. "You know how cute you are?" she asked him, enjoying the feel of his naked back against her hands and his chest against her face.

He still had on his pants, so she pushed back to help him with those.

"Cute?" he asked, smiling at her. "No one has ever called me cute before. Now get the shower started."

He pushed her toward the shower and she obeyed as he slipped off his pants.

Again she could tell he was aroused as she was feeling.

"How about you?" he asked. "People call you cute?"

"Last guy who did," she said, smiling back at him before stepping onto the tile of the huge shower, "ended up with a perfect pattern of holes in his forehead."

He stopped and raised his hands, smiling. "Won't happen from me, I promise."

He looked just silly and wonderful at the same time, standing there in the bathroom with his hands in the air, his wonderful skin and muscles shimmering in the light, and clearly aroused.

"What? You don't think I'm cute?"

He joined her as she turned on the water. He pressed up behind her, his hands finding her breasts, his kisses finding her neck.

"I find you stunningly beautiful and smart," he said, rubbing his hardness against her upper back as he kissed her neck and gently but firmly massaged her breasts.

It took just about every ounce of her strength to stay standing.

He picked her up slightly and moved them both into the warm water cascading down from a dozen showerheads.

The feel of him against her skin, the water cascading all over her, was almost too much.

Then he picked her up, holding her easily under her arms, his hands still working her breasts, her butt against his stomach.

Then, slowly, he lowered her and she slid onto him yet again.

And the release was almost instant.

And intense.

More so than even the one in the pool under the nebula.

She managed to catch her breath as he raised and lowered her, moving inside her slowly yet firmly.

For the first time in her life she loved the fact that she was so small. And she really, really loved the fact that Red was so tall, so strong, and so big.

He turned her so that her head was directly under a shower and she could put her hands on the wall.

She pushed back into him, matching his motion, stroke for stroke.

The warm water washed over her, the feeling of him inside her, pushing against places she didn't know she could feel.

The sensations and him was almost too much to bear.

Then suddenly he pushed really hard and she held him tight as his release came.

And then she followed with a second just as intense and even longer than the first.

There was a shower bench along the back wall of the shower and after a moment he managed to stagger over there and sit down. The water still hit them both, taking away the tension, making them both relax.

She pulled off him and turned to face him, straddling his legs, letting his hardness press against her crotch, but not be inside. Then she kissed him long and hard.

He kissed back and they kept that up until finally she pushed back, looked into his wonderful green eyes, and smiled.

"We have work to do and sleep to get," she said.

"How about sleep first and work second?" he asked. "Give our people time to analyze what we sent them."

She was feeling just about as tired and washed out as she had felt in a very long time.

And satisfied.

Totally and completely satisfied.

"That sounds perfect," she said.

Then she kissed him long and hard again and it took them another five minutes to get out of the shower.

She knew without a doubt that if she didn't stop kissing him, neither of them were going to get any sleep.

But she didn't want to stop.

CHAPTER SEVENTEEN

THE WONDERFUL SMELL of bacon and toast woke her. She glanced at the clock and realized she had slept almost six hours, a long time for her. She seldom slept more than five hours, and could go for weeks on three or four hours per night.

She looked around, stretching her completely naked body under the wonderful sheets, reveling in how the satin sheets felt both smooth and soft against her skin. Red's bedroom suite was designed with his tastes in mind, and yet she loved it. More than she cared to admit.

She was totally comfortable in this room.

Soft indirect lighting ringed the ceiling and the walls were a tan color decorated with different forms of realistic art from the two sectors. She recognized a few of the artists. Chances were the paintings and illustrations and photos all over this ship were all originals.

A long dresser ran down one entire wall with a large mirror over it and the other wall was filled with a huge bed, so big that Red could sleep sideways in it and not touch either side.

They had crawled in after their long shower last night. She had kissed him only once, then turned over and he had curled up against her back.

She had felt safe in his arms.

Safe for the first time in her memory.

She knew for a fact she wasn't going to even think of depending on that, but for one night it had been wonderful.

There was a soft-looking white robe across the foot of the bed, more than likely for her. She put it on, surprised that it didn't drag on the floor and almost fit her.

She found a new sonic-style toothbrush unopened on the bathroom counter and facial soap, plus a comb and brush for her short hair.

After a few short minutes, she padded barefoot down the soft carpet of the main hallway to the wonderful smell of breakfast in the ship's galley.

Red stood there, also in a long white cloth robe, his back to her, working at the stove.

Even though she had come in silently on bare feet, he somehow knew she was there.

"Almost ready," he said, turning to smile at her with that wonderful smile of his. And it reached his eyes, lighting up his entire face. He was actually happy to see her and have her in his ship. That felt good.

"Thanks," she said. "And good morning."

She hadn't realized how hungry she actually was. That wonderful fish dinner last night had been a long time before and now the smells of bacon were making her stomach remind her it needed some food.

"It is a good morning," he said, smiling. Then he pointed to a table and chairs against one wall that was already set with what looked like real silverware and cloth napkins. She liked how Red lived, sparing no expense.

"How rich are you, really?" she asked, sitting down at the table and picking up the silver fork and studying it for a moment. Then she looked at the original art on the wall over the table.

He actually shrugged. "I honestly don't know, never added it all up. But put it this way, building this ship, furnishing it with everything including the original art, didn't even slightly dent the petty cash reserves."

She whistled. "That's rich."

He laughed. "And more just keeps flowing in from investments, land holdings on a dozen planets in two sectors, and Innocence Inc."

"Poor, poor pity you," she said, laughing.

He smiled at her over his shoulder as he worked at the stove. "It's a burden, but someone's got to carry it."

He then dished up part of what he was cooking, walked over, and put a fantastic-smelling plate of bacon, eggs, and toast in front of her. Then kissed her long and softly before turning back to the stove.

A moment later he put a small plate of hash browns beside the other plate and a glass of fruit juice of some sort that was a pale pink color.

"Wow, a rich man who can really cook." She just stared at the food for a moment, not knowing where to start she was so hungry.

"If you like good food as much as I do, and travel as much as I do, you learn."

He moved over to a hidden door in one wall near the table and opened it, showing her a pantry that seemed to go on forever. Just inside the door was a file cabinet.

He pointed to it before shutting the pantry door. "That's full of recipes I have gathered from both sectors and hundreds and hundreds of cultures. So far I haven't tried them all, but I plan to given time."

She just couldn't believe this guy. There had to be something wrong with him. More than likely she would find it before long. She wanted to stand and go kiss him, but instead her hunger forced her to dig into the food.

The eggs were perfect, with just a touch of a pepper-like spice she didn't recognize. The toast was a sweet bread that if she wasn't careful she could eat a loaf of. The hash browns were light and fluffy and spiced with similar spices to the eggs.

She was almost halfway done with her meal before he sat down across from her with his plates and juice.

"Sorry," she said, smiling at him. "I should have waited for you, but this smelled so good and I was so damned hungry for some reason."

"Eat," he said, laughing. "In this kitchen there is no standing on protocol."

Then he dug into his food as she watched for an instant, before going back to eating as well.

He almost caught up to her by the time she had finished and sat back, sipping on the sweet fruit juice that seemed like a cross between orange and grapefruit. Again it was a juice she had never tasted before, but wouldn't mind tasting again.

"Any chance you looked at any of the information yet?" she asked.

He shook his head and finished his toast before answering. "I wanted to wait for you. Two sets of eyes on this stuff are going to be better than one set."

That surprised her. More than likely, in his position, she would have already taken a preliminary look at everything from Sector Force that they got from the ship.

She smiled. "Thanks. I agree."

"Let's get dressed first," he said, picking up his plate and heading back to the counter with it. "Then we can head up to the control room with the big screens to look at everything."

She stared at his back and his legs showing under his white robe. If she saw him naked again, she flat didn't know what she might do.

"How about I get dressed first," she said, "then wait for you here in the kitchen."

He turned and smiled at her. "Why's that?"

"You damn well know why," she said, smiling back. "I see you naked again and I'm not going to be able to control myself."

"How about I just flash you," he said, laughing and reaching for the edges of his white robe.

"How about I just flash you," he said, laughing and reaching for the edges of his white robe.

"Not looking, not looking!" she shouted and sprinted from the galley, his wonderful laugh following her down the wide hallway toward the bedroom.

But luckily, he didn't follow her as well and she managed to get back into her clothes and back to the galley in less than five minutes.

He already had the dishes washing and the table wiped off.

He kissed her lightly as he went past and she sat down at the table again. He had left the remains of her juice and she sipped on it and thought about everything that had happened in the last day.

From Carson's death to the wonderful dinner with Red. She remembered the fantastic sex, the attack in the lobby, the attacker's ship, and the strange occurrence in the lobby of the entire attack gone as if it hadn't happened.

She smiled, remembering the sex last night in the shower and the wonderful night's sleep with her feeling safe for the first time in years. An amazing day, one she would have never expected when she had arrived here.

In fact, it had been a day she had never expected period.

"Ready," he said from down the hall.

She met him and joined him in stride heading for the control room.

She realized at that moment that she felt whole striding beside him. Even though she was much shorter than he was, they seemed to just fit walking side-by-side. Her faster natural strides kept up with his long pacing strides.

She pushed the thought away quickly and forced herself to think of what was ahead. They needed to find out who had killed Carson and why and if there really was a fleet of ships headed this direction.

When they reached the control room, Red pointed to one station. "You should be able to contact Sector Force from there and download everything they have."

He sat down at the station beside her and his fingers flew over the controls, clearly doing the same with the information coming in from Innocence Inc.

The Sector Force researchers had put a summary of all the material at the front, so she scanned that first.

The attacker's ship had no identifiable markings leading it to any one system or group. But it had clearly been constructed in this sector and had many parts from different systems in the surrounding area of the Bodie Station and Resort.

In other words, it had been built in this neighborhood of stars somewhere.

There was a list of backgrounds of the eight dead crewmen, all mercenaries from nearby planets and other nearby sector systems.

Then she got to the heading about how the attackers were greeted on the station at their arrival and that she should use extreme caution on the station.

"Red," she said, tapping him. "I think you need to look at this."

She clicked on the section and a security camera from the attacker's ship came up. Red leaned in beside her to watch as on the screen it showed someone who seemed to be in charge of the ship greet someone at the door of the ship after docking. The time stamp was only a few hours before she had arrived.

"Oh, damn," Red said as the image of the greeter became clear. It was Chief of Security Lovell.

"We both had a sense that was going to be the case last night," she said, shaking her head. "I sure didn't want it to be. I like him."

"I know," Red said, "but now I wonder just how deep this plot is through the entire station and hotel."

"More than likely very deep," she said, watching as Chief Lovell shook the attacker's hand and then left, "we are stuck right in the middle of a very nasty beehive."

She froze the image on Chief Lovell's face. "I suggest we shake the entire thing."

"And kill him in the process," Red said, staring at the face of a man who he felt was at least partially responsible for his best friend's death.

"Exactly," Mattie said. "And slowly if we get the chance. Give him a little time to suffer and maybe do a little talking."

"I like how you think," Red said, touching her arm lightly before pushing back to his station to keep searching the data.

With one more glance at the image of Chief Lovell, she cleared his face from her screen and went back to work as well.

CHAPTER EIGHTEEN

RED WENT THROUGH all the data his people had decoded and analyzed from the attacker's ship and found nothing new. The ship was built in this sector, close to the station, and crewed by mercenaries. A couple had been ex-military from a system close by. Others were just lower-level hires.

As he and Mattie had proven, not a one of them had been a match in the slightest for them.

That puzzled him as well. If the person in charge of all this knew that he was here and that the top Sector Force agent was arriving, why send lowlifes up against him and Mattie. It made no sense and seemed to be a waste of manpower.

However, they had succeeded in killing Carson, but that seemed more like a stray shot than something planned.

Unless this was a distraction. But from what and why?

Or a plant.

Would the man after the Sector Force be willing to kill eight of his own men just to plant some information.

Red suddenly had an idea. Beside him Mattie was deep into studying the information sent to her by Sector Force researchers, so Red pulled up all the information that he could find on Chief Lovell and his force here on Bodie Station.

What he found surprised him.

Chief Lovell had been Special Forces for a small regional protection league that guarded five different planets. He had retired to Bodie Station and taken the job as Chief of Security. Since his arrival two years before, crime had dropped and he had stopped a couple of plots to take over control of the station.

He had on his force a dozen other Special Forces operators, all very deadly, and a few hundred others like the men he had assigned to follow them around yesterday.

This station and resort was heavily armed to defend an attack coming at it from space, had powerful screens, and seemed, to Red's point of view, very defensible from just about any kind of attack.

"I think we're being set up," he said.

Mattie glanced over at him with a puzzled look on her beautiful face.

He indicated she should read the information on his screen. She scooted over against him and did, slowly nodding.

"Sure seems that way, doesn't it" she said, a frown covering her beautiful face. "We are being set up. Someone wants the Chief and his main force out of the way and basically is trying to trick us into doing it."

She went back to her board and sent off the vid of the chief meeting the ship with the instructions to check it for tampering of any sort.

Red did the same with the vid to his people.

Then they turned to comparing notes on the targets, rich targets with military backgrounds that had gotten away from the Sector Force at one point or another. He had to admit, even though he loved working alone, at the moment it felt great working with Mattie.

Maybe a little too good.

He pushed that thought away and tucked it down with all the other things he was going to need to deal with once this was all over.

Red had his list of those who had tried to hire Innocence Inc. for protection from the Sector Force and who they had turned down.

The clients with military background.

The list of targets that had gotten away from the Sector Force was very small. And only one was from this area of the sector with the military background to stage any kind of attack or takeover of any system.

General Jarvis, one of the worst mass murderers in the last hundred years.

And Jarvis had tried to hire his company at one point as well before he vanished. Red's company had turned him down instantly, even though he had offered a large fortune. No amount of money would make Red defend such a human.

The General had been a former dictator of a planet not far from the Bodie Station. He had wiped out over three hundred thousand lives trying to hold onto power before Sector Force stepped in to take him out of commission.

He was extremely rich and even more ruthless.

He had vanished completely and no one at Sector Force had been able to trace him, although the warrant for him still stood. Dead or alive.

For Red, that answered the question as to why a person would go after the Sector

Force. Sector Force was the only sectors-wide group that could harm Jarvis, and would the moment he surfaced.

Jarvis had to destroy Sector Force in this sector of the galaxy to insure his own safety.

Red looked at Mattie and she looked back. Then she said what he was thinking next. "Jarvis built a station in The Emptiness."

Red nodded. "And since he vanished he has been preparing for an attack to take back power and more systems, thus the rumor of the fleet of ships."

"Which is why he needed to destroy Sector Force," Mattie said, nodding to herself, "so he could come back and take command of his new little empire. He knew we wouldn't let him otherwise."

"Exactly," Red said.

At that moment both Sector Force and his people got back to them with the same information. They don't know how they had missed it, but the vid of the Chief had been constructed by an expert and planted on the ship. It hadn't actually happened.

Red smiled at the information. "Looks like we need the Chief on our side, because whatever attack is coming, my guess is that it is headed right for this station."

Mattie agreed and a moment later they had sent an invite for the Chief to come to Red's ship. They had something to show him that wasn't going to make him very happy. Red had no doubt about that.

From what Red had read of Chief Lovell, he would hate getting set up more than anything else.

And he wouldn't much like the idea of an attack coming at his treasured space station either.

CHAPTER NINETEEN

MATTIE WATCHED as Red greeted Chief Lovell with respect at the hatch to Red's ship and then led Lovell in. She was glad they weren't going to have to kill the Chief. From what she had read about him before he got here, he and his team, at least the core part of his team, would make a great addition to any coming fight. And at this point she was glad she and Red had a little help.

But what she was more worried about was General Jarvis's plan to go after Sector Force. She needed to figure out what the plan was and stop it. But she had no idea how she was going to do that.

Both she and Red had sent for top operatives to head this direction. The Sector Force had four major agents that could be here in three days and Innocence Inc. only had two operatives worth calling in that weren't on another assignment. It would take them three to four days as well in travel time.

Mattie had a hunch this might be completely over in three days. If not fewer.

And she had contacted Sector Force, put headquarters on full defensive alert, and told them who was behind it. The Sector Force now had every operative and researcher looking for anything that might give them a clue as to the General's plans or location.

"Wow," Lovell said, looking around the hallway and entry area of the ship. "Got a little money or something?"

Red smiled that wonderful smile that made Mattie melt when he aimed it at her. "A little," he said. "It comes in handy at times."

"I'll bet," Lovell said and laughed.

Mattie really liked the older security chief. He didn't pull punches and she admired that.

The three of them headed back up the wide center hallway of the ship to the control room.

"We had both our organizations go over the information we found on the ship," Red said as they walked.

"And they both found basically the same thing," Mattie said.

"What might that be?" Lovell asked as they got to the control room.

Red pointed to the chair Mattie had used for the Chief to take a seat. "That the eight men who came here were just bait to trick Mattie and me into taking out you and your team. Carson was just a very unfortunate casualty. Not really the target at all as we first thought."

"More than likely a complete accident," Mattie said, feeling the sadness of losing a friend. She knew it was only a tiny part of how Red was feeling. When the time came, she hoped to be able to help him release a little of that grief. But right now he was just holding it in, as she would do in the same instance.

"Take me and my team out?" Chief Lovell asked, clearly puzzled and worried about where he now found himself sitting.

"Don't worry, sir," Red said. "We saw through the ploy. Watch this."

Red keyed up the vid showing Chief Lovell meeting someone from the attacker's ship.

"I didn't do that," Lovell said, leaning in closer to the screen. "But that sure looks like me."

"It's all doctored," Red said. "More than likely someone got a vid of you greeting someone else and just changed out the background and made it look like it all came from the same security image. Top level work."

"And they planted this on the ship so it would be found after you two killed everyone?" he asked, still staring at the screen.

"Exactly," Mattie said. "The attacks were to get us to see this and then go after you."

"Glad your people are on top of this," he said, shaking his head. "So you thought I might have had something to do with the killing of your friend for a moment."

"Only for a short moment, Chief," Mattie said, smiling. "But now we need your help."

Chief Lovell stared at the frozen image of himself meeting a person he had never met, then turned around to face them both. "What can I do?"

"First off, get ready for a major attack on the station and resort," Red said.

"What?" Lovell came to his feet, facing them, his body tense. He was taller than Mattie, but shorter than Red. But Mattie could tell that even older, he would be a tough fight in most circumstances.

"That's why someone spent the lives of eight men to get us to take you and your defense team out," Red said. "They don't want you here to defend this station."

"Those idiots who attacked us sure wouldn't have been able to do it," Mattie said. "So our guess is that there is a more trained force coming."

"You have that right," Lovell said. "I looked into their backgrounds and there wasn't a one a close match to either of you, let alone me or my core team. So you two know who wanted me out and is ready to attack this station?"

"Not one hundred percent," Red said and turned to his screen. He brought up an image of General Jarvis. The general was a square man, thin jaw, blunt nose and beady, rat-like dark eyes. He wore a dark green uniform and a hat with a lot of stars on it in the picture. "We think it's this guy."

"That bastard still alive?" Lovell asked, clearly shocked.

"He went missing about three years ago," Red said.

Mattie nodded. "We think he's been building an attack force and staging out in The Emptiness for an attack on a couple of systems to regain his power. It would be logical to stage from this station and resort if he could take it over."

"If he did that, came back into public, wouldn't your people take him out?" Lovell asked, looking at Mattie.

"They would," she said. "He still has a warrant on him with my organization. But he's also been trying to destroy Sector Force first to make sure we can't fulfill that contract."

"Smart bastard," Lovell said, shaking his head.

"I see you are familiar with him, then?" Red asked.

"He killed my sister and her family," Lovell said, low and mean.

"Oh," was all Mattie could say. She didn't know what else she could say.

It seemed that all of them had a personal stake in this now. That was both a good thing and a bad thing.

CHAPTER TWENTY

RED SAT WITH MATTIE and Chief Lovell for the next half hour in the control room of the ship, talking over ideas. The more they talked, the more impressed Red became with Lovell.

The man clearly was experienced and deadly, even nearing almost sixty years of age. He had a mind for tactics and strategy and could see patterns in human movements that only top police and military even understood. And his core team was filled with younger and just as experienced men and women. He had brought each one in personally to defend the station and run "errands," as he called them, off station.

"So you have a spy network," Red asked, "set up on planets in the surrounding systems?"

"I sure do," Lovell said. "Some of it pretty high up in the governments as well. I figured those planets were the most likely to produce some nutcase that would think of taking over this station. We stopped a few ideas like that before they really got started."

"Makes sense," Red said, laughing. "I really like how you think out ahead of problems."

"I didn't get ahead of this one," he said, clearly not happy with himself.

Mattie was just shaking her head and smiling, which meant she was impressed as well in the Chief.

"So who owns Bodie?" Mattie asked.

"The Bodie family," Lovell said.

Red was surprised. "You mean the Bodie family from the First Sector? The ones that own a couple of planets and do more charity work than anything else? And have ships that are faster than anyone has figured out in this sector?"

"The same ones," Lovell said. "They have their own private wing here in the resort, although they are rarely here. They built this place and pretty much just let me run it. I oversee a staff of managers in the different areas, but I run it and report to old man Bodie himself once per month."

"No wonder General Jarvis wanted you out of the way," Red said.

"And the Sector Force in this sector out of the way as well," Mattie said. "He could take this over and there would really be no one that could go up against him without the Sector Force."

Red agreed completely. "And we almost walked right into his plan and helped him."

"Glad you didn't," Chief Lovell said. "I'm not sure me and my little bunch could take you two."

"Let's not find out, shall we?" Mattie said, patting Lovell's arm.

Red couldn't agree more. Having the Security Chief on their side with his core team was going to be a real advantage.

CHAPTER TWENTY-ONE

MATTIE AND RED were walking the Chief back to the hatch when Mattie asked the Chief one last question that had been bothering her a great deal.

"Chief, you have any indications through your network how General Jarvis could build a staging station out in The Emptiness without anyone knowing it?"

Lovell just shrugged. "I haven't heard of a thing. But not the kind of thing we usually are digging for in our intelligence, to be honest. But I'll have my operatives check if they have heard anything."

"No planets or asteroids or anything large enough to live on out there either?" Red asked, following her line of questioning.

"Nothing," Lovell said. "On the other side of that curtain that is the nebula, it really is a vast expanse of emptiness. It takes almost a year at most ship's top speed to cross into the edges of Sector Four. Not many have tried it that I have heard about."

Mattie nodded, feeling disappointed at that news. Jarvis had to have a base out there somewhere, and far, far closer than a year away. Chances are it just wasn't a bunch of grouped ships either. That would be too vulnerable to attack.

Chief Lovell started to go out of the hatch when suddenly he turned around. "I just remembered. Bodie Station Resort Two is out there, on the far side of the nebula curtain. It was going to be called by another name, but the construction was never finished. It was abandoned almost twenty years ago from my understanding, before my time here. The passenger liners and big transport ships would not go that far out and when the liners declined, the Bodies knew the station was doomed and abandoned the construction."

Mattie knew at once they had found the General. She could feel the surge of adrenalin going through her. Beside her she could tell Red felt it as well, his stance shifting, his entire posture straightening just slightly.

"You have plans and the exact location?" Red asked a half second before Mattie could ask the same question.

Chief Lovell hesitated, clearly thinking. "I should. Give me an hour, let me see what I can dig up."

"Great," Red said.

"But first," Chief Lovell said, "I'm putting the station on high alert and full defensive posture."

"Good idea," Red said, nodding.

"Watch the ships coming in as well," Mattie said. "And the passengers on the liners. Jarvis is going to try to get people inside in a lot of different ways."

Lovell actually laughed. "Don't worry, we have top scanners and no weapons will be allowed on the station until this clears. Except for the weapons you two carry, of course."

With that he turned and headed away from the ship with a fast and purposeful stride.

"Have I said how happy I am that he's on our side," Mattie said, watching the chief for a moment before Red shut the hatch and secured the ship again.

"Yeah, me too," Red said.

Then he leaned down and kissed her firmly on the lips. "And I'm very happy we're on the same side."

His smile made her melt just a little, but then she kissed him in return and pushed him back toward the control room. "We have research to get our people doing on this second station. So no kissing."

He pretended to pout, but couldn't pull it off, which made her laugh.

She couldn't remember a time she had laughed this much before. Or felt this good working with another person on something this serious.

CHAPTER TWENTY-TWO

AN HOUR LATER Mattie pushed back from the control panel and stretched. "I'm starving again."

She glanced over at Red who still worked over his screens. They both had gotten their people to research everything they could about the abandoned space station.

From what Mattie could tell, it sat beyond and behind the curtain-like clouds of the nebula, in a place that allowed for the colors of the nebula and the second sector stars to fill the sky. They had found some early construction images and sales flyers for the station. It would have been spectacular, of that she had no doubt.

But it also made her uneasy just thinking about it. She was used to the depths and emptiness of space, but in the main areas of the sector, and even in the short distance between Sector Three and Sector Two, there were always stars and systems relatively nearby.

Going to the other side of that big nebula curtain was a long distance beyond the edge of the sector, far enough that she understood why the big space liners, the main transportation between systems for most people, would never go out there.

Under normal conditions it would take at least two days to get there around the edge of the curtain, and two days to get back. Just too far out for a resort.

"Hungry, huh?" Red said. "My breakfast not enough for you?"

"That was four hours ago," she said, laughing. "A girl's got to eat to maintain her energy."

"How about we stop by to see what the chief has for us on the station and if he has heard anything from his networks in the nearby systems, then grab some lunch in that wonderful restaurant we ate at the first night."

She nodded. She liked that idea. "Then I really need to go get a change of clothes and some of my own equipment from my suite."

He smiled. "I'll bring the bomb-sensing equipment to make sure none of those idiots got to our rooms before we took care of them."

"Good," she said, stretching some more to loosen up muscles tightened by hours at a computer board.

"You keep doing that," he said, watching her, "and we're never going to get out of this ship before dinner."

She went over and sat in his lap and kissed him long and hard, enjoying the sense of his passion on his lips.

Then, as things started to heat up, she pushed back with every bit of will and self-control that she could muster. "We need food and a plan first," she said.

"How about the plan being that I lick every inch of your body and then make love to you slowly and gently?"

"I like that plan," she said, kissing him long and hard again before climbing off his lap.

"After lunch."

He smiled at her. "You have far, far more self-control than I have."

"Oh, no, not far," she said, turning and heading down the hallway out of the control room before she changed her mind and that smile of his melted what little control she had. "Barely more, and only because I'm starving."

CHAPTER TWENTY-THREE

MATTIE AND RED first stopped at Chief Lovell's office. He loaded all the plans for the abandoned space station and at what level it had been abandoned into both their data pads.

Mattie was impressed that by the time they got there, only about an hour after he had left Red's ship, Chief Lovell had all his top team members in the station and they were coordinating how they were going to check everyone already in the space station and resort for guns and explosives.

The station port was already locked down and one passenger liner was docking and the passengers were going to go through very tough background checks and scans before ever being allowed to come into the resort.

Something dinged in the back of Mattie's mind when she heard that, but she couldn't put her finger on what bothered her. There was no doubt this station suddenly felt a lot safer. As each hour went by it would become more so.

Chief Lovell also introduced them both to his top lieutenants. All four of them had been with him since he took the job. All four seemed intimidated to meet them and said little.

Chief Lovell joked that they had seen the vids of the firefight in the mall and how they had taken care of the three in the lobby. "You two are their idols," he said laughing.

Two of them actually blushed at that, which almost caused Mattie to laugh, but she managed to keep a straight face. What she did learn about them was that all four of them had young families on the station. She had no doubt that would make them defend this station even more.

Chief Lovell gave them all his men's backgrounds as well and asked Red on the side to double check his men with deep background checks through the DI sources. Lovell was taking no chances at all.

Mattie really liked that as well.

They were going up against someone as ruthless as General Jarvis, and someone smart enough to elude the Sector Force for years. They couldn't take any chances at all.

Thirty minutes after arriving at the Chief's office, she and Red were headed for lunch at a restaurant Lovell suggested called Karen's Café.

Mattie was feeling better about the security of this station, but even more worried now that they didn't really have a lead on how General Jarvis was going to attack the Sector Force. Even with the Sector Force on high alert, a good attack could still get through.

Karen's Café looked more like an old-fashioned mall diner that could be found on most any planet. It was tucked off to one side of a small shopping wing near the lifts to one section of the resort. It was clearly the kind of place that employees and those who were regulars at the resort ate at. A normal fresh-off-the-liner visitor would never find this place.

Mattie loved it at once.

There were old-fashioned cloth seats on the booths that could hold six people, soft jazz was playing in the background, and the smell of baking fresh bread filled the air.

At the moment there were only two tables with customers. Two cleaning staff at one small table, clearly in some sort of relationship, and two security staff at another. The two security men saw Mattie and Red come in and turned white, quickly paid and left.

Mattie knew, without a doubt, that she and Red's reputation had spread ahead of them. But that kind of reaction was normal when someone discovered she was a member of the Sector Force. It wasn't something she really ever told anyone except an authority that needed to know. But now, here on the station, it seemed most everyone in the security force knew.

Red just laughed as the security men fled. "Do I need a shower that badly?"

"Don't worry," Mattie said. "I'll help you scrub all the hard-to-reach places later."

"Promises, promises," Red said.

"No promise," Mattie said. "That's a threat."

Laughing, Red led the way to a large booth and a woman wearing a checkered apron with long blonde hair came out of the back, smiled at them and asked, "Water?"

Both she and Red nodded yes and she retreated into the back. Mattie sat across from Red so she could see his face and they could go over the data they had just gotten.

The menu came up under the table surface. Mattie studied it, trying to decide what she wanted. She had become so hungry, she really couldn't decide.

Red, on the other hand, glanced at the menu in front of him, clicked the off button and sat back.

"That easy?" she asked.

He laughed. "The Chief suggested the cheeseburger, made with meat from an animal raised on a nearby planet, and that I should order it with a side of the bread and thin skins, whatever that is."

She clicked off her menu as well. "Make that two."

When the waitress came back, Red ordered for the both of them and then pulled out his data pad.

Mattie did the same and they both started scanning the plans the chief had given them of the abandoned station.

It soon became clear to Mattie that the only area that could have been used fairly quickly and contained was the port area. Most of the construction on the station had stopped far before much more than just the structure was in place. Everything had been left open to space. The port and construction bays were closest to being finished when the place had been abandoned.

Red mentioned that and she said, "A lot can be built in three years," she said.

"But since he was clearly planning on taking over this station," Red said, "why would he have bothered with much more than the basics. No one knew he was out there."

Mattie stared at the images on her data pad, mostly agreeing with Red. "You think he would have fixed the repair bays to build ships and the port area, building living quarters in that area only for workers and crews."

Red nodded. "Exactly. But how did the General get people to follow him out there?"

Chief Lovell had just come in and headed toward them. He overheard Red's question.

He pulled up a chair and sat at the end of the table. "I can tell you exactly how. By threatening families."

"What?" Mattie asked, afraid of the answer, but having a hunch as to what the Chief was about to tell them.

"Every person on that attack ship had a family on a nearby planet. All of them are now dead. That bastard general killed women and children."

Mattie felt her stomach twist into a tight knot.

"Damn," Red said.

Mattie glanced up at the chief. "Are you checking all families of all employees on the station?"

"As we speak," the Chief said. "So far most families are on the station and clean, including everyone who works in this restaurant. Thought you might want to know."

He patted the table and stood to leave.

"Thanks, Chief," Mattie said. "Very good work."

He nodded. "I'll contact you both if I run into anything with any of the

staff here. I have a hunch this is all just starting."

Mattie felt the exact same way.

She looked up at the hurt in Red's eyes that he was trying to push back inside. Innocent families had been killed.

She reached across the table and rested her hand on the back of his. "We'll stop this monster."

He nodded. "Of that, I have no doubt."

The image of General Jarvis's beady little rat-eyes came clear to her mind and all she wanted to do was put a final bullet between them after causing him a great deal of pain first.

Neither one of them could finish their lunch, although they both tried. After that news, it just didn't have much of a taste.

CHAPTER TWENTY-FOUR

RED WENT WITH HER to her suite and helped her check it for any devices or tampering. She felt good with him at her side, sometimes a little too good, but she wasn't going to question that just yet. Between the two of them she felt a lot more confident that they would catch most anything coming at them.

On the way up the lift to her apartment, they had decided, not for sexual reasons, but for strategic reasons, that they should stay together until this was finished. So she was going to move her stuff to his suite.

She had laughed and kissed him when he asked if she minded.

"Silly," she said. "You're the one with the pool."

He had to admit, she had a point.

Then he went silent.

"Come on, admit it, you are remembering me pulling myself up naked out of that water. Right?"

He actually tried not to blush, but failed.

She kissed him before the lift doors opened and then led the way to her suite, giving him time to get his thoughts back on the job at hand, even though hers were not completely there either.

They scanned her room before opening the door. Nothing had been touched in her suite and no one had entered or even tried to enter since she had left. She gathered up her bags and they went to Red's suite and did the same before opening his door as well.

Again his suite was clear and had not been disturbed in the slightest.

She went into the huge bedroom and dropped her bags on one dresser while he stayed in the living room. Then she looked around. His small travel bag was tucked over near a closet. Since his ship was so close, he hadn't brought much here at all.

She desperately needed to change clothes and maybe just lie down and stop for a few minutes, let this problem they were facing sink in. Sometimes she did her best thinking just lying still.

But with Red out there, she also needed to be close to him again. Very, very close, before resting was going to be possible in any way.

She stripped naked, tucking the clothes she had been wearing now for more than a day, back into her bag. Then she headed into the living room with one of the large, fluffy white bathroom towels in her hand.

"I need a swim," she said. "Want to join me?"

He glanced up and his eyes widened slightly. She loved that she had that effect on him.

The pool and the fantastic view of the nebula colors over it felt as amazing as the first time she had come out here. But this time she didn't want to stare up at the colors, because beyond that beauty was someone truly a monster, truly ugly, and she didn't want to think about that right at that moment.

So she kept her focus on the pool and not the wonderful beauty overhead. When this was all over she could enjoy that again.

She had already done a lap of the long pool when his naked body cut into the water and came up swimming on the other side of the pool.

They both did about ten fast laps before stopping at the shallow end.

"That felt good," she said, moving her shoulders around and then leaning into the stone side of the pool and pressing her arms hard against the stone to stretch them even more. "I needed to loosen up a little."

"It did feel good," he said. "Drained out some of the tensions."

She almost made a wise crack about not too much draining she hoped when he moved over closer to her, then behind her, and started to rub her shoulders.

"That feels wonderful," she said, learning her head forward, enjoying the smooth feel of his strong hands on her back and neck.

He clearly had been trained in some aspects of massage, because he knew exactly what kinks to work out, how much pressure to apply where, and how long to work one muscle before moving on.

She was starting to melt under his hands and all she wanted to do was turn around and kiss him. She could feel his arousal moving against her butt under the water.

Finally, when she couldn't take it any longer she said, "Let's do something really unusual this time."

He sort of slowed the wonderful motion of his hands and moved to one side of her. "And what's that?"

"How about we make love in a bed?"

"You sure you want to risk it?" he asked.

She couldn't see his face, but she knew he was trying to keep the smile from showing by the sounds of his voice.

"I know, it's kinky. But I'm game if you are."

With that he laughed and pushed himself up out of the pool, standing above her, clearly aroused. He smiled down at her, knowing full well what he was doing to her, what kind of view he was showing her. Just as she had done to him in the living room yesterday.

Then he offered her a hand out of the pool.

"That wasn't what I was thinking of grabbing," she said as he lifted her with ease with one arm from the water.

"You grab it here and we don't make it to a bed."

"Unless I do this," she said.

She took a firm hold on his manhood and then started toward the door to the apartment, pulling him gently along behind her.

He did not hesitate and she loved the feeling of him in her hands.

A couple places along the short distance to the bedroom she almost decided the carpet was good enough again. But somehow she kept going.

They actually made it to the bed.

Barely.

She lay on the bed, face down and he went to work on her back again, this time rubbing and kissing at the same time, working his way over her neck and then down her spine.

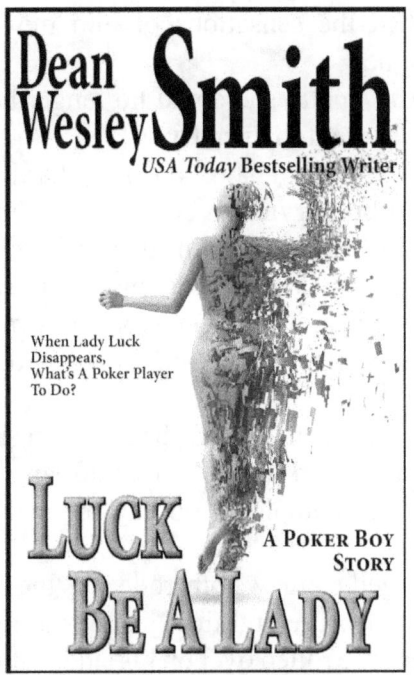

Some Classic Poker Boy Stories
Available at your favorite booksellers.

She felt like she might melt right into the soft bed.

When he reached her butt, he worked both cheeks over gently, rubbing, kissing, then worked his way down her right leg and back up her left leg.

As he came back up he kissed her between her legs and she raised up and pushed back, almost without realizing it, trying to tell him to keep going.

The sensations of his attention on her crotch ran up and down her body, seeming to follow the path his gentle kisses had taken.

His tongue found places and did things to her that she didn't know were possible or even desired.

How was this possible that she could feel like this?

Part of her mind, deep down inside, asked that question and the rest of her brain just shouted that she should let go, enjoy everything he was doing.

That part of her mind won easily, riding with the waves of pleasure he kept pushing her over.

A flick of his tongue here, a lick there, a driving push next, then back to a flick.

Impossible to take for long and she could feel a release coming, building.

She pushed up and against his hands and face and mouth and tongue.

That wonderful tongue.

He held her solidly in place, increasing the tension, the movement, the exacting flicking and touching until finally she came in deep, shuddering waves that seemed to take her from the room completely.

He never stopped, making her release last and last and last until finally it crossed over from pure pleasure to too much sensation and she pulled away.

She flipped over onto her back and lay there, breathing harder than she ever did even after an intense workout in a gym.

He smiled down at her, his face wet with her juices, and then eased down and kissed her, supporting his weight on his elbows.

She could taste herself and him at the same time and she kissed him back long and hard and as she did he moved slowly to a position between her legs and gently entered her.

And she came again, even harder and more intensely as the first one.

He held still, letting her release subside, kissing her gently, and just as she started to relax under him, he started moving, first slowly, then quicker and quicker inside her.

He felt wonderful there, as if he completely belonged inside of her.

It felt as if he had brought every nerve in her body alive for the first time.

His kisses on her lips and face and then neck sent ripples through her that matched the sensations of him moving inside her.

And finally she could no longer hold back, or want to even try.

She came again, pushing hard up against him, trying to be inside of him at the same time he was inside of her.

He joined her, his complete release filling her and sending more and more waves of pleasure up and down through her body.

Never, in all her life, had she lost such control, given herself over to another person so completely in any moment of time.

Together they both rode out the last of the pleasure and then just at the right moment he rolled over on his side, pulling her with him, keeping himself inside of her.

He pulled her close and held her against his strong chest, like he never wanted to let her go.

She felt the same way.

She held him back, hard.

After a moment they both relaxed and he let her pull her leg out from under him.

Somehow he still managed to remain inside of her and she pressed against him, wanting him to stay inside.

A few moments later she could feel herself drifting off toward sleep, being held by a man she didn't know could exist.

For a second she opened her eyes and looked up at his handsome face.

His eyes were closed, his face showing complete trust and relaxation.

She closed her eyes and pulled him close.

And together they drifted off to sleep.

CHAPTER TWENTY-FIVE

RED AWOKE WITH MATTIE still tucked against his chest. She felt perfect there, so perfect that he didn't want to bother her by moving. But they both had far, far too much to do right now to allow for too long of a nap.

Her warm skin felt fantastic against his skin, her soft breathing brushed against his chest like a child's light touch.

He stared at the top of her head where it was tucked against him and then her wonderful, toned body pressed against him. In all his life he had never felt this attracted to, or connected with, another person.

And yet this person sleeping against his chest was one of the deadliest law enforcers in the two known sectors of space. He admired her, liked her, feared her, and was falling for her, all at the same time.

How was that possible?

He would think about that question later.

Right now the two of them had a monster to stop named General Jarvis. There were people to defend against Jarvis. There were innocent people all over this area of space that needed their help. Situations like this were the very reason Red had started Innocence Incorporated.

And if he and Mattie and their two organizations didn't succeed at stopping this monster and soon, a lot more innocent men, women, and children were going to die.

He gently eased away from her, their skin sticking together slightly.

She moaned and tried to hold him, but he kept easing away.

"That's just mean," she said, not opening her eyes as he finally pushed away completely from her. "I was enjoying that."

"We'll do it again," he said, leaning forward and kissing the top of her head. "But right now there's work to do."

He rolled away and off the edge of the bed and stood.

"Slave driver," she said, rolling onto her back and stretching.

He stopped and just stared at that wonderful body of hers. For a moment he thought about just crawling back onto the bed with her, then somehow managed to kill that idea. More hours would go by if he did that and they didn't have more hours right now.

He took the edge of the bedspread and flipped it up and over those fantastic breasts, toned stomach muscles, strong legs and arms, and light-brown pubic hair. "Take a quick nap. I'll wake you when I get out of the shower."

She opened one eye and looked at him. "Afraid we can't shower together?"

"Yes," he said.

She closed her one eye and then rolled over, pulling the bedspread with her. "Spoil sport."

He laughed and headed for the shower, trying his best to clear that wonderful image of her stretching naked on the bed. She had to be the most alluring woman he had ever met. There was no doubt of that.

Now the key was to keep them both alive and stop this Jarvis monster at the same time. And that he had no idea at all how to do.

CHAPTER TWENTY-SIX

MATTIE DOZED for a few minutes until she heard the shower shut off in the bathroom. Her body still tingled from the wonderful lovemaking. But damn it all, Red was right, they needed to focus on the problem of finding a way to stop General Jarvis before more people were killed.

She pushed off the covers and stood. Quickly she ran through a series of exercises to clear her body and senses and get her muscles working again. Then just as Red was coming out of the bathroom with a towel around his waist, she headed in that direction.

She gave him a quick kiss as she went past, then slapped him on the butt and closed the bathroom door behind her. Just safer that way for both of them.

Fifteen minutes later, dressed in fresh clothes that consisted of brown slacks, a white blouse, and a tan vest, she padded barefoot into the suite's living room and sat down on the couch to put on her hard-toed running-style shoes. She had dressed for a fight, just in case there was going to be one at some point.

She had one gun tucked into the holster in the back of her slacks and another smaller gun on the back of her left thigh.

Red was bent over his data pad at the table near a small kitchen area.

"Any ideas?" she asked as she worked to pull on her shoes.

"Nothing," he said. "We have no recent surveillance of that abandoned station."

She had been afraid of that.

"Anything from Chief Lovell? Anyone on the station he's suspicious of?"

Red laughed. "I just got word from him that he has expelled ten people he wasn't one hundred percent sure of, sent them off to the nearest planet under tight security."

"Really?" she asked, surprised and wondering why the Chief hadn't tried questioning them.

"Lovell doesn't really believe any of them have anything to do with General Jarvis," Red said, answering her question as if he could read her mind. "But he can't prove their stories, so he's booting them."

Mattie laughed at that. "I really like the Chief."

Red nodded, not looking up. "Lovell is making sure his people are clean and everyone else on the station is clean and safe as well."

She finished putting on her shoes, then grabbed her data pad and went over and joined Red at the table.

For some reason she felt they were going about this all wrong.

But at the moment they weren't doing anything because neither of them had an idea of what to do.

"Chief Lovell has also done an intensive scan of everyone on board the last passenger liner to dock," Red said. "He is holding five in custody on board. None seemed to be involved, but he again isn't taking any chances. And he had the liner swept for explosives and it's clean."

"Ruining a few people's vacations, huh?" Mattie said.

Red nodded and kept working on his data pad.

Then it dawned on her what he had said. The interstellar passenger liners. Of course!

Over twenty major companies and who knew how many minor organizations and companies ran passenger liners regularly between all the major systems and a bunch of the minor systems. It was the major form of transportation from system to system for most everyone. There had to be thousands and thousands of the passenger liners out there in all sizes and shapes.

A major port for docking liners was in a stationary orbit right over the Sector Force Headquarters. From there an attack would be easy.

"Liners!" Mattie said, working to link up to Sector Force Headquarters as fast as she could.

Red looked up at her, puzzled.

As she waited for the connection to link, she explained what she was thinking to Red.

"Jarvis wouldn't use his own ships and risk an attack that far into this sector. His goal is to just cripple the Sector Force, make sure no one at the Sector Force knows he's behind it, and then retake power here on this edge of space where

he will be safe. And the Sector Force would fall apart or be too busy rebuilding to even notice him."

"Exactly," Red said, nodding, but still looking puzzled.

"So what better way to attack the Sector Force without chance of being traced than send bombs and suicide bombers who are acting because their families are in danger. He would put them on passenger liners destined to be in orbit right over Sector Force Headquarters."

Suddenly Red was following her. "The bombers could come in from fifty different directions, maybe even take over a liner and dive it straight in."

"Exactly," Mattie said. "Jarvis doesn't care how many people he kills. This fits his method of operation."

Red went back to his data link pad, working to contact those at Innocence Inc. to get them started on searching the liners headed for Sector Force headquarters.

Mattie finally got through to the Sector Force headquarters and in less than thirty seconds was talking with the head of the Sector Force.

Mattie took less than one minute to summarize what she was thinking and why General Jarvis might attack the Sector Force in such a fashion, using bombs on the passenger liners. She explained quickly what Chief Lovell had told her over lunch about the eight men they had killed and how their families were now all dead as well for the failure.

"Innocence Inc. is helping on the search for possible bombers on the liners as well," Mattie said.

Across the table Red nodded and gave her a quick thumbs-up signal.

"I would suggest you work with them on this," Mattie said.

Her boss agreed and cut the link.

Mattie sat back, staring at the blank screen on her data pad. "I sure hope I'm right about this."

"I think you are," Red said. "We'll know soon enough."

Mattie sat there staring at the blank screen. Jarvis might have three people heading for the Sector Force, or three hundred.

And they had to stop them all.

She might have just saved the Sector Force, but sitting here completely safe in a suite in a resort on the edge of the second sector, she felt completely helpless. She wanted to be helping find the bombers, stop them.

And of all the things in the world she hated feeling, it was helpless.

CHAPTER TWENTY-SEVEN

RED SNAPPED OFF his data pad and looked at the sour face of the woman he was falling for.

"Oh, oh," he said. "A dangerous enforcer with grumpy face."

His joke didn't even make a smile reach her eyes. It was never a good idea to have the most dangerous woman he had ever met in a sour mood. But he knew exactly what she was feeling. He was feeling it as well.

He too wanted to be in on the massive hunt for bombers that was going on right now. But they had another assignment, and that was to stop General Jarvis, so if Mattie's idea was correct and that's how Jarvis was going to attack the Sector Force, he couldn't do it again.

"You ready for a hop out into The Emptiness?" he asked.

She looked up at him.

"Oh, so jokes don't get your attention, but a trip does."

She just motioned for him to get on with it, so he did.

"Someone's got to get some intelligence on General Jarvis and what he's doing out there. I figure we're the best two for the job. See if we can find a way to stop him before he sends even more attackers."

"Can your ship cloak?" she asked, leaning forward.

"Completely," he said, smiling. "And it's the fastest private ship built. We could go chasing after the Seeders into Andromeda if we wanted to spend a lot of time on it."

She took her pad, walked over to the large vid screen on the wall in the living room. He followed her and with a few clicks she had a map of the edge of this Sector and the emptiness on the big screen.

She highlighted the Bodie Resort in green, highlighted the rough shadow where the nebula curtain was, and then put a red spot where the abandoned station was.

The nebula curtain clouds and all their beauty and deadly radiation were directly between the two space stations.

"How long?" she asked, turning to him.

"If we skirt the edge of the nebula curtain, eighteen hours at my ship's top speed. But leave that on the screen. I want to show you something."

He turned and headed for the door to the pool.

On the deck he switched off all lights so the bright oranges and blues and reds of the nebula came up bright over him.

When she stopped beside him without a word, he pointed to a dark area with some distant stars showing through. It lay between a large green area of the curtain and swirled over into a red cloud.

"I see it," she said. It looked exactly like someone had punched a small hole in the very center of the curtain. "Can we get through there with the nebula radiation?"

"My shields are the best," he said. "I had my people running calculations on that path last night just in case we needed to do this. They think we can make it with minimal risk with my shields on full. It would cut off almost seven hours of flight time. Jarvis would never think anything would come at him through that hole so he would never be scanning for anything in that direction."

"And the nebula radiation would cover our approach," she said.

He glanced down at her wonderful face. She was nodding and again smiling.

And he could clearly hear the excitement in her voice again.

"You game?" he asked.

"Not a damn thing we can do here but make love," she said, smiling up at him. "So we might as well."

"On second thought, maybe we should stay."

"Get packed mister," she said, turning and heading back for the bedroom and her stuff. "But keep this room reserved, would you? I want some more laps in that pool once we get rid of Jarvis for good."

"Deal," he said, following her, glad that they both felt once again they had something to do.

And besides, a happy Sector Justice enforcer was always a good enforcer. And there was no doubt in his mind that Mattie Silks was very, very good at many things.

CHAPTER TWENTY-EIGHT

MATTIE AND RED stopped by the Head of Security, Chief Lovell's, office to talk with him and update him. They both had their packed suitcases with them, plus all their equipment.

Their guns set off the monitoring alarms in three areas on the way down to the security area, but at each area they were waved through by the guards on duty looking terrified to even confront the two of them.

Mattie found that both funny and worrisome. If the Chief's men couldn't even stop the two of them for a moment, how were they going to deal with an attack force if it started at the space station.

More than likely they wouldn't. At least not well.

She and Red reached the bustling security office area and the chief met them near the door.

"I heard you were both headed this way," he said, laughing slightly. "You two can sure put a scare in young officers."

"We don't mean to," Mattie said.

"Yeah, I bet," the Chief said, shaking his head.

"We have a few updates is all," Red said and the chief motioned that they should join him back in his office.

Mattie wasn't surprised by the Chief's office. It was a fairly sparse and standard office, with a large black metal desk that seemed slightly cluttered with paper and tablets, a dark couch that looked like it had seen better days, and two chairs in front of the desk.

Some awards and citations and pictures were the only things on the wall behind the desk. It fit what Mattie thought of the chief's personality. Sparse, blunt, and dedicated to his work. But there was something wrong with the room and she couldn't place it exactly.

The Chief indicated they should take the two chairs and he dropped into his chair behind the desk, leaned back and sighed deeply. Chances are this was the first break he had taken in hours.

Without telling the Chief, Red turned on a sound-blocking device to make sure that nothing would be overheard or recorded. Then he asked the chief if there was any news.

"Nothing," he said. "Just tightening this place down like a loose bolt on an engine."

Mattie just sat and tried to figure out what had bothered her about the office, letting Red do the talking at the moment.

Red nodded. "If any more attackers are found, if there is time, Innocence Inc. is going to work with local authorities on each planet to swoop in and make sure the families are safe."

"I like the sounds of that," Chief Lovell said, nodding. "Better than what happened to those poor families before."

Mattie glanced at Red. He hadn't told her he had that set up. But it made sense. It was the kind of thing they did, and it made her smile. She killed people who were guilty of horrid crimes, such as General Jarvis. Red saved those who were innocent.

They clearly made a great pair.

She pushed that thought from her mind and turned back to the task at hand. "We're headed out to see if we can discover if the General is out there in the abandoned station and scout out what we can."

"That's going to take some time," Chief Lovell said, frowning as if he wasn't sure about the idea. He started to

say something and then shut his mouth.

"It will," Red said, not mentioning the shortcut they were thinking of taking or the speed of his ship. Or the fact that they suspected bombers on passenger liners heading toward Sector Justice Headquarters. Clearly Red didn't want that information out and Mattie was glad he was keeping it close to his chest like that.

Out of the corner of her eye she saw Red reach down and click off the blocking device. He had clearly seen what she was missing and knew something was going on and he wanted whoever the Chief thought was listening to hear the next part.

"You have this place wrapped up tight and defended," Red said. "We just need to see what's coming at us. And see if we can get a shot at Jarvis in the process. So it's worth the long journey out into The Emptiness to find out."

"Good luck on that one," Lovell said, standing and extending his hand to them.

They walked the entire distance to the ship without talking.

Mattie felt very, very uncomfortable about that meeting with the Chief, but she just couldn't put her finger on what was wrong. On the surface it had seemed completely normal. But over the years she had learned to trust her voice and right now that voice was shouting. Something had changed with the Chief in just the last hour.

And clearly Red had seen it.

When Red had the ship scanned for tampering and found none, then had all the sound dampening equipment up and working so they couldn't be heard at all, she finally turned to him. "What did you see in that meeting with Lovell that I missed?"

"His family pictures were missing."

She knew instantly he was right. In her mind she saw it as well. A picture on his desk was gone, a blank area where it had been, and there were three other blank spots on the walls.

"Damn it," she said. "You are right."

She had no idea how she had missed something that obvious. Clearly the Chief was trying to tell them, give them that message without ever saying anything, hoping they could do something.

Ten minutes later they were pulling away from the station and moving off toward the nebula.

The first thing Red did once they were clear of the station was get some of his people on Chief Lovell's family. If the Chief was going to be any good to them in the coming fight, they had to first rescue his family, wherever they were being held.

And do it in a way that General Jarvis wouldn't know about the rescue.

What worried Mattie the most was that Jarvis seemed to have thought of just about everything. He seemed way ahead of them and that worried her a great deal.

CHAPTER TWENTY-NINE

RED SET THE COURSE of the ship on the standard route around the nebula and kept the speed down to normal speeds of most privately owned ships until they left the immediate scanning range of the station.

Mattie sat beside him in the control room, working back and forth with the Sector Justice Headquarters. She hadn't said a word for twenty minutes.

Once they were clear of the station, Red first ran diagnostics on his shields

to make sure they would have no issue going through the nebula radiation fields. They were fine.

Then he ran a diagnostic on the cloaking device and once he determined it was working at all efficiency, he turned it on.

To anyone watching on sensors, the ship just vanished from the screens.

He then altered course, aiming for the hole in the nebula curtain and kicked up the speed.

"Four hours and twenty minutes to the nebula opening," he said, satisfied everything was working.

Mattie nodded. "They found six bombers already on three liners inbound for Sector Justice headquarters." She looked up from the communications equipment at Red. "Your people are on the families of the bombers, working to get them secure where they can."

"Great job," he said to Mattie, smiling. "You just saved thousands and thousands of lives on those liners."

"I'm sure there are more bombers and attackers out there," she said, clearly still very worried.

"And the Sector Justice will find them. Your organization is very, very good at finding people, remember?"

She laughed, but the laughter did not reach her eyes. "They are, but not for these reasons."

"Trust them," he said.

"Do I have a choice way out here?"

"No," Red said, knowing exactly how she was feeling. She was a control person, just as he was. If he couldn't do it himself, he was always afraid it wouldn't get done right.

He picked up his communication pad and indicated she should do the same. Then he stood.

"We need food," he said. "It's been too long since that small lunch and my stomach has been telling me that for the last hour."

She nodded, her mind clearly a long ways away at the moment as she stood and walked with him down the wide corridor toward the kitchen.

His mind wasn't exactly on cooking at the moment either. He just hoped his people could get to the families before it was discovered they had been caught. Otherwise, General Jarvis would discover that his plan wasn't going well and set another into motion.

And that would be a very bad thing for a lot of people.

CHAPTER THIRTY

MATTIE HELPED RED in silence make sandwiches from some sort of spiced red meat and a wonderful-tasting white cheese. He used a white bread that seemed to soften and gain a wonderful fresh smell the longer it was out of its package.

"Drink?" he asked her as she took the sandwiches to the table.

"Same fruit juice as this morning," she said. "If you have more."

"I have plenty," he said.

"And was that only this morning?" She couldn't believe that had only been this morning.

He laughed softly. "Long day so far, that's for sure."

"And I have a hunch it's a long ways from over," she said.

He just nodded, poured them both some of the fruit juice and sat down across from her.

Then they both checked status from their two organizations while working slowly on the sandwiches.

She really, really needed to stay close to the fight to save the Sector Justice. She needed to know what was happening, even though it was a long distance away.

And she liked the news.

Local authorities from four planets were helping as well as dozens of Sector Justice members. The researchers at the Sector Justice said that spotting the bombers was like looking for a red light in a dark room. They were sure they had the immediate threat stopped, but it had been close. All the explosions were set to go off in just twenty hours.

"They stopped two more on the liners," she said, finally closing her tablet and looking over at Red. "They are still searching others due into the planets near Sector Justice headquarters later today."

Red nodded and closed his data pad as well. "My people have safely got everyone's family your people found and have terminated or detained a dozen of the General's soldiers or the people he had hired to hold and kill the families."

"Good," she said. "Now we just have to stop the General before he can launch yet another attack."

"Any idea how?" Red said and then took the last bite of his sandwich.

She finished the last bite of her sandwich as well, enjoying the taste of it for the first time while thinking about his question. "Not a one," she finally said.

"So we wait until we get close to his base to see what we are up against?" Red said.

"You know I hate waiting, don't you," she said. And she did. She hated it more than anything else.

He laughed, this time the amusement reaching his eyes. "I never would have guessed that."

"Can't this go any faster?" she asked, smiling at him. She knew this ship was traveling at a far faster rate than she had ever gone before. And under normal circumstances she would have been impressed.

Actually she was impressed. But that didn't help the impatience.

He glanced down at his data pad. "Two hours and thirty-one minutes to the nebula. "Let's head back to the control room to make sure no one is waiting for us."

She liked that idea, and even though she felt a slight tinge of disappointment that he didn't suggest they head to the bedroom to spend the time, she was happy he had suggested what he did.

At the moment her mind was on the mission. She had no doubt there would be more than enough time for them to be together in the future.

Depending, of course, if they both survived all this.

And at that moment, that was very much in doubt.

CHAPTER THIRTY-ONE

THEY WERE IN the control room of Red's ship, both working at different stations. Except for quick updates or short questions, they had worked in silence since the sandwiches that had served as their third meal of the day. And silence suited Mattie just fine.

She liked how they could do that. Red didn't feel like he needed to keep a conversation going all the time. It made her feel like she was not only working alone, but also with great help at the same time.

She liked that feeling.

The last update she got from Sector Force Headquarters was that they were convinced all the passenger liner bombers were captured and now they were checking other ships inbound or already in orbit.

From the looks of it they had completely stopped this third attack on the Sector Force.

And that made her feel much, much better.

And hugely relieved.

But now they needed to stop the person responsible for it all before he could launch yet another attack. That monster was on the other side of this hole in the bright curtain of the nebula that they were approaching.

Red finished his last update with his people and turned to her.

"My people feel they are close to Chief Lovell's family. They have most of the families of the bombers safe. It seems that all of the bombers were being blackmailed."

"Good," she said.

She glanced up at the big screen showing the nebula approaching. A nebula was nothing more than dust and debris tossed off by a past explosion of a star. But that dust and debris, while beautiful, was full of extreme radiation that would block all communications once they were in it and on the other side.

Getting this close it just looked like a massive wall of colors stretching off in all directions.

"How long do you think we'll be in communication blackout?" she asked.

"Until we come back to this side of the nebula," Red said. "Or move a pretty good distance off to one side of it. The radiation of that nebula curtain won't allow anything through."

He looked up at the monitors and she did the same thing. That was what she had figured. She didn't like the idea of being out of touch with the Sector Force at this point, and she could tell Red didn't much like the idea of losing contact with his people at Innocence Inc. either. But they had to go through and see what kind of forces General Jarvis had massed on the other side.

The large hole in the nebula curtain was starting to grow in size as they approached. In reality it was large enough for a normal solar system to exist inside it, but the radiation was so intense from the nebula, nothing much could even go through it. And compared to the vast size of the nebula, it looked like a small hole.

"Double-checking the shields," he said aloud, just to keep her informed.

After a moment he nodded and glanced at her. "We're set. We'll be on the other side in about twenty minutes and then I'm going to slow us down and move us to one side into a radiation-free pocket so we can safely just observe the abandoned station."

She nodded her agreement to his plan and turned back to the panel she sat in front of. It was a sensor board and she had it on extreme settings, searching for any signs of any ships. So far not one sign of anything on this side of the nebula hole.

More than likely the General never thought anyone would try going through the extreme radiation of this hole. Or had the ability to do it without dying. So he hadn't set up any ships to guard this route.

But who knew what waited for them on the other side. And because of the radiation, they were going in basically blind.

"Here we go," he said.

A moment later the colors of the nebula seemed to dim and everything around the ship sort of went to a dusty haze. Nebulas were always best observed at a distance because they were nothing more than dust and radiation that caused the intense colors.

Mattie watched the screens intensely. There was nothing pretty at all inside this nebula.

They sat in silence, Red watching the readings and shields and she keeping an eye out for any sign of any kind of ship.

Finally, after what seemed like an eternity to Mattie, he said, "We're almost out."

And then they were out.

Suddenly.

Now they were on The Emptiness side of the nebula.

"Magnification on the abandoned station coming up," she said, her fingers moving as fast as she could over the panel. She was relieved that there were no ships at all close to their location, even though they were cloaked. Extreme radiation was known to do strange things to cloaks at times.

Red didn't seem to be saying it had bothered the ships' cloak, though, which was a great thing. A lucky break for them.

Suddenly, on the screen in front of her, she saw what she flat didn't want to see. There had to be thirty ships at least docked at the abandoned space station.

She recognized most as older military types from different cultures around the second sector. And only two ships were like the one they had captured at the Bodie Station.

Plus one was a liner-sized ship, more than likely the General's private headquarters. From what she had studied about him, the guy liked to live in luxury while others around him lived in dorms with little food.

He ruled by terror and threats and didn't care at all about the people who did his bidding. She was going to take great pleasure in finishing him and putting him out of the Sector's mind forever.

"Oh, oh," was all she could say at the image of all the ships.

Her stomach twisted into a tight knot.

Red said nothing at all.

She couldn't believe that Jarvis had managed to gather that large of a force. More than likely this fleet was larger than any planet's forces in the region. Granted, there were always dictators and governments coming and going on planets in both sectors. And regional conflicts on planets that often sprang up.

But very few planets could afford or need large space forces.

After a few moments Mattie finally looked over at Red. He seemed to shake himself and quickly moved the ship to a safe place keeping the nebula behind them, but out of radiation problems. The shields were still solidly in place, so they were cloaked and basically invisible to any form of scanning.

"Let's get readings on all those ships," he said and she nodded, not liking at all what she was seeing.

The two of them went quickly to work, running scans that would not be detected at all by any of the ships at the station.

Fifteen minutes later, when they had finished, she felt a lot better about what they faced.

"Compare notes," she said and Red nodded. "Fire away."

"Five of the older military ships are nothing but dorms for the soldiers and

have been cannibalized for parts. They are never moving or fighting again."

"Agree," he said. "That leaves twenty-five ships that are active."

She nodded so he went on. "A least four of the functioning older military ships don't have any speed at all and would take almost a week to get around the nebula and back to the Bodie Station in the short direction."

"I agree with that," Mattie said, checking her findings as well. The trip they had just taken in a matter of hours would take those ships docked at that station a week. That helped and gave them a ton of options.

"The other twenty-one ships can make the trip in three days," Red said. My sense is that is the General's attack force."

It was her turn, so she started in on the details of the small passenger liner. "From what I can tell, the liner has some decent speed and is in pretty good shape. But it has no defensive capabilities and even at its fastest it would take three days as well to make the trip around the nebula."

"It's no wonder this station and resort was abandoned," Red said. "It's just too far out."

Mattie could nothing but agree to that.

They kept comparing notes, detail by detail. Red had found the same basic information she had, and also he had discovered the fact that almost none of the station had been rebuilt at all. The soldiers were staying on the ships for the most part.

"Did you get a reading of how many are on the ships?" Red asked, glancing over at her with a worried look on his face.

She had tried, but she hadn't believed it and discounted it. The number she had come up with was less than three hundred.

Total.

Among all the ships.

That number was nowhere near enough to even mount any kind of attack, let alone even man most of those older ships.

"I got just under three hundred," he said, shaking his head. "I don't think that's right."

She laughed. "I got the same number and thought the same thing."

"And only fifty people on the passenger liner as well?" Red asked.

She nodded. "Only fifty. Glad I wasn't missing something."

"Maybe we both are," Red said.

So they spent the next fifteen minutes checking it all again, looking for any signs of cloaked ships, or areas of the station that might have been rebuilt to hold more people.

They came up empty. Their initial data had been correct, even though Mattie still couldn't completely believe it. There were very, very few people in that fleet of ships.

Very few.

"So what is his plan?" she asked, trying to make some sort of sense with what they were seeing.

"First he wanted to get the Sector Force out of the way," Red said.

"Got that," she said. "That had to be step one for him because he would never be able to show his face again if he didn't destroy the Sector Force, or at least send its attention elsewhere. Otherwise he would end up dead in a very short time."

"Exactly," Red said.

Mattie went on, trying to make sense of what they had found. "And then he clearly planned on taking over the Bodie Station to be closer to the Second Sector and be able to defend his headquarters with a station that had defensive capabilities."

"Exactly," Red said.

Mattie smiled at Red. "Before we scanned those ships and got the number of people there, it looked impressive, didn't it?"

"It did," he said, nodding. Then he stared at her for a moment before sweeping his hand up at the image of the abandoned station and the ships. "Are you saying that all those ships are just for show?"

"Exactly," she said, now understanding what she was seeing completely. "With that many ships and control of the Bodie Station, the General might be able to take over a standing army on a planet just with the threat of attack from that fleet."

Red laughed. "Even though most of the ships would be harmless and manned with two or three crew. They are an impressive sight."

"Exactly," she said, feeling a huge sense of relief.

She sat back and stared at the fake fleet on the screen. They were a long ways from getting the General contained. But at the moment, knowing he didn't have a fleet of firepower made her feel a lot better.

And also knowing they had stopped the attack on the Sector Force.

Red sat staring at the fleet of empty ships, shaking his head, taking in her idea.

"So now what do you suggest we do?" she asked after letting him think for a few minutes.

"We stop, watch and wait," Red said. "I'll set alarms and recording equipment.

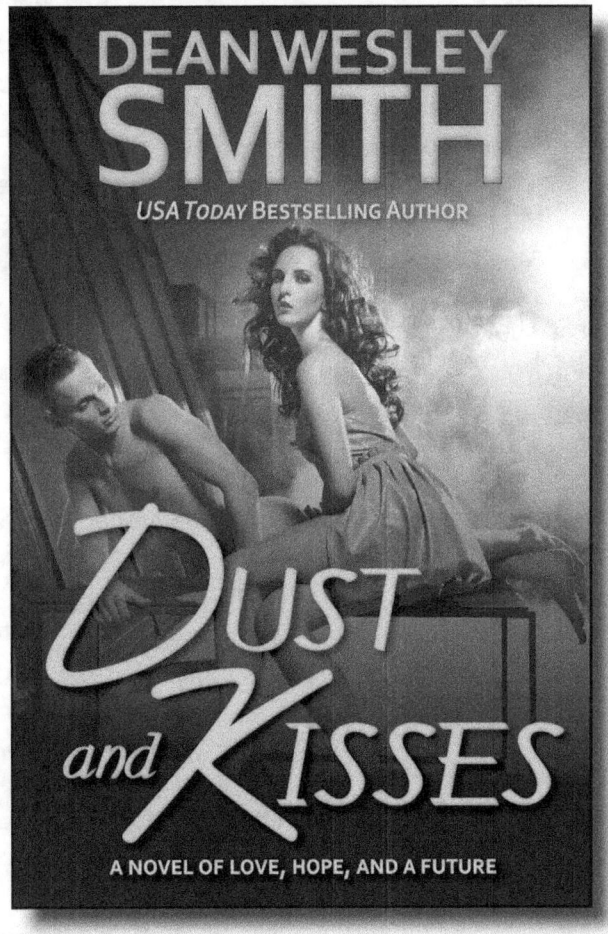

If a ship even moves on that station, or a scanning beam gets close to us, we'll know it."

She nodded. "That will buy us time to decide how to mess up the rest of his plans. But don't you think we need to report this all back to the Sector Force and your people?"

"I do," he said, "but I would rather have hours of scans instead of just one. So better we go back through the hole after we have more data."

That was a really good idea and she knew it. But she wanted action, wanted to sweep into that station and find the General and end all of this now. But waiting and doing more study was the right way to go about it. She knew that.

"Besides," Red said, "we need to get some sleep."

She smiled at him and asked, "Only sleep?"

She was tired, she now could feel it, and she had no idea how long it had been since they had gotten any real sleep. She flat didn't want to think about that.

"And breakfast," he said, smiling at her. "Don't forget breakfast in five hours. That should give us more than enough data."

"Make that five and a half hours," she said, smiling.

"Five and a half hours it is," he said, and started to set scanners and sensor alarms.

She watched him for a moment, then yawned and said, "I'll be in that wonderful bed of yours."

"I'll be right there."

He took too long and she was asleep before he got there.

But she did have a wonderful dream of a handsome man crawling into bed with her and cuddling against her back.

CHAPTER THIRTY-TWO

FIVE HOURS LATER she realized that no warning alarms had gone off as Red slowly woke her by stroking her breasts and waist and back with his firm, but gentle touch. She could feel his hardness against her butt and she pressed back into him, making sure he knew she didn't want him to stop.

He kissed her neck and then moved down slightly and eased himself inside her, filling her with a wonderful sensation of completeness.

She moaned softly and pushed back against him more with her butt while leaning forward and letting him massage her back and kiss her neck.

She was still half asleep and this felt wonderful.

Beyond wonderful.

His movements were slow, easy, slipping back and forth, one moment pressing against her, another moment almost leaving her completely.

And each time he did that she moaned and pressed back against him again, wanting him to stay inside her.

His hands moved around her and worked slowly on her breasts, gently but firmly, making sure that nothing was missed as he continued to kiss her neck and shoulders and then back to her neck.

And then his hand went down to her crotch, forcing her legs open and touching her gently as he moved in and out of her.

The motion with his fingers matched his motion in and out of her and the tension just kept building and building.

His kissing on her neck became more insistent, his fingers moving faster and faster.

Finally he couldn't hold any longer and he pushed into her hard, moving his hand as fast as he could.

And she exploded with him, letting the waves of pleasure float over her and squeeze him over and over and over.

Finally, after far too short a time, yet a time that felt like it had lasted forever, he lay back, pulling out of her.

"Wow," was all he said as he lay on his back and tried to catch his breath.

She rolled over and cuddled under his arm and gently started rubbing his wet manhood that was slick and covered in both of their juices. She loved his smell, a musty clean smell that reminded her of flower gardens.

"If that was what you meant by breakfast," she said, "you can serve that to me as often as you want in bed."

Then, before he could answer her, she stroked him quickly three times, making him jerk upward slightly, and then she climbed over him and headed for the bathroom.

"Your turn to take a nap while I shower."

"The shower is big enough for both of us," he said.

"I remember well," she said, laughing. "And that's why you need to nap for ten minutes."

He sighed and closed his eyes and she smiled at the wonderful picture of him lying there naked. He was an amazing man in so many ways, not the least of which was how he could please her and make her want more.

She stared for just a moment longer and then turned her back and closed the bathroom door.

Just safer that way if they wanted to get anything done in the next hour.

CHAPTER THIRTY-THREE

RED WATCHED from the bed, tucked under the sheet, as Mattie came out of the bathroom completely nude and started to dress. He really, really liked watching her do just about anything. And right now he could still taste her skin on his lips and the smell of her sexual arousal on the sheets.

She was the most amazing woman he had ever met.

It bothered him how much he enjoyed watching her and being with her and working with her and making love to her. It felt like it might be too much, that he was setting himself up for hurt. But right now he wasn't going to think about what would happen to them when this mission was all over.

There would be time to decide that. He had a hunch she felt the same way about him, but she was an enforcer for Sector Justice, and the best one in the business. He was a man who saved people from those who weren't trained, or who didn't have the ethics Mattie and The Sector Force had.

There were no doubt going to be issues between them when this mission was over, but they would cross those problems and work them out or not when this was finished.

Until then he was going to take every opportunity to enjoy her presence and watch her when he could.

She slipped on a pair of dark slacks, leaving her gun and holster on his dresser. At least she trusted him that much, which was going some he knew. She slipped into a tan blouse and slipped a form of vest over the blouse.

Then, with a smile on her face, she came over to the bed and sat down to put on her socks and shoes. Her short hair was still damp from the shower and her face looked scrubbed clean.

He reached for her and she tapped his wrist. "Behave yourself, we have work to do."

He laughed. "You want to check the control room to see if any of my alarms missed anything?"

"Glad to," she said.

"I'll take a quick shower and start breakfast in the galley."

"Anything I can do on that side of things?" she asked, finishing her shoes and standing.

"Just keep me company while I cook," he said. "I might put you in charge of the toast if you are good."

"I might be able to handle that," she said, laughing. Then she reached down and with a snap, before he could react, she yanked the sheets off him.

She stood there, hands on her hips, staring at him, smiling. "Now that's a vision to get a girl's blood boiling for the day."

He liked it when she stared at him like he stared at her. It felt right.

Then she turned and headed for the door. "Hurry up with that shower," she said without turning around. "I'm hungry."

"Aye, aye, Captain," he said, crawling out of bed.

He could hear her laughing as she walked up the hallway toward the cockpit.

CHAPTER THIRTY-FOUR

MATTIE SPENT almost thirty minutes in the control room, double-checking everything and the readings that had come in while they slept. Not a ship had moved and no other ships had joined the other ships at the abandoned station.

The fleet of old warships and one small passenger liner still looked impressive docked at the old station. But all the real information showed it was still nothing more than just a giant deception.

She checked to make sure all the alarms were still on, then headed back toward the galley.

Halfway down the wide corridor she could smell bacon and eggs. It was like walking into a heavenly world. Her stomach growled and she picked up her pace slightly. She really, really was hungry and that smell was so thick, she could almost taste the sizzling bacon.

"Oh, wow," she said as she entered the galley. The table was set, the toast in the toaster, and the breakfast about ready to be dished up.

Red stood at the stovetop, his long hair pulled back as normal, his broad shoulders filling out a short-sleeved shirt that highlighted his strong muscles in his arms. He had on tan slacks that seemed to shape themselves perfectly around his fantastic butt.

"Perfect timing," he said, turning to her and smiling. He pointed to a cold storage door. "Would you pour us both some juice. Glasses up there."

With a spatula he pointed to a cupboard.

She had the juice poured and was sitting at her spot at the table as he set a plate in front of her.

"Same as yesterday," he said, "but figured it would give us a good start and it was easy."

"It's perfect," she said. "And it smells wonderful. Thanks!"

"Eat," he said as he turned back to get his plate. "No protocol in this galley, remember?"

"Gladly," she said, digging into the softly-spiced hash browns and eggs. They tasted as wonderful as she remembered them from their last breakfast. A man who was handsome, competent at everything, rich, and could cook? There just had to be something wrong with him. She didn't know what she was going to do if there wasn't something wrong, something that would drive them apart.

She shook that thought away and kept eating. She hadn't known this man long enough to be thinking thoughts like that.

Red joined her after only a moment and dug into his breakfast as well.

Between bites she gave him the update on the ships and the old station. Basically the alarms were still on and nothing was moving.

"So think we have enough data to dash back through the hole in the nebula?" Red asked as he ate. "Get the information off to our organizations, get them working on this problem?"

"I think that would be a good idea," she said. "And honestly, I need an update on the situation back at the Sector Force Headquarters. It's driving me crazy not knowing."

"You don't look crazy," he said, smiling. "But I agree, we need to be caught up. Also, I want to find out how the situation with Chief Lovell is."

"You like him, don't you?" she asked.

He finished the last of his eggs and nodded. "I do. Don't you?"

"I like him a lot and I think he would be great if we can get him fully on our side."

Red nodded and downed the last of his juice. "Let's go find out what's happening back in the civilized worlds."

They spent the next few minutes getting the dishes into the cleaner and the galley secured for travel, then headed for the control room.

Red cut the alarms as he dropped into his chair and turned the ship back toward the hole in the nebula, checking the screens and shields to make sure they would be safe from the radiation.

She once again scanned for any ships in the area. Nothing. All the ships on this side of the nebula seemed to be docked at the old station and for the moment weren't moving.

"Headed in," Red said as the ship ducked back into the high radiation area and everything around them suddenly went from clear space to gray dust.

She hated this and everything about flying blind into anything.

They sat in silence for the next twelve minutes until finally Red said, "Coming out."

And then all the sensors cleared and they were out of the nebula.

Her fingers flew over the board, running quick scans of everything in the area. Nothing at all looked out of place.

Nothing.

"The area is clear," she reported to him, feeling relieved. She wasn't sure what she was expecting, but she had to admit she felt relieved that the Bodie Station was still there and everything looked normal at the moment.

"I'm going to keep us shielded and cloaked," Red said. "Better to not let anyone know where we are anymore."

"I agree," she said.

"We should be clear enough now from the nebula curtain to contact the Sector Force and my people."

Again her fingers flew over the panel in front of her, making sure that her contact with the Sector Force could not be traced to any one location in space.

After a moment, her immediate boss at headquarters answered the call. Her name was Scipio and she was smiling, something Mattie had seldom seen from her. She had hair shorter than Mattie's and a scar that ran across her forehead. Her dark eyes looked just flat mean most of the time, but Mattie liked working for her because she was all business.

"I want you to know that we intercepted sixteen different bombers on board eleven ships, seven of which were liners. The attack would have wiped out thousands of innocent lives and destroyed the heart of Sector Force Three at the same time."

Mattie felt her stomach relax. For now the Sector Force was safe. She wanted to just slump into the chair, but there was still far too much work to do.

Scipio went on. "There were no injuries and all sixteen carrying the bombs were acting under duress from General Jarvis, who had their families in custody. The Innocence Inc. organization, working with local operatives on each planet, have rescued all of the families and they are being brought to the First Sector and relocated with the bombers to safe havens under new names."

"Thank you," Mattie said. "I am glad this has turned out so well at this point."

"Do you have word on General Jarvis?" Scipio asked.

"All the data we have is being downloaded to you now. We think he is contained on an abandoned space station on the edge of The Emptiness with a small force of men and ships. We do not yet have an affirmative positive sighting."

Scipio nodded curtly. "Other Sector Force members are still a day or more journey from your location."

"I will do my best to end this quickly," Mattie said. "Please have our people analyze the data I have just downloaded about his force and ships and give me suggestions on ways of infiltration and attack."

"Understand," Scipio said. Then she said. "Good luck to both of you and thank you once again, from all of us."

With that the connection was cut.

"That was pretty darned nice," Red said from off to her right.

"It was, wasn't it?" Mattie said, smiling. "Not like her at all. It seems we managed to avoid a major disaster. I'm glad your people could get the families clear."

"It's what we do," he said, smiling. "And we also have Chief Lovell's family clear and on board the station with him now."

She laughed. "I bet he's going to be fun to talk with."

"Opening a secure channel now," Red said.

"It took only a moment before Chief Lovell's smiling face appeared on the screen. "Damn am I glad you two picked up on my hints. I couldn't say a word."

"Red spotted them," Mattie said. "Well done."

"And thank you, Red," Lovell said, "and your people, for getting my family out of that damn monster's grip."

"What's the word on your station now?" Mattie asked.

Lovell laughed. "I took care of the last two of General's men who were left on the station personally," he said. "Those two will never threaten another family again, I can promise you. But try to avoid the space debris heading for the nebula if you are out in that direction. It ain't a pretty sight."

Mattie and Red both laughed. She knew exactly what the Chief had done. He had spaced them, as it is called. Alive. It takes a human thirty seconds to a minute to die in a really ugly fashion in open space without protection.

"All wrapped down now," Lovell said.

"Did you get any information out of them before they made the wrong turn out a wrong door?" Red asked.

"Only that your hunch was right, General Jarvis and some of his men are living on ships at the old Bodie Two space station on the other side of the nebula. Since the men here had no way to communicate to the General from here, the General's plan is to start moving tomorrow morning and be around the nebula and here in about four days."

"That fits what we have seen as well," Red said.

"Trust me," Chief Lovell said. "We have the codes from our dearly departed guests to signal the general when he does get in contact that his people are in charge of Bodie Station. But when he gets in range, he's going to discover just how nasty this space station can be in a fight."

Red glanced back at Mattie, then faced the Chief again. "We're going to try to keep it from coming to that."

The Chief laughed. "Take all my fun away," he said. "But thanks, that would be better if you could. In the meantime I'm evacuating all guests and non-essential personnel until this is over."

"We'll be back in touch," Red said, nodding, clicking off the connection.

Then he turned to Mattie. "We have some planning to do."

She was thinking the exact same thing.

CHAPTER THIRTY-FIVE

MATTIE WATCHED as Red quickly made sure all the ship's screens and cloaks were in place so that nothing could see the ship or track them. And alarms would tell her and Red if another ship was even close.

They were still on the Bodie Station side of the nebula, and they had both figured that was the best place to be for the moment until some sort of solution was figured out as to exactly how to stop General Jarvis and his mostly fake, but still dangerous, fleet of ships.

After getting everything set, they headed down the wide hallway in Red's ship, talking about any idea they could think of as a plan of attack.

So far, Mattie couldn't think of a one she liked much at all. She was best at face-to-face encounters with a target. And that's how she wanted to take out General Jarvis, just to make sure there was no chance he would ever escape and threaten the Sector Force again.

She wanted to kill him and then stand over his dead body. It was going to be the only way she would be satisfied.

"You up for lunch yet?" Red asked, clearly in a very good mood after discovering all the families had been saved and the Sector Force was out of danger and Chief Lovell was back in charge of Bodie Station. There were a lot of reasons to be in a good mood, she had to admit that.

But the job left unfinished bothered her.

Her job.

"How long has it been since breakfast?" she asked as they entered the galley.

"Just under four hours," Red said.

"Then the answer is yes," she said, surprised it had been that long. "I'd love to have a sandwich like the ones we had for dinner last night, if that's possible."

"Very possible," he said, smiling at her and then giving her a light kiss.

Just a soft kiss sent shivers through her.

"Sit," he said, pointing at her chair at the table, "and we can plan while I put the sandwiches together."

She laughed as she sat down. "You really love cooking, don't you?"

"I do," he said, glancing at her as he got supplies out of the cold storage. "And it's a lot more fun when I have someone to cook for."

"Does that happen often?" she asked.

"Rarely," he said. "Usually just for friends like Carson and his wife when I was close to their home."

He buried his head into the cold storage, working to get what he would need and she kept silent, giving him a minute to think about Carson.

When he moved to the counter with an armful of supplies, she spoke up again. "Well, I seldom cook for myself, since I don't have my own ship and when home the restaurants around the Sector Force Headquarters are spectacular. I see no reason to eat anything at home but breakfast and a processed lunch before going out. But I like it when someone cooks for me."

"Great," he said, giving her a wide smile, past the dark thoughts of Carson for the moment. "I like to cook for people, you like to be cooked for. A perfect match."

He turned back to his food preparation and she stared at his back and butt. Wow was this guy amazingly good-looking. It kept stunning her every time she actually stopped and looked at him.

She stared at his back and watched him move for a few moments before he turned around and said, "Out loud. Think out loud so we can plan this attack."

"I was thinking of attacking that cute butt of yours, actually," she said.

"Later," he said, laughing. "Keep your mind on the task at hand. How do we dig the General out of the middle of those men and ships?"

"I honestly don't know," she said. "It would seem logical that the General would be on that main passenger liner, but what happens if he isn't. That could be a decoy as well. We just can't go in blowing up ships without knowing we killed him."

"I agree," Red said. "We have to make sure of the target."

"And I'm betting that many of those men are not loyal to the General," Mattie said, "but just being blackmailed into manning the ships as the bombers were."

"My second big worry as well," Red said, nodding as he finished up the two sandwiches and brought them to the table.

Mattie used her fingers to tick off the problems they faced. "One, we have a fleet of ships we can't safely attack without risking innocent lives, and two, there is no way at all to track General Jarvis's movements in that fleet, or three, to know for certain he is even in the fleet when it starts moving toward Bodie Station."

Red sat a glass of juice in front of her and sat down across from her. "Eat," he said. "This meat in this sandwich is known to be brain food."

She glanced down at the white bread and red meat layered inside it. "It's not actually brains, is it?"

He laughed. "Nope. Honest it's not. Now eat."

She did as he said, and it was better-tasting than she remembered from last night. And slightly sweeter.

"What did you add to this?" she asked after the first bite. "It's fantastic."

A local sector mustard," he said while chewing. "From the brains of the mustard plant."

She ignored the joke and kept eating while he just chuckled to himself.

It was great to see him in such a good mood. She just wished she could match it.

"So," she said between bites, "just to be certain I have the same information you have, run me through the weapons available on this ship."

He did. There was little doubt this ship could do stunning amounts of damage to that fleet without ever being seen. But again, that wouldn't help them much.

Then she had an idea. "How close could we get to a moving ship without being seen?"

"Close," he said. "Almost close enough to touch it, actually. The cloak on this ship is the best ever made. But we can't board another ship without dropping the cloak I'm afraid."

She hadn't been thinking that way at all.

"So what happens," she said, "if one of those battle ships was in motion and we came up behind it and hit it with a really small bomb, not enough to blow it out of space, but enough to make it seem like it suddenly had engine problems."

Red looked puzzled. "You think the General would just keep moving forward with his plan even though he lost a few ships along the way?"

"I do," she said. "And those ships would just be left floating dead and we could come back and get the crews later."

"Or the general's people would come back and get the crews," he said.

She agreed. "That's more likely at first, since he has so few people. And if he didn't think the problem was an attack, but just mechanical. We at least would be rounding them all up on fewer and fewer ships this way."

He smiled and finished the last bite of his sandwich. "I think I've got the exact weapon for this as well. No explosion, just an invisible beam that would melt an engine down to slag given enough time. It could freeze it up something solid in a very short amount of time."

"You have laser weapons on this ship?" she asked, clearly surprised that he hadn't mentioned them as a weapon when she asked.

"Not normally used as a weapon," he said. "They are mounted in the nose area in case this ship runs into something it has to cut through. I used them once to take apart a large asteroid that was headed for a planet and no one there even knew it was coming."

She shook her head. Of course he would do that. And chances are until that moment no one even knew he had done it. Typical of him she was starting to see."

"Industrial lasers take a ton of energy and are usually bright red," she said. "Won't the general or his people see it?"

"I can turn off the color, no problem," Red said. "But you are right, they use a ton of energy and we're going to have to use it sparingly and give the energy supplies time to recharge or otherwise risk losing our cloak."

"As slow as those ships will be moving, we have the time," she said, smiling at Red. "And taking our time will make it look like more normal breakdowns. I think it just might work to knock out a bunch of those ships."

"So how do we get General Jarvis isolated in one ship?" he asked.

"Let's knock down the number of ships he has to pick from first, see how many we can take out of the equation, and figure that out later," she said.

"Perfect," he said. "It seems we have a plan."

"Right now let's tell our organizations what we learned from Chief Lovell," she said, "Maybe, just maybe, instead of letting him get close to the station, some of the surrounding systems can mount a greeting party when he comes around the edge of that nebula with whatever ships he will have left after we're finished with him."

"Oh, I like how you think," he said, smiling at her with that wonderful smile of his.

He picked up their plates and empty glasses and turned to put them in the clearer.

She stared at his butt again. "Have I ever told you that I like how your butt looks?"

He looked back at her and shook his head, giving her that smile that seemed to melt parts inside her that should never be melted. At least in front of anyone else.

"Later," he said. "I have a hunch we're going to have some time."

"I sure hope so," she said, wanting to go over and grab his ass right there. Instead, knowing they had work to do first to set this all up, she stood and turned toward the doorway of the galley.

"Yeah, me too," he said as she headed back for the control room.

How could he make her so hot when they had so much to do?

CHAPTER THIRTY-SIX

RED JOINED HER only a few minutes after she reached the control room. She was just getting hooked up to Sector Force Headquarters again. And once again Scipio greeted her.

Mattie told her of the plan to go back to the other side of the nebula and slowly take apart the General's fleet as it moved around the nebula and toward Bodie Station and Resort.

"We will have agents waiting in ships on this side," Scipio said, nodding at Mattie's request for help to block any chance the General's ships reach Bodie Station.

"Red will have as much help that Innocence Inc. can gather as well," Mattie said.

"Good," her boss said. "Our organizations have worked well so far on this crisis, I see no reason to not continue until this is finished."

"And maybe beyond," Mattie said.

Scipio nodded. "And possibly beyond."

With that the communication link was cut.

Mattie glanced over at Red who was nodding.

"There is no reason why Innocence Inc. and the Sector Force could not work together into the future," Red said. "I like that idea."

"Clearly my boss is not adverse to it either," Mattie said.

"Are you?" Red asked, giving her a serious look.

"As long as I get to stare at that butt of yours, not in the slightest," she said, smiling.

"It must be these pants," he said. "I'm going to have to wear them more."

"Please," she said. And they both laughed.

When was the last time a man made her laugh so much? She couldn't remember any time, actually.

Red turned back to his board to contact his people at Innocence Inc. and tell them to coordinate with the Sector Force. She listened until he ended his communication with the fact that he would be out of contact until this was pretty much over.

That's when Mattie realized exactly what he had just said and it made her stomach twist, not from fear, but from the sheer weight of what they were going to try.

The two of them were going up against a fleet of ships and over three hundred crew. And even though they had the best ship and the fastest ship and best weapons, those kinds of odds did not bode well for their success.

And if they were killed on the other side of the nebula, in The Emptiness, no one would ever know.

That's why she was very glad that the Sector Force and Red's people were going to have a fleet meeting the General's ships. Even if she and Red failed, the General would soon be dead.

One way or another.

"Ready to head back to the other side?" Red asked, turning to face her.

"As ready as ever," she said.

The two of them turned back to their boards and in thirty minutes they were inside the nebula for the third time.

And twenty minutes later they were out on the other side.

And all the General's ships were still at the abandoned station.

None of them had moved in the slightest.

And there were no ships even close to where they had come out, so Red again moved them over to a radiation-free place close to the nebula and made sure the cloak and screens were still up and set perfectly.

She had taken scans of the ships again. They matched almost exactly the scans from before. People had moved around inside the ships, but nothing else had changed at all.

"Any signs of them getting ready to move?" Red asked her.

"Not that I can see," she said.

"That worry you?" Red asked, clearly slightly worried himself.

She shook her head. "He would have waited a day or so after the attacks on the Sector Force to start out."

"How would he know if they succeeded or not?" Red asked, looking puzzled.

She sat back and thought for a moment. "He would have his ways. More than likely a relay station a distance on either side of the nebula curtain."

"Of course," Red said, going back to his board. "I should have thought of that. You want to see if we can find that relay station before he gets the news?"

"I don't think we need to," she said. "And if he doesn't get the news, that might panic him even more."

"How is that?"

She tried to put herself into the thinking of someone like General Jarvis. "If he discovers they didn't succeed, he's going to make a dash for Bodie Station. If they did succeed, he's going to do the same thing."

Red stopped and thought for a moment, then nodded his agreement. "I see what you are thinking. At this point he has no choice, his hand has been played."

"Completely," Mattie said. "He either has to run deep into the emptiness with that liner to try to escape or try to hole up at Bodie Station, which can be defended."

"I would bet on Bodie Station," Red said, nodding.

"And try to take out the Sector Force later," she said. "But we're not going to give him that chance."

"Exactly," Red said. Then he smiled. "Besides, Chief Lovell is so angry, he would blow that entire fleet out of space before it even had a chance of getting close."

Mattie laughed. "But I want us to do it first."

"With pleasure," Red said.

Mattie couldn't agree more to that.

CHAPTER THIRTY-SEVEN

IT TOOK RED TWO HOURS of calibrating the cutting laser and then making sure everything was working as programmed. He finally turned from his board when Mattie said, "Incoming ship."

Red watched as her fingers flew over the board in front of her, bringing up the magnification of the ship coming in from the far side of the nebula. It seemed to be going at its top speed and was a similar make and design of the one captured at Bodie Station.

"At that speed it will take the ship a full twenty-three hours to get to the station," Mattie said. "But it doesn't seem to be aiming for the station exactly."

"What do you think?" Red asked. "Is that the message relay ship?"

Mattie nodded, still focused on the readings she was getting in front of her. "More than likely."

"And it's going to meet the fleet at a future point," Red said.

Red turned back to his board and brought up an image of the nebula and the locations of the General's fleet and Bodie Station on the other side of the nebula.

He drew a red dotted line around the far edge of the nebula to show the most likely and shortest safe path the General's fleet would take.

Mattie overlapped the image of the path of the incoming ship and its speed.

The two lines intersected perfectly.

"In twenty hours the ship will join the fleet at that location," Mattie said, nodding.

"So now we know approximately when the fleet is leaving the station," Red said. He did the quick calculations. "The fleet will be leaving the abandoned station in ten to twelve hours."

Mattie nodded. "How long will it take us to get in behind the fleet near the old station?"

"Two hours from here at a safe speed," Red said. "So we got eight hours to wait before we can move. Seven might be better to give us time to move in behind the fleet slowly."

"So we get to fight in seven hours," she said, nodding. "Finally."

With that he had to agree. He wasn't any better at waiting than Mattie was.

She glanced over at him, her eyes twinkling and a half smile on her face.

"Got any ideas what we should do in the next seven hours?" she asked.

He loved that look in her eyes, that promise of a very, very good time to come.

"I think we need to get some sleep, get some food, and make love for at least an hour."

"In that order?" she asked.

He laughed. "Not necessarily."

"Good," she said, reaching for his hand as she stood. "I'll be in bed. Double check everything here, but don't be too long. Otherwise I'm going to start without you."

Her chuckle as she left the control room clearly must have been in response to the stunned look on his face and the idea of her starting without him and his imagination that went wild thinking about that idea alone.

It took him only one minute to make sure the alarms were set and the shields were up and the cloak was still working.

Then somehow he managed to not run down the corridor.

But only barely.

CHAPTER THIRTY-EIGHT

MATTIE GOT TO THE BEDROOM ahead of him and had her clothes off and was crawling into bed when he arrived.

She kicked the covers back and just lay there naked, watching him undress and enjoying the feeling of being exposed to him. Plus she loved watching him, far more than she wanted to admit. And now she was starting to feel like she had known him for a very long time, even though it hadn't been long at all, less than a few days.

He got his clothes off and joined her, pulling her into his arms and kissing her.

They stayed like that, just kissing, laying with their bodies touching all the way along. She kept her breasts pushed against his chest and she could feel his excitement.

Then slowly she pushed him onto his back and started kissing his neck and working her way down his body, kissing every solid muscle in his stomach, working her tongue through his pubic hair, and then taking the tip of him in her mouth, flicking him with her tongue until he squirmed back and forth.

Then suddenly he sat up, took her waist, turned her around and put her on top of him so that he could kiss her crotch at the same time.

It would not have surprised her in the slightest if sparks shot off her body and lit up the room as his tongue found her and worked back and forth against the lips of her crotch.

She pushed back against him, then eased away, then pushed back toward those wonderful feelings.

She kept him in her mouth, her hand moving up and down on him slowly as she enjoyed every touch of his tongue against her.

Finally, she couldn't take it anymore and she pushed back hard against his mouth and he picked up his pace with his tongue and lips and full mouth.

She pushed back against his face harder and harder and then came in a shuddering, earth-shaking way that made her entire body go limp on top of him.

He eased her over carefully so that she was lying on her back, her eyes closed as she tried to catch her breath.

Then he turned around and before she knew it, he was inside her, his body over her, his weight supported on his arms, his crotch pressing down against hers.

And he moved in and out, the slickness of her last orgasm making his motion easy and smooth.

She wrapped her arms around him and pulled herself up against him, pressing into him.

And as she did he moved faster and faster and she came again, this time with him.

She let go after a long and wonderful moment and dropped back on the bed.

She could feel the last of his release easing and he shuddered once and then eased down so that he could lie beside her.

She moaned in disappointment as he slipped out of her.

"Don't worry," he whispered, softly, as if he didn't have enough air yet to talk fully. "It will be back."

"Soon?" she asked, not wanting it to stop, not wanting anything of this wonderful moment to stop.

"Soon," he said, pulling her tight.

And with that they both drifted off to sleep.

CHAPTER THIRTY-NINE

MATTIE AWOKE to the smell of something wonderful cooking. A light smell of garlic and fresh bread combined with something she couldn't identify, but that made her mouth water.

Around her the sheets were messed up and she had wrapped herself in one of the light blankets. Red was gone and she flat didn't remember him getting up and leaving. But his wonderful musky smell was still lingering with the smell of their passion.

Somehow he had gotten out of bed, got dressed, and made it to the kitchen and started cooking without waking her.

She shook her head and lay back and stared at the ceiling. How had she come to trust one person so much in such a short time? How was that even possible?

Before Red, she never would have allowed anyone to move around her like he must have done without her being awake and aware. She flat didn't trust anyone enough for that to happen. Yet here she was, making love to this man she hardly knew, sleeping soundly around him like she had known him for years.

She had no doubt that such actions were chances she shouldn't be taking because in reality, she didn't know him. Yet with Red, it felt so right.

She was taking chances with him she never thought she would be able to take with anyone. Or want to, for that matter.

And they were chances she flat wanted to take.

Suddenly like a ghost, Red appeared at the doorway of the bedroom. He had on the same clothes as earlier. Black slacks, light shirt, and running-type shoes. His long, dark hair was still wet, so clearly he had also taken a shower without disturbing her.

"Fifteen minutes until dinner," he said, giving her that smile that seemed to melt her every worry about him. "Grab a shower and get ready. We need to be moving in just over an hour."

"Anything changed?" she asked, stretching without showing Red any of her skin. No point in getting either of them started again at this point.

"Nothing," he said. "I just checked."

And then he smiled again. "My alarms would have plastered us against the ceiling as soundly as we were sleeping if something had changed. Thank heavens they didn't go off."

"Good sex can do that," she said, smiling back at him.

"Good sex, hell. That was great sex. Now get showered and come get some food."

With one more smile he turned and headed back toward the galley.

He was right, it had been great sex.

Every time so far.

And from the smells filling the room, it was about to be great food. Now only one thing that would make all this perfect: Putting General Jarvis down for good like a rabid dog.

And that was next on the schedule. That made her smile as well.

She untangled herself from the sheets and headed for the huge shower. Twelve minutes later she joined Red in the galley, dressed in the same clothes she had put on earlier.

And forty-five minutes later, after a wonderful meal of poultry with light garlic sauce, fresh bread, and steamed sweet green vegetables she had never seen before but fell in love with on first bite, they were back in the control room.

Under cloak they headed for General Jarvis's fleet and she could feel the excitement of a coming fight start to fill her. This man had attacked her home and luckily failed. She was so looking forward to stopping him.

CHAPTER FORTY

"DAMN IT," Mattie said, more to herself than anyone.

Red understood exactly how she was feeling. They were both at their stations in the control room and he did not like what was happening with Jarvis's fleet. It

was not what he and Mattie had predicted would happen.

Or at least not all of it.

Jarvis was splitting up his ships.

The passenger liner and ten of the fighters headed off on the path that he and Mattie predicted the fleet would take around the nebula and toward Bodie Station.

Another ten of his military ships headed in almost exactly the opposite direction around the nebula. It would take those ships almost three days longer than the first part of the fleet to get around the nebula and back into Sector space. And they would be nowhere near the Bodie Station.

Red had no idea at all why General Jarvis would do that.

And ten more of the fleet's ships simply stayed at the old abandoned station, including the largest battle cruiser.

And all the ships remained manned and seemingly ready to fight. And worse yet, there was no way of telling from the scans which ship carried General Jarvis.

Mattie shoved her chair back with another couple of swear words, stood, and started to pace. She was angry, very angry right at that moment. And making the most dangerous enforcer in all of the Sector Force angry was never a good idea.

Red had moved their ship up to within striking distance of the old station and put them into a position of hiding. He took what readings he could, made sure their cloak was firm and they couldn't be scanned in any way, then turned his chair around so he could face where she was pacing.

He was smart enough to not say anything, even though he wanted to. At this point it was her conversation to start. And he was willing to wait.

Finally she dropped into her chair again and just sighed. "This is one tricky bastard."

Red decided it was best to only nod.

"He managed to elude the Sector Force for years, almost destroy the Sector Force, and now that we think we know where he is, he's managing to try to get away again."

"He's not going to get away," Red said.

"And if we blow up all those ships out there," she said, "how are we going to know he's actually dead and not just hiding somewhere in the second sector running this like a puppet show?"

"We wouldn't," Red said. "Which is why we are not going in and just blowing up ships."

"We've got to watch this monster die," Mattie said, staring off at the ceiling.

"And we will," Red said. "We both will. He killed my best friend and thousands and thousands of others. He's not getting away."

Suddenly the Mattie he had come to know was back in her eyes and under control. She stared at him. "Suggestions?"

"We stay with the original plan," Red said. "This ship is fast enough to deal with it all. We jab a stick into this nest and see where everyone swarms. And that will tell us where the General is. Then we can go in and clean him out."

"One ship against thirty?" Mattie said, shaking her head.

He laughed. "Yeah, they don't stand a chance, do they?"

For a second she looked at him and then smiled. "You're right. We do this right and they don't."

CHAPTER FORTY-ONE

MATTIE WAS MANNING the laser beam controls as Red eased their cloaked ship up behind a small patrol ship in the eleven ships heading directly toward Bodie Station.

She could feel the tension in the control room because both of them knew that if this didn't work they were in trouble. The idea was to knock out a ship's engine without destroying it and making it seem like the ship only had engine trouble. That way they could disable ships and never have anyone in the fleets know they were even there.

And the hoped-for result would be that the communications after a ship or two seemingly broke down would be that General Jarvis would reveal which ship he was on. So they had all the fleet ships monitored and were ready on that front as well.

"In position," Red said, nodding to her.

Red was the one piloting the ship, doing the tricky cloaked approaches to the other ships. Her job was to fire the laser that would disable the engine of the target ship and monitor the communication as Red got them out of the danger area.

She fired the laser, just a very short and intense burst.

"Done."

Red slowly eased their ship back and to one side.

Nothing showed on the monitor and for a moment nothing seemed to happen. What they hoped was that the laser would burn out parts of the ship's engines, melt it, and cause it to shut down.

Mattie wasn't sure if it had worked or not. She carefully watched the screen and the monitors.

Then the ship they had fired on started to drift slightly and Red quickly pulled his ship even farther back and out of the way.

She did a quick reading. The target's engine was down. From the looks of it, frozen solid.

There were six people on board, and from her scans, three of them went back to the engine area while the other three stayed in the control area.

The chatter over the communications systems seemed pretty normal, but slightly angry. Clearly they had expected some breakdowns in the old ships, but not one so soon after leaving the base.

"One down," Red said, smiling as he turned the ship and headed for the other group of ships going the long way around.

"Keep an eye out on how they handle that problem," he said. "We'll be in position to give them yet another headache in thirty minutes."

"Think of it as a toothache," Mattie said, watching and monitoring the chatter between the dead ship and the others. "We're just extracting them one at a time."

"To make sure the General has no bite left," Red said, laughing.

"Exactly," she said.

Thirty minutes later Red had matched the speeds of the other small fleet taking the long way into the Second Sector. He had decided on a larger attack-style ship to one side of the fleet as the target this time.

The first ship they had crippled still floated in space and no one had turned back for the crew or come from the station to help them yet. The life support systems on that ship would hold those men for almost a month, so they were fine.

"In position," Red said.

Again she fired the laser, this time just a little longer since the ship they were crippling had a larger contained engine.

"Finished," she said.

Red immediately eased them back and away from the ship.

Again, Mattie couldn't tell anything had happened at first. Then after almost thirty seconds the ship seemed to lose ground with the acceleration of the others and drifted back.

"Oh, that got them upset," Mattie said, laughing at all the chatter over the communications links. There were almost two dozen crew on the ship they had just stopped and she had a hunch that another ship would swing back and pick them up. The General just couldn't lose that many men out of such a small force.

She listened intently, trying to get any hint of the location of the general. But orders didn't seem to be coming from any ship directly. And nothing was coming from the passenger liner traveling with the other group.

After five minutes she turned to Red. "No sign. Nothing. But wow are they all unhappy."

He shrugged. "So let's make them a little more unhappy," Red said.

He eased back around to the other side of the slowly accelerating fleet and came up behind the largest ship in this group. And the only one with private cabins of any sort. Mattie figured that if the general was in this group, he would be on that ship in the private cabins.

"Ready," Red said after a moment.

She again fired the laser slightly longer than the last time, directing the invisible beam right into the engine of the big ship. No metal was going to withstand that kind of heat. A large area of that engine had just become slag.

"Done," she said the moment she let up on the trigger.

Red pulled them up and away, moving a distance off to the side of the small fleet.

The big ship started to drop back and then all hell broke loose on the communications channels between the ships.

Mattie put it over the control room system so Red could hear. They both listened for any clue as to the location of the general.

There was a lot of fear, a great deal of anger, and some military types clearly in control and very, very upset.

But no sign of the general breaking in to give orders.

After fifteen minutes Mattie looked into Red's worried eyes. She could tell he was thinking the same thing.

They had forced three major ships in the two fleets to break down dead in space and the General had not said a word

General Jarvis was not out here.

CHAPTER FORTY-TWO

RED COULDN'T BELIEVE the general hadn't said a word after losing three major ships from his attack fleet. That made no sense at all. Had he and Mattie been completely wrong about the general hiding on this side of the nebula?

Mattie had gone back to pacing as Red turned the ship toward the group of ships with the passenger liner. That liner would be their next target; see what happened then.

"Maybe his men are too afraid to tell him what is happening," Red said.

"Possible," Mattie said.

She did two more quick paces back and forth of the control room and then dropped into her chair again.

She brought up the ten ships in the fleet heading directly around the nebula for Bodie Station. "We take out the passenger liner and we'll know for certain."

Red agreed with her. "It's going to take twenty-five more minutes for us to get close enough to those ships. How about you monitor and I go get us a couple of juices and pieces of bread from the galley?"

She nodded. "Thanks."

But he could tell she wasn't really in her mind completely. She was having the same worry that General Jarvis had duped them once again and that the Sector Force was still in danger.

Red had no doubt that Jarvis was clever enough to set up this kind of ruse.

But why?

He kept asking himself that question over and over all the way to the galley and back. And by the time he got back, he had an idea as to why.

He handed her a glass of juice and a slice of the white bread. "Anything?"

"Nothing but anger at the mechanics and so on," she said. "There is no hint at all that they were attacked."

They were still ten minutes from being close enough to the fleet and the passenger liner before he would have to take control and get them into position.

On the screen the ten ships retained formation, filling in the gap left by the one ship they had disabled out of this group. All the warships were around the passenger liner, as if protecting it.

It looked perfect. Too perfect as far as Red was concerned.

On his big screen he brought up an image of the entire area, showing the line of the two fleets around the nebula curtain, Bodie Station on one side and the Three-Planet Alliance where the other fleet would reenter Sector Two space.

Red pointed to small fleets of ships with the passenger liner headed for Bodie Station. "What's going to happen to those fleets if they go charging into those areas now?"

"They are going to be blown out of space," Mattie said. "Chief Lovell on Bodie plus other ships with Sector Force and Innocence Inc. agents will make sure none of those ships make it through. That's why we're trying to figure out where the General is before that happens."

"Exactly," Red said. He pointed to the other fleet of ships."

"What about those."

She looked up and saw exactly where their path was going to take them. "The Three-Planet Alliance fleet will make short work of them. If I remember right, they had a run-in with General Jarvis when he was still in power on his home world."

"Exactly," Red said. Then he pointed to the ships remaining at the old space station, some of which were nothing but hulls that would never move again. "And those?"

She shrugged. "Someone would quickly wipe them out along with the old station."

She looked over at him. "So what are you saying? That all this is a ruse?"

"I'm pretty sure it is," Red said.

"But why?" Mattie asked, shaking her head.

"Because the only way the general is ever going to escape the Sector Force is by having everyone think he is dead."

"I understand that, but where would he go?"

"I have a couple ideas on that," Red said as he took over controls of the ship again and started to ease it in behind the passenger liner surrounded by the fleet of attack ships. "But let's see if he really isn't on this liner and then talk about that."

She nodded and went back to monitoring all the communications and getting another charge built up in the laser.

Eight minutes later Red said "Ready and in position."

"Firing," she said. Then a moment later she said, "Done."

He quickly pulled his ship up and away from the fleet. With normal, modern warships, he never would have been able to get a cloaked ship in that close. But these ships were far from modern nor were they manned in a normal fashion.

As they watched, the liner lost its acceleration, maintaining the speed it had been going.

Mattie looked at Red. "Passenger liner is now adrift. Engines gone."

She made the communications from the different fleet ships fill the command area. Red made one more check to make sure they were clear and completely cloaked. Then he sat back to listen.

CHAPTER FORTY-THREE

RED HAD POINTED OUT to her how these two small ragtag fleets were going to be easily destroyed as soon as they neared Sector space on the other side of the nebula curtain.

She understood that completely. The only reason that General Jarvis would move toward Bodie Station was by thinking he still controlled the station.

But if that had been the case and his plan, he would have taken every ship he could with him, not divide them into three small fleets assured to be destroyed.

Unless he wanted them destroyed.

And now she and Red had disabled the passenger liner and there was still no sign of General Jarvis. Not one word from him.

There was no doubt in Mattie's mind that he was not on the ships. Or on the abandoned station or any ship remaining there.

But he wanted people with this ploy to think he was killed. If that was the case, where was he?

She banged her hand down on the edge of her chair and shut off the communication chatter from the fleet ships. The fleet had only paused for a moment, then gone around and kept going toward Bodie Station, leaving the passenger liner drifting along with the first ship they had disabled. Life support on both vessels was enough to last for over a month, so for the moment they were fine.

"So where is he?" she asked.

Red shrugged, but I have a way we might find out and save all these people and their families in the process."

"You think all this crew is working under threats on their families?" Mattie asked.

"It's the general's mode of operation and can you see any other reason why these ships will continue onward knowing it's a suicide mission?"

"I agree," she said. "So Mister Innocence Inc., how do we save all of them and their families and find out where the general is located?"

"We ask them," Red said, smiling at her.

"You don't think General Jarvis is going to be monitoring all their communications?" She just sort of stared at him. He had lost his mind.

"Oh, I would bet anything he's listening to everything they are saying from wherever he's at, more than likely through relays. That's why they have to just keep going forward no matter what happens to any ship."

"And chances are those ships are scheduled to explode at some point so there will be no survivors," she said, pointing at the ships on the screen that they had disabled. "There can't be any survivors of any of this."

Red looked very concerned, but nodded. "I would believe the same. Which means we can't try any sort of rescue until we have the general in custody or very dead."

"We could do that if we knew what stone he was hiding under."

"So we ask the people on these ships where he is at."

Suddenly she realized what he was thinking. "Short band intercom?" she asked. "Ship to ship with no range?"

"Exactly," he said, nodding. "Sure can't hurt to try at this point."

She sat back in her chair, staring at the screen. It just might work.

She turned to Red. "Let's write down carefully what we plan to say and what we need from them besides the General's location."

Red smiled. "And we need to tell them the exact situation they are flying into. And that they don't have to if they act quickly."

She grabbed her pad and started working on the message.

Beside her she saw him turn back to the controls and ease them in toward one of the fleet ships still heading toward Bodie Station so they would be close enough to send a message that the General would never hear, no matter what rock he was hiding under.

CHAPTER FORTY-FOUR

MATTIE WORKED OVER the message, making sure it say completely and efficiently what she needed it to say to the crew of the small fleets of ships heading to guaranteed destruction. She and Red had decided they were going to try the message on the fleet headed for Bodie Station first, then if that worked, go and repeat it on the ships left at the abandoned

space station and the ships headed toward the Three-Planets Alliance.

Red glanced over his shoulder at her and gave her one of those wonderful smiles of his. "In position and I have ship-to-ship communication set up. No one outside the small area of this fleet will pick this up and I have it directed at the nebula with a directional focus so that the nebula kills anything that might carry."

"Good," she said and took a deep breath. "Here I go."

He tapped his board and then nodded to her that the channel was open.

"Attention crew members of the ships heading in the direction of the Bodie Station. This is a representative of The Sector Force and Innocence Incorporated. We understand you are being forced into this action

Some Classic Dean Wesley Smith Stories
Available at your favorite booksellers.

by General Jarvis. We understand your families are being held hostage to guarantee you carry out this suicide mission. We can rescue you and your families and get you into safe new lives."

She paused and Red nodded and gave her a thumbs up.

"We can help you and save you and your families' lives, but first we need each crew member's name and home planet and any other information you feel we need to rescue your loved ones. We will have them in safekeeping before any of your ships reach the awaiting fleet on the other side of the nebula curtain."

Again she paused to take a deep breath.

"And we need the location of General Jarvis so that we may stop him as well before he hurts or kills or threatens anyone else. We are on the half-dozen cloaked warships that crippled your liner and your other warships to let you know we were here. We will continue to cripple more ships until none of you can fight and the general will kill your loved ones because you failed. Please help us help you."

Red indicated he had cut the transmission.

She leaned back and took a deep breath. She would have rather fought two trained killers in hand-to-hand combat to the death than do that again. She was sweating, her stomach was twisted into a knot, and her palms were damp.

"Copy," a single male voice came back, very weak and clearly on only ship-to-ship.

"This might work," Red said, a touch of excitement in his voice.

"Are they scanning for us now?"

Red glanced over his instruments, then shook his head. "Clearly they are in no mood for a fight with cloaked ships."

"That bodes well," Mattie said. "They also don't want to let the General know we might be out here. No telling what he would do if he thought that."

Red looked a little pale at that and went back to monitoring his board.

They sat and waited, keeping close and paced with the ship they had communicated with.

The other communication between the ships continued as normal, including communication between the three different groups of ships. Although Mattie had to admit, the twenty people left on the few ships on the abandoned space station said the least.

And all the crippled ships were blamed on engine failure and they should be back up and running shortly. Mattie knew that would never be the case, but better to let the General think repairs were possible.

Finally there was a crackle on the ship-to-ship communications channel

Red quickly turned and keyed back in the same crackle to let them know he was still here.

In a moment there was more noise, what sounded like a high whine, then it was gone.

Red laughed and quickly loaded up the sound, then his fingers flew over his board and after a moment the names and home planets of all three hundred and seven humans on this side of the nebula in General Jarvis's fleet appeared on the screen.

Mattie was glad she didn't have to give that speech to the other two groups of ships. They got all the names on all the ships right here.

"The bastard," Red said after another moment as Mattie scanned the names on the screen.

"What?" Mattie asked.

"He's got bombs on all the ships set to explode in exactly three days. He can trigger them early if the fleets stop."

Mattie nodded. "Which is why they couldn't stop and pick up the crew from the stranded ships."

"Exactly," he said.

"So did they say where Jarvis was?" she asked.

"They did," Red said. "He's crossing The Emptiness in a small passenger liner."

Mattie glanced up at the screen full of names. "How long ago did he leave?"

"One week ago," Red said.

"Can we catch him?" Mattie asked, worried about what Red would say.

"We can, given time," Red said. "And we have the time. But first we have to save all these people and their families."

She sat back in the chair and stared at the list of names on the screen. Her desire to kill General Javis, to do her job, was extreme. But Red was right. First save the people Jarvis threatened.

Then kill the monster.

Red keyed in a little static, then said, "Copy. Received."

He looked at her and shrugged.

It was all he could say.

All he dared say.

At least they had given them a little hope of survival, if not for them, for their families.

A moment later, as Mattie watched, Red had the ship moved away from the fleet and headed at top speed for the hole in the nebula curtain. The first of the two fleets would clear the sides of the nebula in less than two days. There wasn't a lot of time to rescue a lot of families on a lot of different planets.

And it would take them seven hours to get to the hole and through to the other side, which cut the time down even more.

Mattie knew that, but she had no doubt that with the combined forces of the Sector Force and Red's people, they could get it done.

And then it would be her turn to do her job and make sure a monster didn't threaten another person.

Ever.

CHAPTER FORTY-FIVE

RED GOT MATTIE to the galley and made them both cups of tea and a snack so they could sit and talk. He was happy she liked the same tea he did, and even got out of her focus on General Jarvis to stop and mention the flavor. It had a faint rich smell of tea, yet had a sweet taste of light honey mixed in.

"Strong stuff," Red said, holding up his cup.

She took another sip. "Doesn't taste strong."

"Kind of like you," he said, smiling at her. "Tastes wonderful but can beat the heck out of you if you're not careful."

She actually laughed. "Now I like it even more."

For the next two hours they sat snacking on some soft bread and cut meat and drinking tea while talking about how they were going to approach the situation on the other side of the nebula.

She just wanted to go through, stay cloaked, tell both Red's people and the Sector Force what the situation was, give them the name, and get them working on it. Then head out into The Emptiness to catch General Jarvis.

But he didn't want to do it that way and he had no doubt it was going to take some convincing for her to come over to his side.

"You know," she said after he told her that they needed to stay for the two days and help in the rescue of those people off those ships before they blew up, "our people and Chief Lovell can handle all that."

"I agree," he said. "On that side of the nebula. But they can't handle the ships and the people we stranded back on the other side of the nebula," he said.

"Damn it," she said.

He pushed on. "Those and the ships docked at the abandoned space station are going to explode at the same time as the others and kill everyone. We need to get those people off those ships as well and we have the only ship in the area fast enough and shielded enough to get back to them in time."

"Damn it, damn it, damn it," she said, pushing her empty cup aside in disgust. "We're going to let that monster get away, aren't we?"

"Not a chance," Red said, smiling at her. "If he's out in The Emptiness, we'll track him down. He can't outrun us."

"If we stay for the days this is going to take, he's going to have a huge start."

"Unless he's got a ship almost as fast as this one," Red said, "it will take him close to a year to cross The Emptiness. It might take us some time as well, but we can catch him."

She shook her head, but he could tell she knew he was right.

"Unless, of course, you don't want to spend that much time with me."

She laughed, stood and went around the table and kissed him squarely on the mouth. "I'd love to spend that much time with you," she said. "But on one condition."

"What's that?" he asked, wondering just what kind of condition she might put on him.

"You teach me how to cook."

"Now that's a deal," he said, kissing her back.

CHAPTER FORTY-SIX

THE MOMENT THEY EMERGED from the hole in the nebula, Mattie contacted the Sector Force. Red got them stopped a decent distance from the nebula and kept up their cloak. Then he contacted his people using a secure communication channel as well. They both sent all the information and their plan on how to save the families.

Then, as Mattie was finished working with her contact at the Sector Force, Scipio came on.

"I understand from what you just sent that the General is headed across The Emptiness in a medium-sized passenger liner."

"Yes," Mattie said. "I'm having the purchase of the liner researched, what kind it is, and the layout."

"Will you be able to catch his ship?"

Mattie nodded. "Easily, from what Red assures me. But it will take some time."

The head of the Sector Force nodded, then smiled lightly. "The side-effect of all this is that the Sector Force and Innocence Inc. are working even closer than ever."

"I hope that continues," Mattie said.

"As do I," Scipio said. "We will do our best to save the families and relocate them as we did the others. Report when the target is terminated. It will be a relief when all this is finished."

Then the screen went blank before Mattie could agree.

When Red was finished with briefing his team and personally contacting the head of the Three-Planets Alliance to ask for his help, Mattie said, "What next?"

"We brief Chief Lovell, then head back to see who we can rescue on the other side of the nebula."

She nodded and glanced at the time. "They had less than twenty-six hours until those first ships cleared the edge of the nebula and started toward the Bodie Station. And nineteen hours later the second group of ships would clear the other edge of the nebula and break into Three Planets Alliance territory.

Not much time at all, especially with bombs ticking on every ship.

It took them only thirty minutes to brief Chief Lovell. Then another hour to get all the plans for the liner General Jarvis had purchased two years before through a series of odd channels. The liner had undergone a year of renovations in the First Sector to turn it into a private space yacht with room for a crew of one hundred. Normally the ship could have carried upwards of a thousand passengers and four hundred crew.

They were sent the new plans and all Red could do was whistle softly. Not only was it a floating palace, it was heavily armed and from the looks of it, not only was there a crew of fifty, but the ship had a military presence of another fifty soldiers on board. Plus a number of short-range secondary ships with a lot of fire-power as well.

Mattie studied the plans for a moment and decided there would be more than enough time while trying to catch that liner to study them.

Both she and Red made sure those were the most current plans. More could have been added on at the abandoned space station, but Mattie doubted it.

"What's the speed of that thing?" Mattie asked.

Red checked, then double-checked with a couple of his people before answering her question.

"It's fast," he said. "Faster than any liner I have ever seen."

"Can we catch it?" she asked.

"We can catch it," he said. "You're just going to be a better cook is all by the time we do."

CHAPTER FORTY-SEVEN

AFTER SEEING the passenger liner plans and calculating the time it was going to take for them to catch it, Red started making lists of the provisions they were going to need. He sent the list to Chief Lovell to have them stocked and ready to be picked up at Bodie Station when they brought in the survivors from the other side of the nebula curtain.

Then he turned to Mattie, who was working over the last of the communication with the Sector Force.

"You ready to go rescue some people?"

"Let's go try at least," she said.

He nodded and set them back toward the hole in the nebula curtain. They had figured there were less than thirty people at the station, another forty total on ships they had left drifting. It would be crowded, but they could handle that many here on the ship for a short time.

But they were going to keep them under lockdown, since there was no telling if any of them were actually loyal to the General and were willing to die for him.

Around the area of the second sector, raids were going in dozens of places, saving entire families. It was a lot of people to save, but the General had paid a lot of low-life enforcers on different planets to hold the hostages. And money talked, but not more than the guns of local police and Innocence Inc. and Sector Force agents.

Red just hoped it all went well.

It took them a silent forty minutes to get to the nebula curtain hole and back through it. Both of them kept working at their boards, going over anything that might happen and looking for anything safer they could try.

He liked the fact that the two of them could work and not feel the need to talk. It was as if he was alone, yet wasn't. A nice feeling.

The entire time all Red came up with was that their initial plan was as good as they were going to get.

On the other side of the nebula curtain, the scene was as they had left it, except that both small fleets were closer to the edges of the nebula curtain.

Red set a course of full speed directly at the abandoned station. They had decided they would get the people there off first, since they would have the best chance of staying hidden in that area.

On the flight to the station, Mattie worked over the containment area and all the scanning equipment they were going to need to make sure no one brought a weapon or a bomb on board.

Red had little doubt that if anyone tried, Mattie would just kill them without a second thought.

And honestly, so would he.

If someone didn't want to be rescued from certain death, that wasn't his problem.

She finished inspecting the storeroom areas that they had emptied to put in the ones they hoped to rescue, and the four extra bedrooms and came back into the control room.

"They won't be comfortable," she said, dropping into her chair. "But it won't be for long."

"Locked in and under watch is all we care about," Red said.

Her fingers flew over her board, bringing up one empty room after another.

"All set."

He nodded. "So we're going to assume that the General has cameras watching everything and his finger on the explosives trigger."

"I would bet on it," Mattie said.

Red had no doubt that they might be killed in this rescue attempt. But it was worth it to try to save so many.

"We put up a natural static to block all communications out of the station, drop our cloak, dock, and get everyone on board. Cloak again and drop the static."

She shook her head. "We have to be away within two minutes or the static would be suspicious."

Red looked at her worried look. "I think we're pushing it at two minutes."

"So they had better be ready or we leave them."

"Exactly," Red said.

Twenty minutes later he eased the cloaked ship up near the largest of the ships still docked. And he hit it with an intercom level message.

It was similar to the one Mattie had read earlier.

Basically the message said that they were part of a cloaked fleet working on saving them. That they had each soldier's name and were working on saving all the families. He told them that the General planned on blowing up the station and all the ships in less than twelve hours, and if they wanted to get off the ships and the old abandoned space station safely, they needed to be within thirty seconds of a certain airlock in ten minutes without arising suspicion. Do not bring guns or weapons of any type.

A moment later a simple bit of static came back and Red nodded.

"They heard us."

Mattie sat bolt upright, her fingers scanning everything she could as he took the ship in within just a few feet of the airlock they were going to dock at.

It was an airlock that everyone on the station and on the grouped ships could get to within five minutes.

After eight minutes she turned to him. "No explosives that I can see, and everyone seems to be headed this direction slowly, as if they didn't care. I'm headed down to greet our guests."

"Good luck," he said. "I'll hit our static cover in two minutes and drop the cloak and dock."

He could see the determination in her eyes as she turned and headed at a medium pace down the hallway.

For an enforcer, she was pretty damned good at this saving people business. Clearly Sector Force agents had gotten a bad rap over the years.

CHAPTER FORTY-EIGHT

MATTIE STOOD AT THE AIRLOCK waiting for the signal from Red. She wasn't sure of all this, but it was the right thing to do. She just hoped that doing this would mean that General Jarvis wouldn't get away from her again.

Then in her ear she heard "Now!"

She felt the bump of the docking with the airlock on the other side.

The red light beside the airlock stayed red for a maddeningly long three seconds, then snapped green.

She cycled the airlock open.

On the other side men and women ran at her. Most were in stained clothes that clearly looked as if they had been living in them for longer than Mattie wanted to think about.

And the smell of human sweat and fear clogged her nose.

She backed up to the main corridor, pointed, and shouted, "Down the hall, doors at the end. Fast as you can! Then get down and hold on!"

Every one of them ran past her, never questioning even for a second.

"Ten more seconds," Red said.

She moved up to the airlock.

Finally one man staggered in. "I'm the last."

"Clear!" she said to Red and hit the airlock close button.

A second later she felt the ship disconnect with the station.

She glanced at the time. "One minute and seven seconds."

The man who smelled of grease and body odor leaned against the wall, panting.

She glanced at him and he nodded his thanks.

"Thank us when we get everyone out alive," she said, pointing down the hall to the large storage room where everyone else had gone. "Tell everyone to stay down. It might get rough before we're done."

He nodded and did as he was told.

When he went in, she made sure the door was closed and locked, then quickly put a dampening field on the room to make sure no weapons or explosives could be set off or signals sent out.

After a short scan it was clear there were no weapons or explosives or anything in that room but a lot of dirty and terrified people.

But she didn't trust anyone at this point, so she left the dampening field on and headed back toward the control room with Red.

As she entered, she could see that they were speeding away from the station, heading for the passenger liner and the other ship they had knocked out. And the station and ships were still there and intact.

"How are our passengers," he asked as she dropped into her chair and brought up the image of the large room full of fugitives sitting and laying on the floors.

"Smelly," she said, glancing over at him. "But at the moment alive."

"About all we can ask for at this point," Red said, smiling.

CHAPTER FORTY-NINE

MATTIE WAS AMAZED at how good she felt. They had managed to get to all four disabled ships and get everyone off without a problem. Right now they had a ship-full of very dirty, tired, and happy soldiers and civilians from a dozen different second sector planets.

Red had them headed at top speed back through the hole in the curtain nebula. They both knew the fleet was just rounding the edge of the nebula near the Bodie Station.

In thirty minutes exactly, those ships of both fleets on both ends of the nebula curtain would be blocked completely from all incoming and outgoing signals and just as she and Red had done, ships would quickly unload the crews.

Then the ships would be blown out of space.

"We're clear of the nebula," Red said.

On the screen the stars of the second sector became clear, filling the viewpoint.

Both of them, without a word, gave a report to the Sector Force and to Innocence Inc. Then they heard the good news.

Without fail, every hostage had been rescued without a casualty. All three hundred families.

Mattie couldn't believe how she felt at that moment. Elated, satisfied, and completely grinning from ear-to-ear. She had not believed it was possible.

And they had saved the Sector Force as well.

"Tell our passengers," Red said, smiling at her with just as wide and happy a smile.

"I think both of us need to do that," she said.

She moved over beside him and clicked on the communications link that opened a channel to all of the rooms where they had locked the crew.

"Your attention, please," she said and everyone in every room turned to them.

"My name is Mattie Silks with Sector Force and this is Red Simms, the cofounder of Innocence Incorporated."

At learning their names there was a buzz around each room, but Mattie just waited for a second and everyone gave her their attention again.

"We are very happy to inform you that all your families have been rescued from General Jarvis's henchmen and hired guns. And also all the families on the ships still headed for the station and for the Three-Planets Alliance. A rescue operation will be starting in just a few minutes to get them off those ships as well and then, as General Jarvis wanted, all the ships will be destroyed. Only none of you will be on them."

There was massive cheering and hugging in all of the rooms and she and Red both just sat and watched the celebration.

After they calmed down, she asked for their attention one more time.

"After we have unloaded you all at the Bodie Station, we will be going after General Jarvis to make certain he can never do this again. If you have information about that passenger liner, the crew with him, or the destination, please let one of the officers know who will be helping you at the Bodie Station and they will get the information to us."

As everyone nodded and looked tired and relieved, Mattie finished by saying, "Welcome back. We should be arriving at Bodie Station within two hours."

Then she cut the link.

Red looked at her with a huge smile. "Great idea to get information from them."

"If they have any," she said, leaning back in her chair.

"We'll get him," Red said.

She said nothing. She hoped he was right, but after spending all this extra time, she wasn't so sure any more.

CHAPTER FIFTY

RED WATCHED SILENTLY with Mattie the rescue of the other crews from General Jarvis's doomed fleet, then watched as the now empty ships were blown out into(?) space by numbers of ships from nearby planets' military.

"If Jarvis is watching at all," he said, "he's going to think his ploy worked."

"I sure hope so," she said.

Red looked at the woman he had fallen for. Now that the rescues had been pulled off, her only focus was on the target. And so was his. But if she stayed in this mood, it was going to be a very, very long trip out into The Emptiness.

They sat in silence for a short time and for the first time, Red felt uncomfortable with the lack of talking.

"Carson would be proud of all this," Red said, finally, thinking of his friend. "The two organizations he worked for, that he believed in, working together to save thousands of lives."

"It wouldn't have gotten started without him risking his life and giving his life," Mattie said.

"I know," Red said, the feeling of sadness just below the surface. "And now we go get General Jarvis and make him pay for taking our friend's life."

"And so many thousands of others before this," Mattie said. "The reason for the Sector Force target on him."

Red nodded, then he turned to Mattie. "I want to watch you kill him for Carson."

She smiled at him for the first time in hours. "Deal."

CHAPTER FIFTY-ONE

IT WAS ONE of the longest twenty-five hours Mattie had ever spent on any space station ever.

They had docked, let off their passengers, then had a meeting with Chief Lovell, who said that numbers of the General's crew were coming forward with information they might use.

So as they had their supplies loaded, they talked with many who had information about the General's passenger liner, how it had been modified, who the crew were, and so on.

It seemed that everyone on board the liner were General Jarvis loyalists who had been with the general since his empire collapsed. And that there were just under one hundred total.

She and Red learned where the General's living quarters were, where the control room had been moved to, what types of engines and environmental systems were on the liner, and so much more.

It had been worth the extra time to interview everyone, but it had driven Mattie crazy. She knew that with every passing minute the general was getting farther and farther out of reach. They had to catch that passenger liner before any of this information mattered at all.

On the next to the last interview, however, her mood brightened completely.

"He's headed toward the Single Cloud," an older man named Hustorn said. He had a beard and had showered and been given fresh clothes, but clearly he hadn't eaten well in the last six months.

Mattie looked at his file and saw that he had two grown children and some grandkids, all of whom had been threatened by General Jarvis's people.

"And how do you know that?" Red asked Hustorn.

Mattie quickly brought up the Single Cloud information on her pad.

"I'm a navigator for the Three-Planets Alliance," Hustorn said. "I was taken by the general and forced to help his people set the course on the big passenger liner. They are not a bright bunch on that ship."

He shook his head in disgust and Mattie couldn't help but smile at him.

"So why do you say that?" Red asked, pulling up a map of the known areas on the other side of The Emptiness on a screen in the room. It showed the Single Cloud group as well. A bunch of stars close together and seemingly on the edge of The Emptiness.

"Because even though the Single Cloud group of stars look to be closer on an image like that, they are actually four months travel time farther away and don't have a livable planet among the thirty systems in the small cluster."

Red looked puzzled.

Hustorn smiled. "The Three-Planets Alliance is on the edge of that Emptiness. Trust me, we know what's on the other side of it. Turn that image ninety degrees and you'll see the optical allusion."

Red did and suddenly the Single Cloud group of stars was a distance from the edge of the Emptiness.

Mattie really laughed. "And you didn't tell him that, of course."

"Not a chance," he said, smiling. "I figured if I was going to die, he and his idiots might as well too."

"Why are they going to die?" Red asked, now really shocked and still staring at the star field on the screen.

"Because they don't have the food supplies to get to the Single Cloud at the speed that ship can go and the number of people on board. Let alone go any farther."

"Our information tells us it's a pretty fast passenger liner and was modified to be even faster."

Hustorn again just smiled. "You can't kidnap a person's family and get good work out of anyone."

"You sabotaged the ship?" Red asked, looking stunned.

"I wouldn't say sabotaged," Hustorn said. "Me and a few of his most trusted kidnapped mechanics just slowed it down some is all."

Mattie looked at him and knew that Hustorn wasn't telling them everything.

"And?" she asked, smiling.

"We also sort of made sure about a year's worth of food supplies would spoil very, very quickly."

Both she and Red just broke into gales of laughter and after a moment Chief Lovell came into the room to see what was wrong.

Mattie was laughing so hard she couldn't even begin to tell the Chief what was wrong.

Hustorn just sat and smiled.

Finally Red indicated that Hustorn should tell Chief Lovell and then the Chief started laughing. Finally the chief managed to get out another question for the smiling Hustorn.

"How much food do they actually have?"

"They should realize their problem about twelve weeks out," he said. "They will be out completely by week sixteen or so."

"So," Red said, "you made sure they wouldn't have any real speed in the ship, then made sure they would be far enough out into the Emptiness that they would starve even if they tried to turn around and come back."

"Pretty much," Hustorn said.

"You two need to hire this man," Chief Lovell managed to say as he too just couldn't stop laughing.

Finally Red said, "Chief, can you put Hustorn here and his engineer friends in my suite while they wait for their familes

to join them. Let them stay as long as they like. On me."

"You got it," Chief Lovell said.

"Come on," Mattie said. "Looks like we got a dictator to put out of his misery."

"Not too fast I hope," Hustorn said.

"Oh, trust us," Mattie said. "It's going to be slow and painful and really, really fun to watch."

"Wish I could be there," Hustorn said.

"Get in line," Chief Lovell said.

CHAPTER FIFTY-TWO

MATTIE SAT WITH RED in the control room as they went through the hole in the curtain nebula once more. If she never had to go through this radiation-intense area of space again, she would be very happy.

On the other side, she saw what she was expecting, but it still surprised her a little. The ships they had rescued the crews from were gone, destroyed completely with nothing remaining but expanding fields of floating metal.

The abandoned space station was mostly gone as well, and all the ships that had been docked there had vanished into a large cloud of debris.

She and Red both took some scans of the area before moving on toward The Emptiness, making sure nothing had been missed. General Jarvis had made sure that no one would find any evidence of his little plan.

After scouring the area, they both worked on scanning outward as far as they could as they moved out into The Emptiness. Red had a very powerful scanner on his ship and with the help of knowing in what basic direction General

Jarvis's ship had headed, they were able to spot their target after only an hour.

That made Mattie almost giddy with happiness and relief. She had been so afraid that the effort to save all the hostages would cause them to lose General Jarvis. But it seemed like they hadn't.

It took another hour, but they finally confirmed it was the passenger liner. "How fast is it moving?" Mattie asked, worried that their sources were wrong.

"About the same as a normal passenger liner," Red said after a moment. He turned to smile at her. "In other words, moderately slowly compared to what it should be doing. Seems the sabotage worked."

She loved when he smiled at her and gave her good news at the same time.

"Price of the help you hire," she said, smiling back at him.

"Or kidnap as the case might be."

She laughed, feeling better and better by the moment. "How long until we catch them?"

"Reasonable speed so we take no chances of engine failure, four weeks. Another week to come in slower and cloaked."

She nodded. "That's only a few weeks before they discover they will be running out of food."

Red nodded, smiling.

"Perfect timing," she said, laughing. "We can pace them and just watch and listen."

"A perfect plan by me to start with," Red said. "So, are you ready for an adventure?"

"Are you saying that hanging around with you for six or seven weeks or longer will be an adventure?"

"I can only hope so," he said, giving her that evil smile.

"Then get us on the way," she said. "I'll be in the shower if you'd like to join me."

With that she kissed him and turned and headed down the hallway laughing at the stunned look in his face.

CHAPTER FIFTY-THREE

MATTIE COULDN'T BELIEVE how she felt. The days with Red were wonderful. They settled into a routine she couldn't believe she enjoyed. She did her exercises every morning alone in his full gym. Then helped him with breakfast.

He kept his promise to teach her how to cook and by the second week she flew solo on an easy dinner of game bird and rice. It actually tasted good and she and Red both ate their entire meal. She had gone into the meal making Red promise that if it was bad, he would cook them something in replacement. He had promised, but thankfully hadn't been held to that promise.

Every afternoon they worked out together as Groff martial art masters, sharpening their skills.

They often napped and often had sex. But the intensity had grown into a longer, more intense love-making.

Over meals they talked about each other's families, history, and goals. Over one dinner she learned about his first fiancée named Sarina who dropped him and changed his life in the process.

Mattie was very grateful that the woman had been a total idiot. But she said nothing.

And a couple times they talked about Carson. Good conversations, remembering a friend and a good man.

But even with the great routine and company, the actual nothingness of The Emptiness slowly wore on Mattie, as well as their inability to even come close to figuring out a way to board that passenger liner without putting their own ship at complete risk. If they had been close to a number of star systems, that might not have been a problem, but this far out into the emptiness, it was another matter completely.

Help would be a very long time in coming, if ever.

Behind them, the huge curtain nebula had shrunk down to nothing more than a tiny light after a couple of days and then had completely vanished. The entire second sector of millions of stars was now nothing more than a white hazy cloud stretching out in a slowly narrowing band.

Ahead there was nothing but more blackness.

And the General's fleeing ship.

She had been on an ocean on a planet once that had felt like this. The smaller ship she had been on had developed engine troubles and been dead in the water for a number of hours until rescue came. It had bothered her more than she ever wanted to admit that she couldn't see any land in any direction. She was a good swimmer, but being so far out that land was not visible had really bothered her.

It gave her a feeling of helplessness she hated beyond any other feeling.

And now she was feeling that same thing in The Emptiness. There was nothing out here.

They had been in contact with both of their organizations for the first number of days out, but as they went farther and farther, and without signal relay stations, after a time all they could do was send out updates. Conversations were not possible.

If they needed to call for help, they would not even have a way of knowing if the call got to anyone who could help.

At the point where the instruments on the big passenger liner might have detected a ship following them, Red had cloaked the ship and slowed down slightly.

Mattie knew that now there would be no chance of The General knowing they were approaching.

But they still hadn't figured out a way to get on board that liner, even though almost every evening it was part of their dinner conversations.

Finally, after five weeks, they caught the passenger liner.

Red put them into a position to one side and slightly behind the big ship and set a speed to pace the ship.

Mattie again felt excitement and utter frustration. General Jarvis was so close, yet for the life of her she couldn't figure out a way into that big ship. All of the crew on board were loyalists to the General and wouldn't help them. And the moment Red made his ship visible and they tried to dock, the big ship would open fire.

And both she and Red had the same fear. They didn't want the big liner to be destroyed until they could prove, without a doubt, that General Jarvis was on board.

So they decided to wait.

And that made both of them irritable and impatient, not a good thing to be considering they were both deadly killers and both feeling trapped in the middle of nowhere on a small ship.

Patience came hard.

CHAPTER FIFTY-FOUR

RED COULDN'T TAKE much more of the waiting. So that morning he had promised her a good dinner that night and a solution to their problem. She might not like it, but it would be a solution.

They had spent the rest of the day apart, including skipping their normal Groff training in the afternoon. Since both of them were so frustrated, it had gotten pretty rough at times.

At dinner, she had arrived, kissed him lightly on the cheek and sat down at the table.

"Smells wonderful," she said, smiling.

He knew she was just doing her best to lift both their moods. But now, after almost seven weeks, two weeks trailing the big liner without a sign at all that General Jarvis was on board, both of them were fed up, both with this mission and slowly with each other.

For two loners, being forced into something like this was more than both of them had bargained for.

He had cooked them a sizzling beef dish and a salad with a light wine dressing. He had to admit, it did smell wonderful.

He sat the plate in front of her with a glass of good red wine, then joined her.

She took a bite and her eyes lit up slightly, the first time in days. "Wow, this is good. You got to teach me how to cook this."

He smiled at her and her sudden excitement at his meal. "Glad to, on the way back."

She shook her head. "Won't that feel good to be doing that?"

"As much as I love spending these weeks with you," he said, smiling. "I have to agree."

She looked up at him, clearly worried. "It's not you. You know that, don't you?"

"That's what they all told me," he said, trying to keep a straight face. Then he laughed. "I'm having the same problem, you know that, and it certainly isn't anything to do with you either. It's this emptiness and the frustration of not being able to get in that ship and do our jobs."

"Exactly," she said, nodding.

"So let's get this show on the road, kill a monster, and head back to bright lights of the sector."

"Suggestions?" she asked. "We've gone over and over this."

"I know," he said. "But now we have another weapon we didn't have two weeks ago."

She looked puzzled and almost angry. "What might that be?"

Red smiled at the woman he had fallen for and her angry stare. "They are about to find out that their reserve food is worthless and that we are their only hope."

"How are we their only hope?" she asked.

"We aren't, of course," Red said, laughing. "But they won't know that until we put a hole in their foreheads."

Then, as they finished their sizzling beef meal and sipped their wine, he outlined the plan he had worked on for the last week.

And when he was finished and they had agreed, she was again laughing.

"You know," she said, smiling at him and standing. "For being the one to come up with such a great plan, I think you should be rewarded."

She reached for his hand and pulled him to his feet.

Then, leaving the dirty dishes until later, she pulled him down the hallway to the bedroom, slowly undressed him, and managed to not miss one inch of his body with her kisses.

If he had known that coming up with a plan would be this much fun, he would have done it weeks earlier.

CHAPTER FIFTY-FIVE

MATTIE LOVED THE IDEA that Red came up with. And he had been right, they didn't dare try it two weeks ago because there was a chance that some of the liner's extra food could have been saved if those on board the passenger liner realized the problem. They were betting none of them had checked those supplies since they left.

But by waiting the extra two weeks, from the information they had gathered from the hostages who sabotaged the food, all of the reserve food would be spoiled and most of the food available in the kitchen area would have been used.

By Red's count, even on rations, General Jarvis and his loyalists were soon to discover they only had a few weeks to live.

The next morning, after breakfast, she and Red worked intensely at creating a cover story. He was going to be Red Canworth, in charge of the Three-Planets Alliance mission to bring General Jarvis back to trial.

There were eight ships in their mission, all smaller cloaked ships converted to hold prisoners. They would tell the general that their entire fleet had enough food and water among them to get the entire crew back to the Second Sector.

After she and Red finished with their cover story, they worked out the plan that would allow them to get on board.

Mattie had no doubt that they were going to have to fight their way on board because once the crew realized the food situation, they would not take a chance on destroying any of the ships. But they would try to capture the ship. And that would mean a fight.

And wow was Mattie ready for a fight.

"So you ready for step one?" Red asked, smiling at her.

She leaned over her control board. "I've had a little practice at this. Let me know when we are in position."

He nodded and began to ease the ship around behind the large passenger liner. They were going to disable the engines, put the big liner adrift in the middle of The Emptiness. Granted, the liner's forward momentum would eventually take the ship past some star on the other side of The Emptiness, but that might be hundreds of years.

In other words, not only was General Jarvis about to realize his attempt to escape had failed, but that he was going to starve to death. And everything about Mattie loved that idea, even more than she wanted to put a bullet in his head.

But she had to know, for a fact, that General Jarvis was on this ship.

"Ready," Red said.

She fired the laser into the engines of the big ship, giving it just a fraction of a second longer than she needed before saying, "Clear." She had to be very careful with the laser shot because the last thing she wanted to do was cause the ship to explode.

Red quickly dropped their ship back and to one side to get out of any danger zone.

Mattie watched her scans as the engines of the big liner froze up and shut down.

"The engines are nothing more than slag," she said, laughing. "No one in a thousand years will be fixing those machines."

Red rose and kissed her, then dropped back into his chair.

"Great shooting."

"Shall we tell them about their food today or tomorrow?" Mattie asked, again actually enjoying all this.

"I think now might be the best time," Red said, laughing.

"Well then, get dressed," she said and went back to work over her board, making sure that the signal they were about to send could not be traced back to an exact location, but instead look like it came out of a dozen different places around the big liner.

"Ready when you are," she said.

She glanced around. Red was wearing what looked to be an official, yet casual military jacket with his long hair pulled back and tucked into the back collar of the jacket. It made him look very military and formal.

"Nice," she said, smiling at him.

Red nodded, tucked the small script they had written for him on the front of his control panel, then took a deep breath. "Ready."

She started the transmission to the passenger liner with an image of the Three-Planets Alliance insignia on the screen. Using that, she checked to make sure her signal could not be traced to them.

Then after about fifteen seconds she dissolved the insignia to Red.

"Attention General Jarvis. My name is Red Canworth of the Three-Planets Alliance Defense League. Your ship has been disabled and your food will be running out within the week. There are eight cloaked ships surrounding your liner ready to destroy it. We would rather accept your surrender and transport you and your crew for trial in the Three Planets Alliance. General Jarvis, we will be awaiting your response."

Mattie cut off the signal and made sure it had not been traced in any fashion while Red took them back and out of firing range of the big liner just in case someone on board went crazy and started firing without reason or aim.

"Perfect," she said, laughing. "I would love to be a fly on the wall on that ship as they discover they are without engines and without food."

"As would I," Red said, laughing.

CHAPTER FIFTY-SIX

MATTIE EXPECTED no response quickly, if at all. But the general was not fool enough to start a fight with them. He knew he at least had a chance back in the Three-Planets Alliance. Out here in The Emptiness, without power or food, he stood no chance of survival at all.

But she also had no doubt that he would try to capture their ship. And Red knew that as well, so they worked out a fool-proof method that in case the two of them were killed, this ship would explode and the general and his men would starve to death.

Mattie's target was going to die one way or another very soon. And considering what a monster he was, that just made her smile.

Six hours later the signal came in that General Jarvis was trying to contact them. They had been in the galley having a light dinner and both of them just smiled at each other.

The conversation over dinner was on the topic of letting the general and his men just starve to death instead of killing them outright.

Both of them liked the idea more than they wanted to admit, but first they needed to know that the general really was on board.

When they got back to the control room, Red again put on his Three-Planets Alliance look.

She made sure that the signal could not be traced in any fashion and that it appeared to come from more than a dozen sources. Then she put up the Alliance symbol again for a long five seconds before signaling Red that he was visible.

A secondary commander's face appeared. "We have considered your terms and—"

Red cut him off. "We will not discuss any terms or conditions with anyone but General Jarvis."

Mattie cut the transmission.

Red quickly moved their ship slightly farther away and into an almost blind area for the big, drifting liner.

She was disappointed, but not surprised the general had not appeared.

Suddenly there was a page back to them.

"Wow, that was quick," Mattie said, quickly checking again that the signal could not be traced.

Again she put up the Alliance seal for a few seconds before letting Red go live.

The other man was still at the screen. "I am afraid the general is not available. I am now in charge."

Red looked at him, his stare intense, his voice cold and mean. "Then send us a vid of the general's dead body and we will talk. Otherwise we will leave and you and all your men will be left to starve. Your choice. Trial in the Alliance courts or a long slow death out here."

Again Mattie cut the transmission.

"Wow, you are good," she said. "You don't think the general is actually not in command any more?"

"Not a chance," Red said, moving the ship even farther back and away from the liner and out of any kind of fire range just in case they were spotted. Then he turned to her. "Now, let's go finish that dinner."

CHAPTER FIFTY-SEVEN

MATTIE STAYED IN HER ROUTINE as they waited for the general to contact them. Clearly he had to be planning something, but she had no idea what it might be. His options were limited to say the least.

They had gotten a decent night's sleep, Red had cooked them both a good, solid breakfast, then she had done her exercise and taken a long shower.

After that she had spelled Red in the control room while he took a long shower and got cleaned up as well.

The ship was completely out of firing range of the defenses in the passenger liner and from what Mattie could tell from her scans of the big ship, a lot of people had gathered around the food storage areas for a time yesterday. And even more had gathered in the engine rooms.

It seems that they were proving to themselves just how bad a situation they were in.

Also, during the last twelve hours, the big liner had tried dozens of scans, changing wavelengths, trying to get even a glimpse of the fleet that seemed to surround them, but could not be seen.

Finally, the big liner sent them yet another page.

Mattie made sure their response could not be traced in any fashion and that the incoming message was not dangerous in any fashion.

"What are we going to do if this isn't General Jarvis?"

"We tell them we are leaving and wish them luck," Red said, smiling. "Then stand back and watch the panic for a time."

Mattie loved that, but at the same time she just wanted to see Jarvis's ugly face on that screen, just to make sure he really was there.

They waited a good ten minutes before Mattie put up the Alliance shield again. And then let Red go on screen.

Facing them was the same man again.

Mattie felt intense disappointment.

"The general will not allow us to record him or put him on screen in any fashion," the man said, clearly not happy. "I am afraid the general said that you must negotiate with me."

"Not acceptable," Red said. "We will be returning to Alliance territory in twelve hours if I have not spoken directly to General Jarvis in that time."

Mattie cut the link.

Then she said, "The general has gone completely crazy and his men know it."

"Seems that way," Red said as he again moved the ship to a different location. Then he turned around to Mattie with a smile. "Your turn to cook lunch."

She loved that smile, but she had to ask a question she had not asked before. "At full speed, how long would it take us to get back into civilized space from here?"

"Bothering you, is it?" he asked. "Or is it my company?"

She took a deep breath and said, "Just answer the question."

"At this ship's top speed, if we pushed it, nine days. Normal fast speeds, just over two weeks."

"Nine days?"

He nodded. "Once we hit that speed, even if we lost the engines, we would still be in civilized space in that same amount of time."

She could feel herself relax. It often took that long to get from one area of one sector to another. She understood nine days.

"Thanks, that made me feel better. And how long would it take if we stayed and watched the general starve to death?"

"Two more weeks headed out into The Emptiness at this pace?" Red asked, then quickly checked his board. "Eleven days to get back at top speed."

"Wow does that make me feel better," she said.

He laughed. "I've been checking that same number now for a week."

"And you didn't think to tell me?" she asked.

He shrugged. "I thought about it, but you never asked until now."

"That's it," she said, standing and heading out of the control room. "You cook lunch."

Behind her all she heard was a light chuckle and then "Ahh, the punishment, the punishment."

She laughed all the way to the galley and by the time he joined her, she had lunch mostly ready.

CHAPTER FIFTY-EIGHT

RED WAS NOT SURPRISED that it took almost the entire twelve hours before they got another contact from the passenger liner. In fact, if it had come earlier, he and Mattie would have both been surprised. But the general waited until just one minute before the deadline.

They had talked a lot during the afternoon about the value of even going on board that ship. They both agreed the risk might be too much, considering that everyone on board would be dead in a short time anyway.

But they also both agreed that they somehow needed confirmation that General Jarvis was on board.

If they general didn't come on screen, then they would go to Plan B and stage an assault on one airlock. Red hated that idea. There was just too much of a risk that one or both of them would be injured or killed. But if they had no choice, they would do that.

Red glanced over at Mattie as she worked to make sure their response could not be tracked or traced in any fashion.

"They are going to beg for more time," he said.

"Listen to him," she said, "get them to kill the general for us."

"Wouldn't that be nice," Red said, smiling.

Then as Mattie sent them the Alliance Seal, he turned to face the screen.

And then the image cleared and he couldn't believe it.

He somehow managed to not let his mouth fall open. He was staring into the face of one of humanities worst monsters, General Jarvis.

The general had on his uniform, pressed and clearly recently washed. He had on his hat and had a fresh shave and haircut. His thick nose and beady eyes glared through the screen.

After the surprise had passed, Red managed to also not scream at the man.

Behind Red, Mattie muttered, "Well, what do you know?" It was soft enough that only Red heard her.

He was feeling the same way. Stunned, disgusted, and angry all at the same time.

"What are your terms?" the general asked.

The bastard had enough gall to ask what their terms were. He was clearly an insane monster right to the end, without any grasp of reality.

"We have already started back, general," Red said. "I'm afraid you missed our deadline."

The general actually started to look panicked, beady eyes glancing at someone beside the screen. Sweat broke out on his forehead, but he managed to maintain a little composure.

"Let me check if that decision can be cancelled?" Red said.

The general only nodded.

Red indicated that Mattie join him.

"General, I would like to introduce myself. I am Red Simms of Innocence Incorporated and this is Mattie Silks from Sector Force."

"But…" General Jarvis said, his eyes filling with panic.

Red smiled, feeling better than he had felt in years.

"General, we first would like you to know that we rescued every person from your decoy fleet and saved all their families as well."

"And general," Mattie said, "we stopped your attempt to destroy the Sector Force and we saved all those families as well."

Red went on, smiling right along with Mattie. "You are so incompetent a leader, we have now rounded up your entire following on one ship and killed you all, letting you think it was all your idea."

"You can't leave us here!" he shouted at the screen, his face growing red.

"We can," Red said.

A shot exploded over the communication link and the side of General Jarvis's head exploded out to the right in a shower of red.

Red was actually impressed.

"I hope we have all that recorded," he said to Mattie, who only nodded. "We'll play it back in slow motion for most of the two civilized sectors to watch. That was almost as much fun as being able to do it myself."

"Almost?" Red asked, smiling.

"Almost," she said, laughing.

A man pushed the general's body aside and it landed with a loud thump and crash on the floor, clearly knocking something over.

The man sat down in front of the camera, the same one that Red had talked to before. "The general is dead now. Would you please come back for us? Please?"

Red glanced over at Mattie who wore a smile so large it looked like it might hurt.

"What do you say?" Red asked her.

"The Sector Force would not like the fact we brought back so many killers who helped General Jarvis. You would just have to all be targeted and tried and then killed. A huge waste of time and effort. So I would vote no."

Red looked back at the screen, his anger building. "You and your general and your little private army killed my best friend and one of the nicest people I have ever known."

The guy on the other side looked like he might pass out his face was so white.

But Red did not care. All he could see was Carson lying there in that mall, dead.

"My organization, Innocence Inc., sides with Sector Force. We believe that some people should not be defended or rescued from their deserved punishment, which in your case and in the case of the rest of the crew, is death."

Red clicked off the communications link and flipped the ship around and headed even farther away from the passenger liner.

Then suddenly he had the most dangerous enforcer in all of known space holding him, hugging him, kissing him, and climbing on his lap.

"We got him," she said after letting Red come up for breath from a very long and passionate kiss.

"That we did," Red said. "And we saved a lot of innocent lives in the process."

"Somewhere," Mattie said, "Carson is smiling at us right now."

"I hope he doesn't watch too long," Red said, working at kissing Mattie's neck, "because very shortly I plan on doing some very rude and wonderful things to your body."

She laughed. "A promise I will hold you to."

And she did.

CHAPTER FIFTY-NINE

MATTIE COULDN'T really believe General Jarvis was finally dead. They had stayed close to the liner for another two days until on board there was some sort of revolution and gunfight and about half of the remaining crew and followers of General Jarvis were killed.

"What are they fighting for?" Red had asked more as a rhetorical question, because he knew the answer just as much as she did. They were fighting over food.

And all that would do would delay the inevitable. That liner would become a ghost liner in very short order if someone inside didn't blow it up first.

They had sent the video back to both their headquarters and would continue to send it every day on the way back until they got a response. The Sector Force and Innocence Inc. needed to know General Jarvis was finally dead, the threats were over.

On the day they both decided it was time to just head back, Red had asked how fast she wanted to get back.

She had been thinking about that same thing. She wasn't sure what awaited the two of them back in civilization. And she wanted to know some answers to that question before they got there.

"Normal speed," she had said. "I have a bunch of cooking to learn."

His smile in response to that eased a lot of worries. Clearly he wanted the same thing.

He set their speed to take them just under four weeks to return. She hoped that was enough time to figure out just where they were headed, and get to know each other better without the pressures of a manhunt and threats of death around every corner.

And it did. In all her life she had never imagined getting to know another person as well as she had come to know Red.

And even more frightening to her when she allowed herself to think about it: She loved everything about him. And she had a hunch that being trapped in a tin can in deep space for weeks at a time would bring up any bad habits she might not like over time.

The man had none. She had no idea how that was even possible.

USA Today *bestselling writer Dean Wesley Smith returns with a second novel to the world of* Dust and Kisses *from the first issue of* Smith's Monthly.

Together, Callie and Fisher work to discover the secrets of a galaxy that have been hidden in plain sight, even from the powerful humans who had rescued millions. And in the process, they just might change everything.

Now Available
from all your favorite booksellers in trade paper and electronic editions.

CHAPTER SIXTY

AS THE STARS OF THE SECTOR grew from a thin line to a wide band and then filled the viewport, she got more excited about being out of the emptiness. And worried at the same time.

In four weeks since leaving the General's ship, they had not talked about what they were going to do next. She was afraid of bringing up the topic and Red didn't bring it up either.

Red took his ship around the edge of the big nebula and docked at Bodie Station. When that final click and bump echoed through the ship, she felt the largest sense of relief she could ever imagine.

Chief Lovell and his men give them a military welcome and in all her life of staying out of the limelight and just doing her job, this kind of ceremony just felt strange.

They headed eventually up to Red's big suite after having a drink with Lovell in his office. The pool looked wonderful and all she could think about was taking off her clothes and jumping in, enjoying the feeling of being back in civilization.

But when Red suggested they go get some dinner first in that wonderful café in the trees, she realized just how hungry she was and said yes. There would be time for the pool later.

And she wanted to sleep next to the man she loved for a good twelve hours, make love, eat something, and then go back to sleep again. She felt that tired.

But first, she wanted to ask Red what they were going to do next. No one at Sector Force had even suggested she

might have another assignment quickly. So she felt relieved to be back and at the same time sort of at loose ends.

She needed some answers.

But mostly she needed to know what Red was thinking about their future.

The restaurant was as beautiful as she remembered it, tucked in and around huge trees off to one side of the large lobby. As they came out of the elevators and walked to the restaurant, dozens of people had nodded at them and a couple people said, "Well done."

When they reached their table, Red smiled at her and pulled her chair out like a real gentleman. Could the man get any more perfect?

Or more handsome.

She was so much in love, she didn't want to even consider a future without him in it. She knew that much for sure.

He ordered a bottle of wine. After very little deliberation, she ordered the same meal she had had with him that first time.

And he did the same.

Then before she could even say a word, he reached across the table and took her hands gently in his.

"So what do you want to do next?" he asked.

"My topic of conversation exactly," she said, smiling at him.

"I have a suggestion," he said. "Why don't we come back here every year on this same date to celebrate."

The feeling of disappointment slammed into her stomach. She didn't want to only see Red once a year. Was that how he felt about her?

She pulled away from his hands and sat back.

"The head of Sector Force will be offering you a new position as the liaison between Sector Force and Innocence Inc."

That shocked her more than she wanted to admit. And made her happy. But how had he known?

He smiled at her and motioned that she not say anything just yet. He was up to something, but darned if she could tell what.

Chief Lovell walked over to their table and handed Red something. Then he said, "Enjoy your meal."

But she noticed he didn't go far before stopping and turning around.

And all over the restaurant and huge lobby, others turned to stare at them.

What was happening?

She glanced back at Red as he stood, moved around and knelt on one knee facing her.

If felt like the entire room was spinning.

"Mattie, would you do the honor of marrying me?"

He opened the package that the Chief had handed him, showing her the most beautiful diamond and ruby ring she had ever seen.

She wasn't sure if she could catch her breath.

She looked at the ring, then into the handsome face and smiling eyes of the man she loved more than anything.

Around them in the trees and out in the lobby area, hundreds of people watched in silence.

She leaned down and whispered to him, "I could kill you for this, you know?"

"I know," he said, smiling at her. "But I would rather you just say yes so we can go back upstairs after dinner and take a swim in that pool."

She laughed, pulled him to his feet and kissed him harder than she had ever remembered kissing someone before.

Then she pulled back from him just enough to say, "Yes."

Around them the lobby and restaurant exploded in applause and cheers.

She didn't care. She was kissing the man she loved and that was all that was important.

～

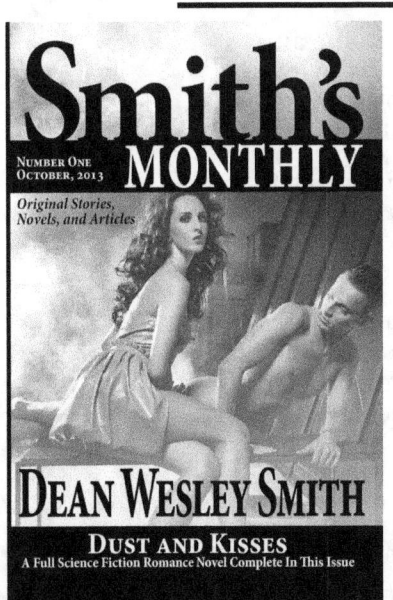

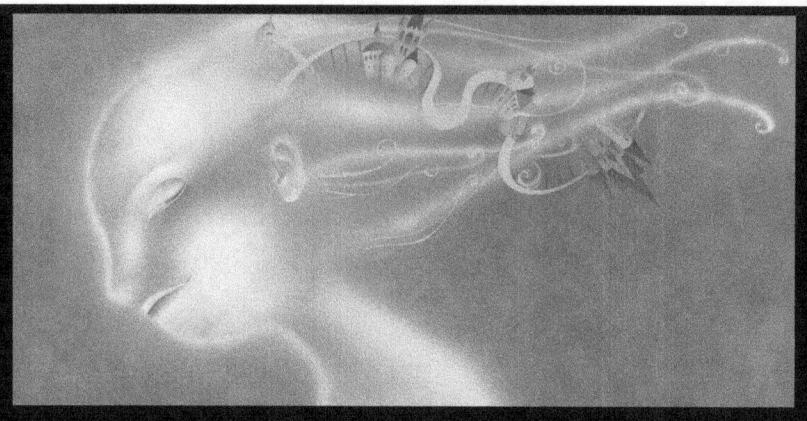

Poems by DEAN WESLEY SMITH

Born to Be Weightless

She was born six weeks early,
on International Two, the space station,
one day before her mom was to take the transport
to the surface.

She was healthy, a little light,
but the zero gravity caused no complications
a moisture suction hose couldn't handle.
Mom, biologist Susie Maxwell, did fine as well.

But then came the question.
What should the first child in space be named?
The parents had no preference,
so they opened the choice to the world.

Computers set up at major universities
kept the nominations
as everyone wanted to have a say
in the name of the first human child born off planet.

A picture of her floating in the air,
weightless and smiling, her eyes twinkling,
sealed the vote. There was no other name close.
Star Maxwell it would be.

Star returned to Earth a week later,
and was soon forgotten by everyone but her family.
and the record books.
On her eighteenth birthday she turned down an interview.

She grew to love floating in pools,
seeming to want to return to space and weightlessness.
At seventeen Star had a drug problem,
telling her mom it made her feel light and free.

At eighteen she was arrested for swimming nude
in a public pool.
At nineteen she died sky diving,
just not bothering to open her chute.

www.ingramcontent.com/pod-product-compliance
Lightning Source LLC
Chambersburg PA
CBHW081247210626
46818CB00016B/3104